Bound
by
Faith

Book III
Psychotherapy with Ghosts

Joseph S. Covais

NewLink Publishing
2022

Henderson, NV 89002
info@newlinkpublishing.com

Bound by Faith
Joseph S. Covais
Copyright © 2022
All rights reserved

Contact the publisher at info@newlinkpublishing.com

Line/Content Editor: Janelle Evans
Interior Design: Jo A. Wilkins
Cover: Janelle Evans
E-pub Design: Richard Draude

p. cm. — Joseph S. Covais / Paranormal
Copyright © 2022/ Joseph S. Covais
All Rights Reserved

ISBN: 978-1-948266-53-6/Paperback
ISBN: 978-1-948266-54-3/E-Pub

1. Fiction / Ghost
2. Fiction / Fantasy / Paranormal
3. Fiction / Fantasy / Romantic

NewLink Publishing
Henderson, NV 89002

Info@newlinkpublishing.com
Published and printed in the United States of America

1 2 3 4 5 6 7 8 9 0

Bound
by
Faith

Chapter 1

April 1842

The room smelled of coffee, coal fire, and tobacco. Sandborne observed the two men smoking long clay pipes, playing a game of checkers. They stopped, regarding his aged form in the doorway.

"Good day, gentlemen. My name is Emmet Sandborne."

The more portly one rose and extended a meaty hand. "I'm Jack DeGroot, this here's Henniker. Are you seeking a room?"

"I am, yes."

"You read our motto over the door, so you know this is a temperance house?"

"Aye, I do."

Sandborne eased his bundle to the floor and rolled his aching shoulders.

"No guests upstairs. No spirits of any kind — that goes without saying. No swearing. Two bits per week for a bed without meals, or a dollar if you want coffee and bread in the morning and a full meal at midday."

Sandborne accepted the terms without question and handed DeGroot a silver dollar. The man was about to lead him up a winding, narrow staircase to the third floor, but stopped and turned to stare at him.

"Can you climb stairs?" DeGroot said, staring at his cane.

"One flight, yes."

"Good. I have a bed on the second floor." DeGroot explained that a washerwoman lived at the end of the block. "You can take your laundry to her," he said. "Are you from hereabouts Albany?"

"No, up on the lake in Essex County."

"Willsborough?"

"Yes."

"You don't say," said DeGroot with a smile. "I have a good friend from there, he and his new bride left for South Carolina a few months ago. Maybe you know him? His name is Danny Dwyer."

Though his talkative host deserved to know more, Sandborne couldn't bring himself to say anything beyond, "Yes, I knew Daniel."

Of course it was Dwyer's description of this boarding house that brought him here in the first place, but hearing that name spoken aloud so soon and so suddenly was jarring.

"Well, as it turns out, this was Dwyer's room when he stayed with us. You'll be sharing it with Henniker, you met him downstairs. He's a good fellow. He don't say much, but he's clean. I think you'll like him."

Sandborne dropped his bundle on the bed and scratched at the gray stubble of whiskers on his face.

"If you've no objection, I'll retire now. It's been a long journey."

"Of course," said DeGroot.

"I'll see you downstairs for breakfast then." At the door he turned around. "Did you know his girl? I think he told me she was from Willsborough too. What was her name?"

"Almira Hamilton."

"That's right. So you knew her too."

"I did, yes."

"I never saw a fellow more in love," DeGroot said. "But small wonder why — she was an unusually pretty girl, wasn't she?"

Chapter 2

June 1972

"Doctor Weis, please do wake up."

David opened his eyes and saw a familiar face, but before he could comprehend anything further, he coughed up water, followed by convulsive vomiting and a series of dry heaves.

"Is it really you?" he said, still gasping for air.

"Yes," Almira said. Her voice sounded calm, coming from an indefinite point above him. "It is I."

David thought he felt a hand wipe away hair and particles of pond scum from his face. "Am I dead?"

"No, you're quite alive."

"You've come back?" He shook his head. "Why?"

"To save you. You see, doctor, you once saved me in death, now I must save you in life."

She began to fade away, growing transparent and floating toward the heavens.

"Please don't go yet." He pleaded with her. "I need

to talk with you."

"Don't worry, I'll soon return to my room. You'll see…" She ascended upward — the stars visible through her vanishing form. "We shall have a nice visit. Now lay your head down to sleep."

By the time he woke, morning sunlight had dried David's face, though much of his clothing was still wet and muddy. Feeling wretched, he looked to the side. His shoes rested where he'd placed them the night before, complete with keys, wallet, and an empty vial of Valium tucked inside.

Years spent as a psychotherapist had taught him that the arrangement of personal effects of suicides was highly idiosyncratic. What did this arrangement say about him? A need for order, even in death? A dramatic, self-absorbed gesture, intended to elicit sympathy? Or an unacknowledged urge to continue living, a subconscious knowledge that replacing his ruined driver's license and lost keys would be supremely inconvenient when he resumed his dreary life?

Last night he had polished off a bottle of slivovitz, puked into the toilet, then cracked open a fresh bottle and hammered down most of that one. All the while, Sinatra's "My Way" played on the stereo over and over. That was how it started, but what was the train of thought that led him here? Oh yeah, he would see his life through if he could swim across the lake and back, relying on the cold water and physical exertion to keep him from drowning in a drug-induced sleep. Last night the idea seemed inspired and heroic. But lying here on the bank of the lake in the harsh light of morning, it did not seem so at all.

Grudgingly, he admitted his actions were typical of any other drunk and depressed person. Stupid too. So, filthy and tired, David rose and walked home.

It wasn't until David stepped onto the dirt lane that Almira's visitation reentered his mind. What was it she did? What was it she said? It was a struggle to remember, in the same way it was hard to remember a dream. Something about him saving her, or she him. No matter. It had been wonderful to be with her, however briefly, and have the confirmation that there remained some thread of connection between them.

Yet, he felt ashamed. He'd disturbed her resting spirit. Helping her to gain that peaceful state had been one of the few things David felt good about, and now he had screwed that up too.

David slept a lot over the next few days, but he did a lot of thinking too — about his life and what to do with it. He had always struggled with his on-again, off-again history of depression. Over the years those despondent moods came and went, but attempting suicide was an ominous escalation of the cycle. Really, were it not for Almira, he would be dead.

Most persons who commit suicide first isolate and have already tried to end their lives at least once before, gaining courage and proficiency with each successive attempt. David knew all this, and that the house by the lake only facilitated his tendency toward unhealthy isolation. If he didn't get it together, there would be another successful attempt in his future.

It was shocking to think back that not long ago he had been David Weis, Psy.D., a Manhattan psychologist and rising star in the profession, about to achieve licensure and establish a lucrative practice of his own. That seemed like a long time ago, more than the few years it really was.

Chapter 3

April 1842

"Miss Becca, you been quiet these days," said Tildie as she finished brushing her mistress's hair. "You missing Miss Almira?"

"I am." Rebecca shrugged. It was true. After each of her many letters sent over the course of the endless winter went unanswered, she had abandoned further hope of ever communicating with her dear friend again.

Matilda began parting Rebecca's hair with a horn comb. "It sure real strange the way nobody hear nothing from Miss Mirie, like she just disappeared."

It was strange indeed. Despite their friendship, and despite their promises to correspond, Almira had vanished. She, and soon after, Daniel, had left without a trace. Surely they were married by now, somewhere. She hoped so, but she also knew their plans to open a daguerreotype establishment in Charleston were as yet unaccomplished.

How much she missed her home. That seaside city with the gentle weather and its gentle society. It would be such a relief not to be regarded as alien because of her religion, accent, or customs.

Why she had insisted on Albany despite strong suggestions that Philadelphia would be a better school for her seemed a mystery now. Daddy said it was just to irritate Mother, and he was probably right.

Seated on the edge of the bed, Rebecca reviewed the previous year, just as—she supposed—soldiers might pass in review before their general. Since she'd arrived in Albany from South Carolina to attend the Female Academy, so much had taken place. At Mrs. Bright's boarding house Rebecca enjoyed the company of other young ladies, some from very good families. True, some few of them were anti-Semites and let their views be known. That wasn't surprising, but to most her religion didn't matter. More awkward was having Matilda with her. Slavery irritated these northern girls more than she had expected. To keep peace, required her discretion at all times.

For the first few months these problems were made less imposing by a new friend, Almira Hamilton. The mysterious and beautiful girl from even further north than Albany, and one of the few who had accepted her unfamiliar Carolina ways without judgment. In return, Almira entrusted her with secrets of her own. Within their alliance of two, the disapproval of classmates counted for little, and that was such a comfort in this unfamiliar city.

Rebecca mulled over the course of their brief but intense friendship. Her suspicions of the pregnancy had been confirmed by Almira's embarrassed confession. She then found herself planning an elopement with Almira's lover, Daniel. The whole thing had fallen apart when Almira's father appeared and took her away in a rage.

Since then, so many letters had gone unanswered or undelivered, she knew not which. Had all this transpired over the course of a few short months? It didn't seem possible.

"Tildie," she said, "are you lonely here?"

"Me? No, miss. There's lots of people here, and you, and now Mr. Jack too."

Soothed by her maidservant's grooming, Rebecca lapsed back into quiet.

"How about you? You lonely, miss?" said Tildie, braiding each bundle of her mistress's hair.

Rebecca welcomed the chance to complain. "I am. I think these northern girls don't much like us. Some exclude me because I am a Jew, and the rest hate me because I've brought you with me."

Tildie continued to work her mistress's hair, humming to herself.

"I'm sorry. I shouldn't have said that," Rebecca said after a period of silence. "It wasn't very nice, and they don't all hate me. Phebe's been very kind, and Emily too, but I do so miss the South. Here it is, the middle of April and the nights are still fretfully cold."

"Yes'm, it's sure enough cold here."

Rebecca looked over her shoulder at her servant. "Tildie, do you remember one winter in Charleston, the time my daddy slipped on the ice?"

"I surely do, miss."

"Daddy was a sight, wasn't he?"

"Oh Lord, yes. Poor Master Carvalho," said Tildie with a giggle. "He split his britches right up the middle, and when he try to get up, he slip again and smash his tall hat flat."

Their giggles grew into laughter.

"Do you remember—" Rebecca sputtered again. "—remember how angry Mother was? She called him a clumsy lickspittle, but Daddy laughed and laughed. Goodness, I miss him so."

"He a good man, your daddy. He always was kind to Tildie."

The girls settled down, wiping the tears from their eyes. The laughter felt good, but now that it had passed, Rebecca only grew more homesick.

"Do you think you could conjure up a spirit for me?" she said, looking upward over her shoulder. "One that could tell me what happened to Almira?"

"Miss Becca, why you want me to do this?"

"Because I fear something terrible has happened to her—I'm just sure of it. I thought

maybe one of your negra spirits could tell me."

"It hard to say. But it sure was spooky the way her daddy come for her, weren't it? And never a word since."

Tildie pulled some loose hairs from the comb. "I could maybe try, but Jesus don't like us to conjure spirits, except we do it in his name."

"And I am a Jew," said Rebecca with a sigh. "So it would be meaningless."

Chapter 4

June 1972

For the first few nights, David waited in the quiet room where Almira used to materialize. He had his pen and legal pad at the ready, in true psychotherapist style. Every minute or two he glanced up in the hope of seeing the first glimmer of her emerging form, but the daybed, with the memorial commemorating her birth and death hanging from the wall above it, remained unoccupied.

A week went by. At first it seemed worthwhile, but now standing watch for a ghost who didn't appear seemed as pointless as the rest of his life.

Tonight, he started reading a new book: Townshend's 'Facts in Mesmerism with Reasons for a Dispassionate Inquiry into It,' published in 1840.

He must have fallen asleep from the dense text, for a voice startled him awake.

"Doctor, would you receive an old friend this evening?"

His head snapped up—sure he would see Almira seated on her daybed. But it was empty.

"No, Doctor Weis, I'm behind you."

He turned in his chair to find Almira standing beside the fireplace mantel, fully materialized.

A smile spread across his face. "You've come back."

"Of course," she said. "Didn't I promise you I would?"

Remembering to be sensitive to her nineteenth century manners, David got up from his chair and gestured toward the daybed. "Excuse me, there's so much I have to ask you, but please first make yourself comfortable."

She took a step closer but hesitated. "No. I think it's you who ought to take the settee. You look so very tired."

She was right, but he still protested.

"Please," she said. "I insist."

David eased himself onto the daybed. Leaning against its single cushioned arm, he couldn't help but release a groan of relief.

"There, isn't that better?" said Almira. She glided to the klismos chair. "And I shall take my place here."

Having collected himself, David studied Almira seated across from him, smoothing the folds of her dress. Her ensemble was that of a more mature adult—a plain blue dress, starched white cuffs and collar, hair pulled into a simple bun held in place with a modest comb. And, of course, she wore her signature coral necklace. But there was more than a change of wardrobe, Almira's demeanor was also different. Gone was the forced serenity, attempting, not always successfully, to conceal her internal turmoil. Gone as well was the girlish carriage of a budding young woman. A flower in full blossom had replaced it.

"There's so much I'd like to talk about," he said. "But

14

first, I have to apologize for disturbing your peace."

Almira raised her hand. "Please, don't apologize, doctor. I was disturbed only to see you so disconsolate."

"Well, I'm sorry anyway. It wasn't right for me to involve you in my problems, but I never thought you'd be aware of what I was doing." He took a quick breath and returned with momentum. "There's another important thing. I also have to thank you for saving my life. I don't know how you did it, and I don't even know why…" David looked at her in earnest. "Why did you stop me?"

"I had to," said Almira. "You were trying to force the hand of God, and I couldn't allow it."

"The hand of God," he repeated. "When I left you at the lake last winter, I was starting to believe in Him, but I guess I got lost along the way."

"Doctor," she said. "Each of us is asked to turn the misery of this physical world into heaven. A heaven on earth, you might say. God wishes it so, not for ourselves but to glorify him through serving others. That is why we are here. When you tried to end your life prematurely, you were squandering the opportunity of that end."

"You mean through good deeds." The words were said with a hint of sarcasm.

"Precisely, and those deeds may yet be accomplished."

Ashamed, David looked down and picked at his well-worn corduroy slacks. "And that's why you saved me. Is it that simple?"

"Yes."

Almira had dumped the meaning of life in his lap, and in simple terms no less. How many hours—no, how many years had he searched for that answer? Now, irrefutable as the source was, he would have to give it thought. And there were still so many other things he was curious about.

"If you're united with God, can you tell me what that feels like? What is the afterlife like for you?"

"Not just now, Doctor Weis," she said, waving him off. "I will return soon, and then we will converse more, but presently it's time for me to leave." Almira stood, walked to the mantel, and turned back toward him. "There is one last thing before I go. It's a bit of advice for you, doctor, if I may be so bold."

"Yes, please."

"You will recall our first conversation. It was in this very room. I told you then that woman was meant to be man's moral protector, and man her physical protector."

David nodded. "Yes, I remember that."

"This is my advice to you, Doctor Weis. Every man needs a woman's softening presence. Take a wife. Without a woman's leavening influence, there is nothing to check your animal nature."

In much the same way a candle is blown out in the wind, she flickered and disappeared. David stared at the empty space, trying to assimilate the visitation. Feeling very, very tired, too tired to get up from the daybed, he unlaced his boots, pulled them off, and lay down to sleep.

All through breakfast and the day's chores, Almira's words about serving God through serving others bounced around in David's mind. He wasn't sure he wanted to hear it. What he wanted was to be left alone, not challenged to dedicate himself to a humanity which he knew to be corrupt and rotten.

Almira's parting words dogged him too. 'Take a wife,' she'd told him. Well, it wasn't that simple. If she knew how royally he'd messed up things in the past, especially this last time with Angela, Almira wouldn't have made that suggestion.

Thinking about her left him feeling lousy anyway. Angela really did love him, and for all he knew he may have loved her too but preoccupied as he was by this house and its ghostly inhabitant, there wasn't much room left for her. Besides, Angela hated it up here, and now he hated the city, so that was that.

He didn't need a relationship, much less a wife. The phlebotomist in Dannemora was quite enough. She enjoyed sex for its own sake. She was a distraction when he wanted it, and for now that was all he wanted.

Anyway, in the midst of all this rumination over the meaning of life and the opposite sex there was still an auction in Saratoga to hit. He turned the truck onto the road that led out of town and a cardboard box on the passenger side shifted across the footwell. He eyed the package. It was full of things Angela left behind — a pair of jeans, a pair of platform clogs, that red dress he really liked, and a bunch of cosmetics. For a while, he held onto these things thinking maybe she would come back for them. Once it became obvious that wasn't going to happen, David intended to mail them back. It seemed the most reasonable thing to do, yet too impersonal. He threw his jacket over the box and turned on the radio.

Chapter 5

April 1842

Tildie gazed into the flame burning at the end of the candle.

"What do you see?" whispered Rebecca.

"Don't see nothing yet."

It was nearly midnight, and everyone else in Mrs. Bright's house was asleep.

"Hold out your finger, Miss Becca."

She extended her hand. Tildie poked it with a straight pin. She yelped, then sucked in the pain.

"Sorry 'bout that, miss, but Jesus say you got to have blood." She squeezed the finger until a large crimson bulb hung heavy at the tip. It clung for a moment before dripping into the flame, causing the candle to gutter.

"You got that piece of paper?"

Rebecca slid a small sheet across the table. It was one of Almira's unfinished compositions, the day Mr. Hamilton took her back to Willsborough. Rebecca found it lying on the floor of her friend's hastily evacuated room.

"Now I gonna take some more."

This time the drop of blood spattered onto the paper with Almira's handwriting on it.

Tildie took the paper and moaned softly — something between a chant and a melody as she held it up.

"Someone is here," Tildie said in an expressionless voice.

Rebecca glanced around the room. Except for the two of them, it was empty.

"She here now."

"Who?" said Rebecca in a hushed tone. "Is it Almira? Who is it?"

"Uh huh, Miss Almira. She's here."

Tildie was breathing like someone in a heavy sleep.

"She want to know why you don't send letters."

"But I have. You must tell her so."

Tildie's chin dropped to her chest. Her head lolled from side to side. "She says she miss you."

"Please," she begged. "I have to know where she is."

Tildie's hands flew in the air. With a shriek, then a dull thud of dead weight, she fell to the floor.

Kneeling at her servant's limp body, Rebecca could already hear excited voices outside her door as the other boarders spilled into the hallway.

"Who screamed?" said Mrs. Bright, pounding on the door. "Rebecca, open the door."

Before Rebecca could get up, Mrs. Bright used her passkey. Phebe and Harriet followed her with candles held high.

"What is the meaning of this?" Mrs. Bright said. "What is Matilda doing in your room, on the floor no less?"

"Y'all don't know this, but Tildie walks in her sleep.

She wandered in here and frightened me out of my skin. I screamed and she fainted."

Mrs. Bright was doubtful. She looked around the room, noticed ashes and the remnants of a burned piece of paper on the writing table and frowned. "Are you sure?"

"Yes ma'am. It's happened before. It's nothing at all, truly it isn't."

Phebe knelt beside Tildie and wiped her face with a dampened towel.

"Mrs. Bright," said Harriet, "oughtn't we call for a constable?"

"No, she's fine now," Rebecca said, snapping back over her shoulder at the constant troublemaker. "There's no need of it. Can't you see she's waking up?"

"She is that." Phebe helped Tildie to her feet.

"Harriet," said Mrs. Bright, "you and the other girls go back to bed. Fetch Rose and tell her to come help Matilda back to her room. Get along. Phebe, you too please."

Mrs. Bright stayed to scrutinize the still groggy Tildie, who now sat on Rebecca's bed. Rebecca herself looked badly shaken.

"This is very odd," she said. "You're quite sure she was sleepwalking?"

"Oh yes Mrs. Bright," Rebecca said. "Tildie does this sometimes.

That night, Rebecca lay awake for hours, thinking about what could possibly have happened to Almira. Tildie's conjuring hadn't provided any clear answers. Had she felt Almira's presence, or was that her imagination? Left with more questions than ever before, she tossed, first this way, then the other, until slumber finally brought an end to her inquietude.

Sometime in the pre-dawn hours, Rebecca woke amid sheets too tangled for comfort. Still feeling the dream in which she'd been immersed, and desperate to capture its images before they flew from her memory, Rebecca thought hard. She'd been sleeping, then awakened with a start. There, standing in the moonlight beyond the foot of the bed stood Almira dripping with water, her skin white as marble, her hair clinging to her body. She pulled off her wet chemise and let it drop to the floor.

How real it had seemed when Almira stood nude beside her on the mattress with one hand on the bedpost, proudly displaying the roundness of her new mother's belly. Rebecca had brushed her lips across it, kissed her there, and pressed her face to her taut skin.

Rebecca remembered turning back the covers, inviting her shivering friend to join her where, naked and cold, she lay enfolded until Almira's living warmth rekindled.

Someone spoke loving words in the dark. Who was it? She'd had daydreams before of these same whispered promises, and would have told Almira about them, but she'd always held back, afraid that those bold words would offend her friend's innocence. Now she regretted her hesitation.

Pulling the feather bolster to the length of her body, Rebecca remembered more. How did she touch her? Like this, and here, and there as well. Bringing her hand to her face, Rebecca could faintly smell the lingering scent of Almira's hair, perfumed with lavender. Was that possible if it was only a dream?

Chapter 6

July 1972

In the vestibule, David buzzed Angela's apartment but there was no response. He pressed the buzzer again and was about to leave disappointed when Tina's voice broke over the speaker.

"Who is it?"

"It's Dave Weis."

Another long silence, then the lobby door clicked.

At the second floor he knocked. Tina's voice called to him from inside.

"Come in, it's open."

David entered a bit sheepishly, since he didn't expect a warm reception.

"Hey. I'm in here. Just lock the door behind you, Okay?"

It was Tina's voice again, along with the sound of kitchen cabinets being opened and closed. He turned the bolt and placed the box of Angela's things by the door. He stood searching for signs of her—an article of clothing, her keys, something, anything.

"Is Angela home?" David said, entering the kitchenette.

Tina had her back to him, wearing her blue stewardess uniform but barefoot. An empty glass with a lipstick-smudged rim sat beside her on the counter. "Nope, she's gone."

"Will she be back soon?"

"Angela doesn't live here anymore."

"What? She moved out? When?"

"A couple of months ago." Tina took an aluminum ice cube tray from the freezer, yanked on the handle, and refilled her glass with ice. "I'm drinking vodka. What'll you have?"

"Nothing for me. I'm cool."

She ignored his response, broke the seal on a fresh bottle of Smirnoff, and upended it. "So what took you so long?"

"What do you mean?"

Tina turned around. Perfect make-up, blue eyeshadow, mascara, albeit in a heavy way. Holding two fresh drinks, she stepped very close to him and pushed one into his hand.

"Nothing," she said. "I just got in from Heathrow an hour ago, so I'm still getting my head together."

"Where did she go?" David asked. "Where is she living?"

"How should I know? She left in a huff."

David tried to retreat but his back was to the stove. "Well...I brought by some of her things. Maybe you can give me her address so I can return them."

"Yeah, sure," Tina said, sounding disinterested.

Taking a deep drink from her glass, she examined one of his shirt buttons between French manicured nails.

"Look. Really, I'd better go." He protested, feeling awkward about the whole scene.

"No, stay. At least finish your drink."

He took a sip and winced. Vodka, straight, with the slightest hint of orange juice.

"So, doctor, where have you been hiding?"

"At my place upstate." He regarded her Max-Factored face. Tina was a handsome girl, even with too much makeup, but he didn't trust her. Neither did he care for the implied mockery of the way she called him 'doctor.' "I don't get down to the city very much anymore."

"Well maybe you just need a reason."

"So, you don't know where she's living?" David said, eager to return to the subject of Angela.

Tina took another drink. Ice tinkled. "Like I told you," she said into her glass. "She left in a huff. If you ask me, you're better off. That girl had a lot of hang-ups. I, on the other hand, have no hang-ups at all. None whatsoever."

"Look, if you don't have her address, I really ought to go."

"What's the matter?" Tina said, walking her fingers up his shirt. "Don't you like me?"

"It's not that."

"All right, then there's no problem, is there? And the way she told it, you like to fool around. Well, I like to fool around too."

David sat his drink on the counter and tried to slip past her. Tina blocked his escape.

"Hey, don't run away," she said in a breathy voice. "You know the rumors you've heard about stewardesses? Well they're true—all of them."

David felt a tug on the belt loop of his jeans.

"Come on over to the couch and I'll show you," she whispered into his ear.

A good-looking stewardess, one he'd had his eye on for a long time, drunk and up for anything. God, and she was still in her uniform. That was so sexy. But whether out of loyalty or the memories in this apartment, it was too unprincipled, even for a fink like him. So David cursed his luck and pushed Tina aside.

"What the hell?" she said as he made for the door. "She never told me you were some kind of fairy. Is that why she left you? Is it? Well, take her shit and get the hell out."

David barely made it into the hallway and slammed the door before glass shattering on impact sounded right behind it.

Chapter 7

April 1842

At the breakfast table the flurry of speculation and questions about the previous night's commotion was brought to a quick conclusion by Mrs. Bright's announcement that Matilda had had a fainting spell, was upstairs resting, and that everyone else needed to attend to their own affairs.

Later that day, Rebecca and Phebe sat outside, eating their lunch on the academy's portico. Enjoying the first spring-like day of the year, they chatted about their morning Phrenology class.

Rebecca, unconvinced of the science, said, "Do you really think we can tell a person's character by the bumps on their head?"

"Of course," said Phebe. "You can see it everywhere. Miss Meigs has the broad forehead in harmony with her intellect, and Professor Horsford's character is abundantly evident in his noble profile." She smiled and sighed. "I think the better word is, regal." Recovering her focus, she said, "*Parlons Français ensembles?*"

Rebecca was not disposed to the idea. Though they often had fun in this way before, she was too fatigued by the previous night's events. "Very well, *Par l'anglais.*"

Both girls wiped their hands with moistened napkins and reached for their apples.

"Rebecca," Phebe said, "that was a most peculiar thing last night. Does Tildie really often walk in her sleep?"

Rebecca stopped mid-bite. "Only now and then."

"To be honest, I thought it was your Matilda who'd screamed, and not you."

"Come on now, you don't think I was telling a fib, do you? When I woke up and she was there I naturally screamed. Goodness, wouldn't anyone?"

Judging by Phebe's fixed stare, Rebecca knew she'd been found out. It wouldn't do to lie. After all, she liked Phebe, and, with Almira gone, the Gardiner girl was her only real friend at the academy. "Very well…" She looked right then left to ensure no one hovered nearby. "But you must promise not to breathe a word of this—especially to Mrs. Bright."

Phebe extended a tiny pale finger. Rebecca curled hers around it, and the pact was made.

"Now we have an unbreakable promise," Phebe said with enthusiasm.

Rebecca swallowed, then spoke in a low voice. "Tildie and I were conjuring spirits—"

"Conjuring spirits!" Phebe sounded delighted by the revelation. "Tell me everything. I abhor secrets to which I am not privy."

"Well, it has to do with Almira. Over a dozen letters have I written, yet not one has been answered."

"I wrote to her as well—though but once," said Phebe. "When I never heard back, I thought it just impolite, but what has Tildie to do with Almira?"

"I was hoping she could summon one of her negro spirits, maybe tell me what has happened," said Rebecca.

"Was she successful?" Phebe squirmed in place with anticipation. "Did you find out where Almira went to?"

"Goodness, no. Tildie went into some kind of spell, and then she screamed and fainted away."

Phebe bit her lip as if in deep thought. "Rebecca," she said with conviction, "I think Tildie may have been practicing Animal Magnetism."

"What's that?"

"Animal Magnetism is a proven scientific method to achieve somnambulistic ecstasy." Her statement had the ring of memorization, as if she were reciting from one of their textbooks. "My sister Mary and I have been reading about it this past year since."

Rebecca knitted her brow. "I don't think it was that. I think she was just conjuring spirits the way her people do."

"Whatever it was," said Phebe, "you and Almira were such close friends. That she hasn't answered you in particular is most strange."

"It's more than strange, and I know from my family that she and Mr. Dwyer never arrived in Charleston. They've disappeared. Vanished. And I'm terribly concerned."

Immediately on returning from the academy, Rebecca sought out her servant.

"Tildie," she said, hastening her with the motion of her hand. "Come with me. I want to speak to you."

Once within her room, Rebecca closed the door. "Are you feeling better?"

"I'm alright." Tildie shrugged.

"Last night, before you fainted, what did you see? Did you see Almira?"

"Please don't ask me to talk about that, miss."

"Come on now. You know how desperate I am over her absence," said Rebecca. "If you know where she is, then I just have to know."

"Miss Becca, I swear I don't know where Miss Almira is, ain't nothing more to say."

Rebecca tilted her head and put on her best pouty face. "Not even if I say 'please?'"

The effort had no effect, though she had humbled herself. It was humiliating. Rebecca's dark eyes blinked with outrage.

"What can you mean? You must tell me."

"Don't want to talk about it." Tildie shook her head.

Rebecca set hands to hips and pursed her quivering lips. "It isn't a question of whether you want to." The two stood immobile until Rebecca said, "Does this mean you are refusing me?"

Tildie lifted her face. "Yes ma'am, it does."

"B-but..." she stammered. "You must tell, you must."

"Why?" said Tildie. "Because I'm a slave, that why?"

"Well, yes."

Tildie remained silent. Having no experience with opposition to her will, Rebecca was disarmed. What would her father have done? She took a deep breath.

"Perhaps it was unkind of me to remind you of our relationship, but couldn't you tell me something?"

Tildie shook her head. "I swear it, miss. I don't know where she is. All I remember is a big empty space, and cold, the devil's own cold, like being dead. I don't want to call it up. I'm afraid of it."

"But wouldn't your Jesus want me to know if Almira is in danger?"

"No. Jesus doesn't like his people doing this. You made me do it once, but you can't make me do it again."

It was true. Overcome by a sudden weakness, she sank to her chair. In Charleston this would never have happened, but here in Albany she could no more bend Tildie to her will than she could the sun or the moon.

"Goodness," Rebecca said, resigned to this new situation. "How things have changed."

"Yes, miss, things a lot different here. Like Mrs. Bright, she pays me to do things for her just like she pays Rose, or anybody else. Sometimes you ask me to go buy pretty little trifles you want, and now I got a little money of my own, so I buy something pretty too. That makes me feel good."

Rebecca looked up. "Like that new lace collar you're wearing?"

"That's right," said Tildie. "You see, miss, out on the Broadway people don't know who I am. They think maybe I'm white. Fact is, up north here, half the time I don't know whether I'm black or white either."

Rebecca got up from her chair and stood beside her servant. She took Tildie's hand in hers. It wasn't as soft, her nails weren't buffed, and her complexion was a little darker, but the hands were the very same proportion. "Tildie, I won't ask you to conjure again, I promise."

"Thank you, Miss Becca," she said. "Now I got to go. Mrs. Bright got me and Rose taking up carpets for the summer."

31

Chapter 8

July 1972

"Hey," he said when the telephone was answered. "It's me, Dave."

"Hey yourself," Gail replied. Her voice had the husky quality of someone who'd been woken from sleep.

"Are you busy later?"

"Maybe. That depends."

"Well, I thought we could meet for drinks, and after that… you know." He heard noises suggestive of someone getting up from bed and pulling on a robe.

"This sounds like a medical emergency," she said. "Do you need to have your blood drawn?"

"Something like that, yes."

"Fortunately, I am a trained medical technician."

"No kidding."

"Alright. I'll meet you at Boom's at four o'clock. *Ciao*."

When he got to the bar, Gail was already there, halfway through what might have been her second Grasshopper. David climbed onto the stool beside her.

Right away she informed him of the situation. "I can't stay out late tonight. I have to be at work at seven, so we only have a couple of hours."

He was always impressed by her sexual efficiency. No strings, no entanglements, no encumbrances. Very goal oriented. So they finished their drinks, he paid the tab, and they left.

It was a well-established routine. She'd follow him to the motel and park away from the office. He'd go in, rent a room and, once inside, leave the door unlocked. She'd wait ten minutes and come in without knocking, by which time he'd have the covers turned down and his shoes off.

The sequence of events didn't vary much, except for the time they got the room with the coin-operated, vibrating bed. In selected positions, the effect was a sensual novelty, but mostly too distracting. Afterwards, they sometimes got something to eat, but a lot of the time she would shower and leave — today in her nurse's uniform.

The long nap he took after Gail left had him up late that night. He spent a few hours refinishing furniture in the carriage house, ate a can of soup, followed by reading more from Townshend's *'Facts in Mesmerism'*. That brought him past 2a.m.

Brushing his teeth, his thoughts drifted to Gail, the phlebotomist. What a queer duck she was. Unlike other women he'd been with, she didn't want to talk at all. The few times he'd attempted to engage her personally, emotionally, or intellectually for that matter, ended in failure. Like the day he told her about the Phrenology Bust — that was a good example. He was excited. It was a great medical antique, something he thought they'd both find interesting and could talk about. But she showed no interest in his life and made it plain she didn't want him prying into hers.

After wiping out the bathroom sink, David became cognizant that Almira was back. No sensory clue, just an awareness. And since this awareness had always proven reliable, he made some Sanka, took up his legal pad, and made his way upstairs.

He entered the Quiet Room to find Almira already seated

in the klismos chair, embroidering. She looked up at him, smiled, set her needle, and placed her work in the sewing basket on the floor.

"Good evening, Doctor Weis," she said. "I was expecting you."

"Don't you want to sit on your daybed?"

"You forget this was my chair too, and besides, you looked so much at ease on the settee when we last spoke, I thought you might like it again."

David thanked her and sat. He placed his notepad beside him on the velvet cushion.

"Please begin," she said. "I know that you have many questions for me."

"I do." He took a sip from his mug, placed it on the floor, and cleared his throat. "Honestly, I don't know where to start. I'm really very confused. I thought you and Daniel were gone to heaven or someplace like that."

"Your curiosity is anticipated. Our existence is something of a mystery to us as well, but I'll attempt to describe, if not explain it." Almira stood and walked to the window. "To begin, you are correct that Daniel and I were reunited when you brought me back to the lake. You saw us together. You saw me mount his horse before we left."

"Yes, I did. I saw the two of you disappear into the snowstorm."

Almira brought one hand up to the glass panes. "That night was much as it was when we tried to run away. Of course we knew how it would end, but it was enough that we were together. Having accepted our destiny willingly, God was merciful. This time we were not called upon to suffer. Instead, we woke side by side on the clover hill on a most wondrously beautiful day. So much like paradise was it we thought we must be in heaven. Even though we perished, in reward of our faith, God had given us a life together."

David knew he ought to be taking notes, but the story was too riveting even to glance away from her for a moment. "It sounds like perfection."

"Indeed, it was. We were as free to enjoy each other's

company as two lambs in a meadow." Almira turned her back to the window. "Except not quite the heaven it seems." She glided back to the klismos chair and sat, leaned forward and rested her chin in her hands. "You see, when we were interrupted, we were destined to have children. Indeed, we were surprised to learn I would have given birth to twins. The little birdies, as I like to call them. Of course, our birdies remain unhatched, and that is a great sorrow to us."

"Then if it's not Heaven, and it's not Hell," David said, struggling to formulate a sensical question. "What is it? How do you and Daniel pass the time?"

"We spend our time here together, going where we both are familiar and have happy memories, walking hand in hand, picking flowers, taking picnics on the clover hill, with mutton chops and apple pie if we wish." Almira turned to look over her shoulder, toward the window again. "Often we ride. There was a path along the lake we enjoyed. I do not know if it exists in your time as it was for us, but we mount our horses and take that path to our favorite places."

"Day after day?" David asked. "Over and over?"

"Yes, but time is oddly irrelevant to us. So, while Daniel and I have each other, eternity calls us to stay here torn between the joy of each other's company and mourning our unborn children."

"But an eternity sounds cruel. Isn't there any way for the two of you to be released?"

Almira shook her head. "But that our children be born, no. Until then, we remain in this purgatory."

David sat listless, finally looking up at her, his eyes glazed over with moisture. "It's too tragic."

"Don't be sad for me, doctor. I have much to be thankful for. Because of you, I am no longer trapped alone in this room, bewildered and lost. Instead, I am together with Daniel. And in this way, we pass our days, somehow carrying on as things might have been. I admit, it is very queer, but I assure you it is a full life—of sorts."

His mind reeled. He picked up his mug, but the coffee had turned cold and bitter. Reminded of the thoughts which drove him into the lake, he frowned. His tendency was to favor inanimate objects over real-life relationships, shutting down emotionally whenever that pattern was threatened.

"You are so unhappy, doctor. Why?"

David looked up. "What makes you think I'm unhappy?"

"It's obvious," she said. "Tell me, have you thought about my advice?"

"To take a wife? Yes, I have, but it's not practical."

Almira shook her head. "Come, doctor, you know better. We are not speaking of the mind but of the heart."

Thus corrected, he scratched his nose. He threw his ankle on the other knee and scratched his nose again. Finally, he said, "There was someone, once, but she's gone now."

"The lady with dark hair?"

"Yes, the lady with dark hair," he repeated. "She's not very happy with me these days."

"Don't be frightened."

"You think I'm frightened?"

Almira didn't answer his question but reassured him instead. "She loves you. That is all you need to know."

Chapter 9

May 1842

Rebecca, just back from shopping with Phebe, turned from the pegs where they'd hung their mantillas. She noticed Mary Gardiner seated majestically in Mrs. Bright's wing chair no less, surrounded by the girls of the boarding house, the youngest of whom sat adoringly at her feet.

"It's you!" Phebe cried as her sister rose. Amid the rustle of petticoats, the Gardiner girls flew into each other's arms. "My dear, dear sister."

They embraced and petted each other's hair until Mary lifted her face from Phebe's shoulder.

"You must be Miss Carvalho," Mary said in a soft but confident voice.

Rebecca inhaled sharply, for Mary's attention took her breath away. *She so resembles Almira*, she thought, taking in Mary's thick, lustrous brown hair and oval face. The resemblance was undeniable. It provoked in her the same flurry of butterflies as Almira so often had. But Mary Gardiner also seemed much more confident and more polished.

When searching Almira's gray eyes, it was always clear, to Rebecca, at least, that the modes and manners of polite society were new to her family — acquired through careful study and imitation. That fact lent to her endearing innocence.

By contrast, Mary Gardiner exuded a history of culture, accumulating generation upon generation into this perfectly formed example of *la femme ideale*.

"Phebe has told me so much about you," said Mary. She slid out of her sister's arms and kissed Rebecca's cheek. "You don't mind, do you? From Phebe's letters, it feels like I already know you so well."

"Me?" Rebecca said, touching her finger to her collar. "Why? I can't imagine what she could have told you?"

Never before had anyone, man or woman, so disoriented Rebecca. "I'll, I'll let y'all visit," she stuttered and fled to her room.

At six o'clock, everyone assembled at the dining table. Given the time of year, it was still daylight. Windows were open, shutters folded back, and strips of fly ribbon hung at strategic locations.

Changed and freshly powdered, Rebecca felt much refreshed as she took her usual seat. There were ten of them at the table. Mrs. Bright sat at the head, with teaching assistant Emily Wilcox opposite. The youngest girls, little Betty Wheeler from Vermont and the Skinner twins from Plattsburgh, all still children really, sat nearest Emily. Mary and Phebe Gardiner sat at Mrs. Bright's right hand, while Rebecca, followed by Susannah and Harriet, sat on her left.

Thanks were given, platters of meat, potatoes, and bread made their rounds. Once everyone had taken a few bites, Mrs. Bright offered a suggestion.

"Mary, since it concerns all academy students. Won't you tell everyone about the reasons for your visit?"

Mary put down her fork and incidental conversation ceased while she finished chewing the tiny piece of food in her mouth. Swallowing, she dabbed her lips with a napkin before speaking.

"Sister Scholars, if you are not already aware, members of the class year of 1841 are founding an association for graduates of the Albany Female Academy. It is the first such organization for women ever established. We call ourselves the 'Alumnae Association.' The term 'alumnae' is the proper word since 'alumni' indicates the masculine and 'alumnae' the feminine plural in Latin."

"My sister tells me," Phebe said, adding in another detail to the conversation, "it was our own Professor Horsford who brought this point of Latin grammar to the association's attention."

"Is that so?" said Mrs. Bright. "That is very astute of the professor. We thank the Lord for his guidance."

"Some of us," Mary continued, "feel that the ties of friendship and the pursuit of knowledge often fall by the wayside after graduation. We're hoping to reverse this by formalizing our connections."

Rebecca listened to Mary's voice, admiring its controlled modulation, even tone and practiced cadence. A flawless delivery. In comparison, the mindless prattle of others seemed but the buzzing of captive flies on paper.

"Mary," said Mrs. Bright, "do tell us about your special role."

"Hopefully, this isn't immodest," she said. "But I've been recognized as Poet Designate of our alumnae. As such, I shall be reciting a special poem of commemoration at Friday's ceremony."

"I can add sums all day," said Emily, "but my poetry simply fails to inspire. What advice would you offer?"

Mary gave the question consideration. "My answer is simple. Dip your pen in your heart and write. That is the only thing for it."

Amid sighs of agreement, Mrs. Bright murmured, "How true, how true."

"I'm so proud of my sister," said Phebe.

"We can all see why," Rebecca said, feeling her own pride in her relationship with the Gardiner girls. "It's truly an honor to have such a talented poet counted among us."

"That's so kind of you, Rebecca, but the honor is all God's. I write my poetry because I'm called to it. It's God's talent, and I am only his vessel."

Tildie took up the dinner plates, and Rose replaced them with cherry pie—Mrs. Bright's favorite. The conversation turned to the summer vacation. Susannah and the Skinner twins were excited to be returning to their Plattsburgh homes, and the Wheeler girl to her village in Vermont.

"Maybe," said Susannah, "I'll hear something about Almira whilst I'm up the lake. She doesn't live very far from me, you know."

"Yes," said the Skinner twins. "We liked Almira. She was nice. Why haven't we heard from her?"

There was an awkward silence. The older girls looked at their plates.

"I trust you will both be summering at Shelter Island?" said Mrs. Bright to the Gardiners, making a blatant attempt to move on from the tender subject.

"We will. Our Papa insists."

Susannah had a mischievous gleam in her eye. "Mary," she said, "I can think of one gentleman who'll be heartbroken to see you leave Albany."

Mary smiled modestly but said nothing. Meanwhile, Mrs. Bright reminded all the girls against idle gossip at the table.

"Rebecca, what about you?" asked Phebe. "Are you going back to Charleston?"

"No, my parents are hoping to spend a month or more at Saratoga Springs to escape the summer heat. If they do, I shall join them. But until such time, they wish I remain here."

"You would be all alone then," said Mary.

"I hope not, but, if so, I can't imagine a finer home to stay for the summer than this."

The card read:

> *The misses Mary and Phebe Gardiner request your*
> *presence for tea this evening. They will be happy to*
> *receive you at 8p.m. No prior response is necessary.*

The invitation was electrifying. Rebecca threw open her

trunk and bureau drawers searching for the perfect chemisette, the perfect lace collar, and the perfect cuffs. *But perfect for which dress?* She mustn't overdo it, but the Gardiners were elegant girls. To appear in a simple muslin frock might outrage their sensibilities, and rightly so.

"Tildie," she called from the top of the stairs, trying to be discreet and yet heard. "I need you right away."

Returning to her room, Rebecca surveyed the mess she'd made in such a short amount of time and felt helpless. Where to start?

"You called me, Miss Becca?"

"Oh, Tildie, I'm just so glad you're here. The Gardiner sisters have invited me for tea tonight. I need your help picking out something to wear."

Tildie wiped her hands with her apron. "Alright, Miss Becca, but Mrs. Bright's got me helping with tomorrow's supper."

"Do you think my blue silk would be too formal?"

"You're only going down the hallway, Miss Rebecca. Wear your green dress. That always looked nice on you."

Half an hour later, Rebecca, carrying a modest fan, made her way to the Gardiners' rooms as the parlor clock sounded.

Her tap on the door was answered by Phebe's voice. "Rebecca? *S'il vous plaît entrer.*"

She entered and Mary rose from her chair. Gliding over, she kissed her again. "What a lovely dress you're wearing."

"Why, thank you," said Rebecca through her blush. "You don't think it's *trop formelle*, do you?"

"Not at all." Mary took Rebecca by the elbow and guided her further into their sitting room. "Green is very becoming on you. Now, won't you sit and visit with us."

Phebe poured tea and offered her a tray of molasses cookies. Rebecca took one, bit off a piece no larger than her fingernail, and began the process of polite conversation. "Mary, have you been at your home on Shelter Island since graduating?"

Mary swallowed her sip of tea. "Yes, for a few weeks I was, but afterwards I went on to Providence as a guest of

Miss Lynch—our past governess with whom I stayed until coming here."

Phebe, who had taken a seat beside Rebecca on the settee, patted her arm. "You would adore Miss Lynch, I'm sure," she said with excitement. "She's accomplished in so many things." She turned to Mary. "My dear sister, wouldst thou not agree?"

Mary nodded. "Poetry, painting in oils, sculpture, the sciences. Aside from my sainted mother, it is she who taught me everything about being a lady."

The remark obscured more than it revealed, causing Rebecca to wonder if she'd been taught "everything" too.

"Rebecca, Phebe and I have a proposition for you," said Mary, as if calling a meeting to order. "At yesterday's dinner you said you might remain here in Albany all summer."

"Maybe. It all depends on whether my parents come to Saratoga."

"Well," said Mary. "We'd love you to stay with us at Abbey Manor, our home on Shelter Island."

"Yes," said Phebe. "Can you not stay with us and be our guest? Do, do."

Chapter 10

August 1972

At the New York Public Library, David saw Angela standing behind the circulation desk at the far end of the central reading room, or rather her long, black ponytail. He crossed the open space between them as quickly as he could without attracting attention. When she turned in his direction, he saw her speak to a coworker and exit the counter. He lengthened his stride and tried to catch up before she reached some area off limits to patrons.

"Angela, wait."

"Please, leave me alone," she said, keeping herself turned away from him.

There was something wrong. He didn't know what, but he was certain. "Look at me."

When Angela turned her face, he saw that her nose was crooked, and one side of her face bore signs of recent abrasions.

"My God! What happened to you?"

"I got mugged."

"What?"

"Yeah, walking home from the subway after work."

"What do you mean?"

"I mean two guys jumped me. They beat me up pretty bad—at least that's what the cops said. I don't actually remember that much."

David searched her expression.

"No, they didn't do what you're thinking," she said. "Evidently the cops got there before they had enough time."

An older librarian walked past and glared with disapproval.

"Look, I've got to get back to work."

"Can I see you when you get off?"

"I don't think so."

"Angie, c'mon. I'd really like to talk to you."

She looked down and away and exhaled.

"Please."

"Alright, I get off at 5:30. Wait for me by the employee's exit. You know the spot."

With a couple of hours to kill, David ducked into a bar and, not expecting them to have it, asked for slivovitz. To his surprise, the bartender nodded and placed a shot before him. He ordered a second and took them both to a booth, where he settled in with a copy of the New York Daily News.

He needed a drink, unnerved by the whole encounter with Angela. Poor kid, her bruised face and broken nose were painful to look at. God, he hated this city—the filth, the corruption, the crime, the way it hardened people. Even the song on the jukebox was threatening, sick and kind of evil.

At 5:30 he was waiting for her. "We could go to Fong's. Get something to eat."

"No, let's not do that. There must be someplace else. I don't want to slip into old habits."

"Right. Sure, I get it. There's a deli around the corner. I think they're still open."

Seated at a table, they placed their orders. Angela specified separate checks. For the first time, David could see her face fully in the bright diner lights.

"Those bruises must have hurt."

"You should have seen me ten days ago." She filled him in on the basic facts, but when their sandwiches were on the table, she changed the subject. "So, how's your ghost friend doing?"

"She's gone, mostly."

"Mostly," she said, hitching up one of her penciled eyebrows.

"Yeah, well, she has materialized a couple of times, but it's different. She's — don't laugh — doing a lot better."

"Oh really?" She took another bite of tuna salad sandwich. "Well, that's nice."

"You think I'm crazy," said David. "You think that was all bullshit."

"Something like that, yeah."

"Well, she was real. I actually found evidence that she was a real person who lived in the house, and in other places too."

"Okay, whatever you say." Angela set the tuna salad aside and lit a cigarette. David sensed the same skeptical vibe from her during their pre-break-up conversations six months ago.

"You don't believe me."

"Look, I don't know what to believe, except that this stuff is all pretty weird, and you were a whole lot more into this ghost chick than you were into me. So, you know, dead or alive it was a competition, and I lost."

The waitress stepped up, asking if she could get them anything else.

David, irked at having the momentum of the conversation interrupted, said, "Not right now. We're fine."

There was an awkward silence. To get their talk rolling again, he said, "How's your dissertation on Poe coming?"

It's not," she said with a snort. "Not very well anyway."

"Angela. Do you remember once telling me that I couldn't believe in ghosts and not believe in God? That I couldn't have it both ways? Do you remember that?"

Rather than comment she slumped back into the booth.

"Well, in any case, you were right. But it applies to you, too. You can't believe in God and not believe in ghosts, or at least be open to some kind of spirit existence— whatever you want to call it."

She put out her cigarette in the coleslaw. The butt sizzled for a second.

"Well," said Angela. "I don't believe in either anymore, so it's a moot point, isn't it?"

Finding a comeback to that wasn't easy, so he said something trite. "It's been a lousy year for you."

"Yeah, you could say that." Angela drew another cigarette from the hard pack in her purse. "But it could be worse, right? Like my brother—he stepped on a landmine."

"He wasn't—"

"Killed? No, but he's pretty messed up." Angela finished her Coke. "Look, let's not talk about it, alright?"

He took a drink of iced tea, thinking it might cleanse the conversation. "Where are you living now?"

"How did you know I moved?"

"I stopped by your old place a few weeks ago. I had some of your stuff. I thought you'd like to have it back, and maybe we could talk. Anyway, Tina told me you moved out."

"I'll bet she did."

David ignored her remark. "She said you moved out on bad terms."

"Oh, did she?" Angela blew smoke through her nose. "So, did you get in her pants?"

"C'mon. I know I'm a rat, but I'm not that bad."

"I'm sorry." She looked down. "I shouldn't have said that. If you haven't already noticed, I'm not myself these days. Everything bugs me. Everybody gets on my nerves. I feel like I hate everybody."

"What about me? Do you hate me too?"

"No," she said. "Actually, it's kind of nice to see you, even though I'm still mad at you."

"I'm sorry."

"Don't be. It's over and done with."

Chapter 11

June 1842

Rebecca lingered behind. Maybe Professor Horsford knew something about what had become of Almira and Daniel. After all, both gentlemen were involved with daguerreotypes.

"Professor," she said on approaching his desk. "Do you remember Almira Hamilton? She was a student here last fall."

"Almira Hamilton," said Horsford to himself. "Yes, I do recall her. Why do you ask?"

"I know that you were acquainted with her intended, Mr. Dwyer."

"Yes, Dwyer was employed by the studio. Mr. Cushman and I made him the gift of an old daguerreotype camera. A nice young man. Why do you ask?"

"Because Almira and Daniel have never been heard from. Not one of my letters has been answered, not even the littlest note."

Horsford tilted his head. "Come to think of it, I've heard nothing about Dwyer either. Perhaps I ought to have inquired after them. Since the death of my dear friend Cushman, I've disengaged from daguerreotyping." He stroked his chin, mulling something in his mind. "Of course. It does seem a bit odd. Perhaps we shall receive word of the young couple this summer. Is there anything else?"

His words brought her audience to an abrupt end. "I'm sorry, professor. I apologize if I've disturbed you, and I do thank you kindly."

She turned, and was about to leave the room, when Horsford spoke again

"The studies did not come easily for her," he said, as if to call Rebecca back. "That happens sometimes when girls aren't ready for scholarship. They become discouraged, abandon the quest for knowledge, and leave for home."

She turned in his direction. "Do you believe, sir, that is what happened?"

"No," he said, and after another awkward silence added, "but I am confident that your friend and her gentleman are safe. Let us pray it is so."

Back in her room, Rebecca found their conversation disappointing. Horsford seemed disinterested. Or was it that he knew her to come from a family of slaveholders? Perhaps he knew she was a Jew and was predisposed against her on that account. It was impossible to tell, but one or both of these circumstances sometimes complicated her intercourse with northerners. The old question reasserted itself — should she have listened to her parents and attended Madame Grelaud's in Philadelphia instead of coming here?

"Tildie, I have wonderful news. We've been asked to spend this summer with the Gardener sisters at their home."

"What? Where's that?"

"It's called Abbey Manor, on an island somewhere along the seacoast. I think it's a sort of plantation."

"Why we got to do this?" Tildie asked.

"Come on now. It'll be fun, and we won't have to stay in this ugly town."

"Don't think it's a good idea, Miss Rebecca."

"You're being silly. Whatever could be wrong with this?"

"Mrs. Bright, she says to me that since she got me and Rose both she wants to do big house cleaning this summer. If I'm gone, how's she gonna do that?"

"She can hire another girl and pay her just as she would you."

"What if I don't want to go? Why can't I stay here?"

"Tildie, don't get in such high dudgeon. It'll be a lovely time. We leave next week, so you'll have to see that our trunks are packed and ready."

Tildie cast about the room, making a show of attending to her mistress's things carelessly, muttering to herself. After the phrase "stupid plantation" was twice repeated, Rebecca lost her composure.

"If you don't stop your insolence, I swear I'll stop your allowance. What do you think of that?"

"That's alright. I got money of my own. I don't need no allowance from you."

"Very well," Rebecca shouted. "You stay here and do drudgery for Mrs. Bright if you want. I'll do nicely without you. The Gardiners have plenty of proper help."

Rebecca stormed across the room to her bureau,

yanked open a drawer, and took out a fresh chemise. "I'll just do for myself. It'll be good not having you around. You think it's so easy for me? Having to explain to all these Yankee girls why I have a Negro following me everywhere? Do you think it's easy? Well it isn't."

Tildie ran from the room in tears.

Rebecca threw herself on the settee, wearing the face of someone at the end of their patience. Phebe offered her a cup of tea.

When she declined, Mary blotted her pen and said, "Rebecca, you look in a state of nervous distraction. Does steamboat travel frighten you?"

"No. It's Tildie. I'm afraid my girl is being terribly unreasonable. She refuses to go with me to your home and cannot be persuaded. In recent months, she's become so incorrigible."

"But why ever would she object?" Phebe asked.

"She says that it would be a hardship on Mrs. Bright," said Rebecca. "But I think it's because she has formed an attachment."

"Attachment?" Mary said.

"Yes, DeGroot, the gentleman who maintains a Temperance House on Hudson Street. Phebe, you might remember him? Almira's cavalier, Daniel, boarded there. The bald fellow—he's a bit rough and ready, but I think honorable."

Phebe nodded in agreement and set down her teacup. "Yes, I've seen him come to the back door. He's the bald, chubby gent with whiskers, is he not?"

"That is him."

"There seems no need for concern," said Mary in a calm, conclusive voice. "Let your girl stay if her absence be a perturbance to Mrs. Bright."

"But nor can I be a burden on your family."

"Don't be silly. You won't be. We have plenty of help at Abbey Manor to attend you. It is settled. You'll stay with us at Shelter Island."

Chapter 12

August 1972

"Being in spirit is more like being alive than dead."

Almira's words only confused David more.

"Let me try again," she said. "I can well recall that in my physical life I viewed death as a passive, sleeping state, but in fact I've found one's perception is greatly sharpened. Imagine being alive, though in an unusually aware fashion.

In death I found a greater understanding. Somewhat like what one might expect having reached the top of a great promontory. I'm now able to see the span of my life, and the lives of others. The point is, whilst you live, you can yet change the course of tortured lives. Through your acts, sad lives can be made happier and selfish lives more generous."

Feeling like the identified patient, David moved forward on the settee before remembering it was poor form to come near to her. He quickly changed motion and settled back.

"See," he said, seized by the urge for self-revelation, "I'm the kind of person who feels more comfortable on the outside looking in. Do you think that's unhealthy?"

"Unhealthy to separate yourself from others?"

"Well, yes. Sure. I guess I just prefer to be apart. Alone with my things."

Almira walked to her trunk, knelt and opened it. "Here," she said with a sweep of her hand. "All my life might be represented by these things. But they are mere trifles, are they not? You can see that. You're an educated man, are you not?"

David nodded

"As a doctor, have you not the responsibility to help others?"

"Yes, of course, but it's—"

"Then you understand our common responsibility," Almira said, cutting his excuse short. "That is what God wants for us, and you can yet help God turn hell into heaven. Will you do it, or must you be bought?"

David took his ringing phone from the hook.

"Hello, Doctor Weis?"

"Yes, that's me."

"It's Maureen Todd, Doctor Koenigsberg's secretary."

He was glad to hear her voice. Maureen was always the bright spot in Koenigsberg's office—cheerful, freckled, ridiculously efficient, more than the perfect girl Friday, but she didn't sound right, she sounded upset and addled.

"It's after seven o'clock," he said. "Isn't it late for you to be working?"

"I'm calling with bad news. Doctor Koenigsberg

passed away."

"What? When? What happened?"

"This morning. He didn't come out of his office for a long time, and, well, I—" The voice on the other end of the line cracked.

"Maureen, are you okay?"

"I'm sorry," she said through sniffles. She blew her nose and went on. "Don't worry, I'm okay. Anyway, like I said, he didn't come out for a long while, and it was just too quiet in there, so I tapped on the door. When he didn't answer, I knocked harder, then opened it. At first, I thought he was sleeping. But when I saw that his cigarette had burned down to his fingers, well…I knew he was gone."

"Poor Doctor Koenigsberg. He was a real mensch."

"David, the weird thing was he had a smile on his face. You know Doctor Koenigsberg, he was a serious man, but he was smiling."

"My God."

"I know." Maureen cried freely now. "I'm sorry."

"Don't be. He meant a lot to both of us."

"No," she said, "it's more than that. Dr. K. was like a father to me. He saved my life." Maureen blew her nose again. "Nobody knows this, but back before you came to us, I'd only been working for him for a few weeks—I was in a really bad marriage. My husband used to get drunk and abusive. It was horrible. I had nowhere to go and nobody to turn to. I used to come into work with all this makeup on, trying to hide the bruises."

"Maureen, I never knew."

"Nobody did. So this one day Doctor K. asked me into his office. He started to talk to me. He asked me if something was wrong. Naturally I said everything was fine, which was a big lie of course. He said to me, Mrs. Fontana—that was my married name—he said, Mrs. Fontana, I think it is not so. Is there something you'd like to tell me? It was all in that German accent of his. So I spilled my guts. Doctor K. was so kind to me. He gave me his handkerchief and gave me one of his cigarettes. I remember I was shaking so bad he had to steady my hand so I could get a light from him."

David would never have suspected any of this. Maureen had always seemed so happy, sitting at her electric typewriter, in her sleeveless dresses. She would kick off her office shoes and sit barefoot behind her desk. As far as he knew, or could possibly have imagined, that was the extent of her secrets.

"Anyway, I told him everything," she said. "And at the end, he took out his personal checkbook. He wrote out a check payable to me. He put it in an envelope. He sealed it and slid it across his desk, and you know what he said? He said, Mrs. Fontana, this is three thousand dollars. I wish you to keep this in your desk. When you are ready to change your life, it is yours. A gift, you see. I must tell you though, we cannot have a receptionist who is a battered woman. It would be subliminally upsetting for our patients, many of whom are already in a distressed state of mind. Take a few months to think about this, but if things have not changed, you must take the check with you and find another place to work.

You know, I kept that check in my desk for ten weeks, and then I used it to hire a lawyer and get an apartment. I tried to pay him back, but he wouldn't let me."

Inside David, two emotions competed for primacy. One was pride in Koenigsberg's generosity, particularly at a time in his life when David knew him to have been a staunch atheist. What a privilege to have known such a supremely decent man. The other emotion embarrassed him. It was jealousy. David liked thinking that he and Koenigsberg had a unique relationship—like he'd been specially selected among those in Koenigsberg's professional circle. Koenigsberg was more than a mentor, he was a father figure. But hearing this story of Maureen's showed that he wasn't the only one. He now had to share that status with someone else—and who knew how many others?

She had more to say. "I have to tell you, this morning, when he came in, he said to me, Maureen, remind me to dictate a letter to David Weis this afternoon. There is something I wish him to know."

"Do you know what it was?"

"No, he never said, and when I checked on him next, it was too late," she said. "Anyway, there's a funeral service the day after tomorrow. I'm sorry it's such short notice, but I guess Jewish people don't believe in embalming." Maureen spoke again, sounding afraid of having offended him with the remark. "Don't mind me. You already know that of course."

He got the particulars and hung up the phone. David considered not attending. There would be a lot of people there he would rather not see. To his former colleagues, he would be like Lazarus back from the dead.

Chapter 13

June 1842

Professor Horsford was at his desk correcting papers. Rebecca tapped on the door jamb.

"Yes?" he said without looking up.

"I'm sorry to interrupt you, professor, but might I please speak to you for a moment?"

"If you're inquiring after Miss Hamilton and her young man," Horsford said. "I have yet heard nothing."

"It's not that, sir. It's something else." Rebecca hesitated. "It's a difficult thing, but Miss Phebe and Miss Mary told me I could trust in your utmost discretion."

At the mention of the Gardiner sisters, Horsford capped his mechanical pencil, rose from his chair, and closed the classroom door. "You may trust, miss, they've told you correctly. Do have a seat and believe me, your sincere confidant."

Rebecca went to a chair at one of the instruction tables.

Horsford joined her. "Now, what is your question?"

Rebecca mustered up her courage. "I am from South Carolina."

"I know you to be southern—your accent readily identifies you as a lady of that region."

"Is it that obvious now?"

"Forgive me," said Horsford. "I didn't mean to embarrass you. Your accent is charming."

"Perhaps it is. Yet not all my southern ways are so well received. This is why I have come to you."

Rebecca stalled, running a fingertip along the edge of the table, searching for the words to describe the most ordinary circumstance of her life, though one in which she never spoke of openly. "Very well," she finally said. "You are unlikely to know about this, but I have brought with me from Charleston my...servant-girl, my slave, if you prefer."

Horsford leaned back in his chair, crossed his legs and sniffed. "Please go on."

"Her name is Matilda—I've always called her Tildie. In any case, she was bought for me when I was just a little girl, to be my lifelong maid and companion. I hardly remember a time without her."

The professor re-crossed his legs, sniffed again, and spread the fingers of one hand across his raised knee. "And what, might I ask, has this to do with your visit this afternoon?"

Rebecca sensed disdain. It wasn't surprising. She'd often felt the sting of Yankee opinion since coming to Albany, but it was disappointing nonetheless, having hoped that the professor might hold his judgment until he'd heard her out.

"Do you know what should happen, were she to suddenly leave my service?"

"You mean run away," he corrected.

"Yes. I suppose one might call it that."

"Have you reason to believe she would, or that she is considering such an action?"

"Not really. And, of course, it's not the sort of thing I could ask her. We don't talk about such things with our people."

"No, I don't imagine you do," said Horsford. "Why are you concerned now?"

"There are two reasons, professor. Firstly, since we arrived here in Albany, my girl has been exposed to northern customs. They confuse her. She is a quadroon and easily mistaken for white. What in Charleston we call 'high yellow.'"

"High yellow?"

"Yes. It's a southern term, and I blush to use it. It means she hardly looks at all black."

"And the other reason?"

"The other reason is that Tildie has made the acquaintance of a local fellow — a white man."

"And," Horsford said. "You suspect they have developed an affection for each other.

"I surely do."

Horsford rubbed his temple. "You do understand that I cannot do anything to perpetuate another person's bondage."

"I understand that. It would be foolish of me to expect otherwise. But would you be so good as to investigate what the law is up here in the north, just in case she was to leave?"

During meals it was Mrs. Bright's habit to tap her spoon on the table if she wished to capture the attention of her boarders. So it was that evening, after the supper plates were replaced with those of cherry pie, she retrieved a piece of paper from her desk and sounded the call to order.

Being seated close by, Rebecca glanced at the six or seven items written there, in a bold hand, large for a woman.

"Girls, ladies. Over the coming days, most of you will be leaving for your summer vacations, and while I know traveling isn't a novelty to any of you, I feel there are some points worthy of reminder. Now do pay attention to this, especially you younger girls."

She paused until there was complete silence. "Firstly, whatever the conveyance be, traveling affords an easy display of character and breeding. A true lady will be known at once as genuine or simulated. Therefore, take care at all times to conduct yourselves in a way which reflects well on both our academy and your families."

"Yes, Mrs. Bright," they responded as if in class.

"Good," she said. "Now I want each of you to write clear forwarding directions and paste them to the ends of your baggage, in case some item be left behind."

"But Mrs. Bright," protested one of the Skinner twins, "won't that ruin our bandboxes?"

"Better ruined than lost," said Mrs. Bright. "Take a second trunk, and pack them within, lest you plague everyone with your paper boxes."

Emily volunteered to help the youngest girls prepare.

Mrs. Bright thanked her and took a bite of pie. She followed it with coffee, stirred it and took another, deeper drink. "Mary, you and your sister have been quite a bit on steamships. What would you have our younger sisters remember?"

The Gardiners glanced at each other. Mary spoke first. "Because there are persons of all classes aboard, one must remain aloof and self-possessed at all times."

"Quite true," said Mrs. Bright. "Though, this is essential in every situation, not only on steamboats."

"Also," Mary added, "my papa always told us that should there be some accident, we ought never to rush with a crowd to any one part of the boat."

"Yes," said Phebe. "By following the crowd, one is apt to become infected by their panic."

With the flick of her pencil, Mrs. Bright crossed out one of the items from her list. "Here's another thing," she said. "I believe all of you will be spending at least one night in the ladies' cabin of a steamboat. It is difficult for ladies of refinement to accomplish their toilet amongst strangers. I suggest you don't completely disrobe. Remove your outer garments, set them close to hand, and loosen your stays. If you sleep thus, should some accident take place, your natural helplessness as ladies will be greatly diminished."

Mrs. Bright looked around the table. "Do any of you have a last suggestion for those of us less experienced travelers?"

Rebecca spoke up. "There is one thing I can think of. It was a long way here from Charleston, on several different boats. I found that it was preferable to be among the second seating for dinner. That way there was no need to feel hurried or be part of the undignified scrambling for seats at the table."

"Truly," said Mary. "Who would not rather lose their dinner than their self-respect?"

Chapter 14

August 1972

With Koenigsberg gone, one of the few people he admired, David felt lost at sea.

Two months ago, he might have gone to his desk drawer for a valium, but David was trying not to do that anymore. Instead, he poured some slivovitz into a coffee mug, dropped in an ice cube, and went upstairs to the Quiet Room.

It was still daylight, so he wasn't expecting Almira, but the Quiet Room always calmed him. And if the phone rang, David could simply pretend he didn't hear it.

Sitting on the daybed, he thought about a fantasy he'd entertained recently in which he drove to the city, picked Koenigsberg up at his office, and brought him back to the house.

David would show him the buildings, the renovations and restorations. Impressed, Koenigsberg would clap David on the shoulder and say something like, "David, it is good you did this thing. *Ich bin sehr Stoltz auf Ihnen.*"

At least while that fantasy could have still happened, it kept him afloat during periods when the whole house restoration and antiques business seemed ill-conceived. Maybe his whole life was ill-conceived. Comparing it with that of the real-life Doctor Koenigsberg only stirred up those doubts which had been quiescent for a long while.

There was guilt too—a lot of it. David's mind lapsed into a review of his dead patient's last visit.

February 3rd, 1969. It was a three o'clock, Monday appointment.

David swallowed the last of the slivovitz. By now it was mostly meltwater anyway. He placed the mug on the floor and leaned forward, elbows on knees. His memory replayed the session. It was easy. He knew it by heart.

First, he looked up from his swivel chair. Cheryl Jankowsky stood in the doorway, dressed to the nines—heels, fishnet stockings and everything.

"Hi Cheryl, have a seat. How have you been since last week?"

Ignoring the question, she stepped across the office and placed a small white paper bag on his desk. "I know how much you like Chinese food, Doctor Weis, so I brought you an order of eggrolls."

"Thanks," he told her. "You know it's not necessary."

"I know," she said. Keeping her knees together, she lowered her bottom to the sofa and crossed her legs. "But it's not wrong for a girl to show appreciation, is it?"

In truth, David considered Jankowsky to be a tiresome manipulator. He was annoyed by her constant efforts to personalize the therapeutic relationship. Worse, several sessions back she had initiated a pattern of overt flirtation. The clinical term for this: 'being a tease.'

He started over. "How has your mood been?"

"Lousy."

"Last time we were talking about the events leading up to your arrest for assault."

"Were we?" She flicked a speck of lint from her shoulder. The gesture was theatrical and very effective. "Oh yeah," Jankowsky said, feigning a recovered memory. "I was upset. Who wouldn't be? That back-stabbing bitch."

"You felt betrayed?"

"Of course I felt betrayed. Wouldn't anybody?"

"Not necessarily, no. Is it possible that you contributed to that situation?"

Cheryl glared back. "No, it isn't."

The usual back and forth, back and forth repartee ensued. It was boring and, in his opinion, of limited therapeutic value.

"Alright," he told her. "What I'd like to know is, are there other ways you could have handled it?"

"I could have shot her."

David did think the comeback was funny, especially considering her conviction for assault with a deadly nail file.

"See, I made you smile, didn't I?"

"Come on, let's try to keep on track. Was there some other way you could have handled this?"

Cheryl took a moment to bask in her success of getting a reaction from him. "Maybe, I don't know."

"But it cost you your job."

"So what? I'll find another modeling job. I always

do. They were a bunch of two-faced shits at that agency anyway."

David thought he was back in charge, driving the session where he wanted it to go, when she crossed her legs again, tugged the hem of her skirt down her thigh to the top of her stockings, and started running her fingertips along the sofa cushion. It was quite distracting, her very long fingernails painted pale pink to match her heavy lipstick.

Cheryl looked up at him and seemed pleased to see she'd gotten his attention. She smiled with her sticky lips. "You know I had another dream about you."

Against his better judgment, David took the bait. "Would you like to talk about it?"

She did, of course. "Yeah, Doctor Weis, it was scary. I dreamt I was lost in this really bad neighborhood. These creepy guys were making lewd comments about me. I mean really raunchy stuff. One of them grabbed me by the elbow. I tried to get loose. They were all laughing. But I knew if I could find your office, you'd protect me."

One of Cheryl's high-heeled shoes dangled from her toe. David knew he should have interrupted the show, but instead he prompted her to go on.

"Yeah, David—is it okay to call you that?"

"It's probably better if we stick to the rules."

"I knew that's what you'd say. You're such a professional. I really like that."

Feeling the session slipping away, he said, "Let's get back to your dream."

Cheryl smiled. "Sure. I understand. You want me to get to the part with you in it, don't you?"

Outfoxed—she'd done it again, seized control.

"So," said Cheryl. "All of a sudden, the dream changed,

and we were together in my apartment. We were, you know, doing stuff."

"Cheryl, wait a minute. Before we go on, it's important you understand that the content of your dreams is symbolic. It's not me but what I represent that you were dreaming about—"

"I climaxed in my sleep," she said, cutting him off. "What do you think of that?"

David tried to ignore what she'd said but doubted that his face didn't betray him. He pushed on. "So the question is, since you don't actually know me, what is it I represent to you?"

From what he knew about Cheryl, she had a history of sexualizing all of her relationships with men, including her numerous therapists. Small wonder. Cheryl Jankowsky exuded sex like a lawn sprinkler. If David didn't have any ethics, he thought ruefully, he could have gotten away with murder.

"Doctor Weis, do you ever think about me when I'm not here?"

"No." It was a lie, so he tried to redirect the conversation. "Miss Jankowsky, I think you're splitting. Right now you see me as all good, but tomorrow you might see me as all bad."

"Do you ever think about me, when you're alone? At night, when you're lonely. Do you?"

"Stop it," Weis said sharply. Therapeutically speaking, he was never, ever supposed to let a patient get to him like that. Now, on top of it all she was crying—or pretending to anyway.

"C'mon, I'm sorry," he said. "But we've talked about this before. Your tendency to see all relationships in black and white terms—a victim, a villain, a rescuer—in reality, that's not the way it is. People aren't all good or bad, guilty or innocent for that matter."

Jankowsky wasn't having any of it. "I guess you're just not going to let me in, are you?" she said, with a long-suffering upward tilt of her face.

Borderlines and their histrionics. He reached for the appointment book. "Is next Monday at three o'clock still good for you?"

"Sure. Whatever you say." Cheryl got up and slung her bag over her shoulder. "You know, Doctor Weis, I'm different. You shouldn't ignore me. You'll be sorry," she said and walked out.

Those last words were seared into the soft tissue of his brain. The next time David heard Cheryl Jankowsky's name was when the detectives told him she was dead.

Chapter 15

June 1842

A few days later a carriage arrived to take Rebecca, the Gardiner sisters, and Mrs. Bright to the landing where their journey would begin. Already in the coach were two other academy girls—Charlotte Nichol and Eloise Hunting—who were also from Shelter Island or nearby. Something of a holiday atmosphere filled the morning. Even as they stepped out of the house, Charlotte hailed to them from the coach with a waving handkerchief. Everyone climbed in, but it took several minutes more to hand up or strap down baggage and start off with the usual lurch.

"Rebecca, is it true you're spending the summer at Abbey Manor," Eloise said to her.

"I surely am."

"Then we must all visit," Charlotte said. "Won't it be fun?"

Everyone agreed.

Reaching the Albany docks, the party found organized chaos. Dozens of ships, both steam and sail, were tied to the docks or navigating the river. Continual cries of recognition, goodbyes, shouting of orders, loading, unloading swirled about the scene, and amid it all, gangs of ragged children begged to handle baggage for a penny. Mrs. Bright dispensed a few cents to them with firm instructions to handle the girls' trunks with care.

They had only just boarded the Eureka when the whistle sounded, and the steamship engaged its paddlewheels.

Charlotte made an unnecessary show of excitement when the boat was well on its way. Mary and Phebe went below to the ladies' salon, and Rebecca found herself alone at the railing.

It felt like a rare privilege, and such it was, since being without an escort on city streets or public transportation was seldom acceptable for a lady of her age. She faced into the wind and admired the romantic Hudson River landscape. Lottie and Eloise came up to the railing and, like bookends, positioned themselves on either side. She didn't know them well, but well enough to know both were notorious gossips.

"Rebecca," Eloise said, standing to her left, "Where is your girl?"

"Tildie asked permission to stay and help Mrs. Bright for the summer," said Rebecca, who was immediately thrown another question from her right by Lottie.

"What kind of name is Carvalho? It sounds exotic."

"It's Portuguese," she said. "I'm from Charleston."

"That's what the other girls told us," Eloise said. "They all say you've never been north before. Can that really be true?"

Pivoting between her two inquisitors, Rebecca felt on display and very aware now that she'd been regarded as something of a curiosity at the academy. She chose her words carefully. "No, until coming to this academy, I've never left South Carolina."

"Well," said Lottie with a tisk, "all summer at Shelter Island. It won't be very exciting — not like New York." She leaned in closer. "But you're staying with the Gardiners. That ought to be interesting enough in itself."

Her secretive tone had Rebecca's attention snapping back to her in a dramatic gesture.

"Those poor lambs," she lamented. "With their mother taken from them at so young an age."

"Yes," said Lotttie. "Thank God Miss Lynch was already living at the manor and instructing the sisters. She was a great comfort to them."

"And their father," said Eloise. "There was a rumor that the following year, while Miss Lynch was teaching at Madame Grelaud's in Philadelphia, Mr. Gardiner proposed marriage."

"How bold of him." Lottie's eyes widened. "And that despite their great difference in age."

"Did you say Madame Grelaud's? My parents wanted to send me there," said Rebecca.

"Perhaps I still will."

"Miss Nichol, Miss Hunting," a stern voice said, interrupting the girls' conversation, "You're not engaging in idle talk about affairs which are no business of your own, are you?"

"No, ma'am. We wouldn't do that."

"Good," said Mrs. Bright. "I didn't think you would. Now move along."

Mrs. Bright took Lottie's place and leaned against the

rail. A lively breeze came blowing up the Hudson. "Miss Hunting and Miss Nichol sometimes forget to govern their tongues. I could see you were besieged and came to rescue you."

"I do appreciate it, ma'am."

"Rebecca, while I have the opportunity, let me also say that you are a credit to your race, in spite of those who would be ill disposed toward you on that account."

The words were blunt but offered the chance for a frank conversation.

"Mrs. Bright," said Rebecca. "Don't you think it strange that Almira and her cavalier have never been heard from?"

After some seconds, Mrs. Bright raised her attention from the rushing water to look directly in her eyes. "In some confidence, I will tell you that I knew more of Almira's particular dilemma than you may have thought — the poor girl. I can only assume her father sent her off somewhere, to relatives perhaps, and forbade her correspondence with anyone. It was all something of an embarrassment to the academy and, I might add to me personally."

Rebecca looked down and played with the ivory stem of her parasol, rolling it between her gloved fingers. She imagined Almira riding side by side with her lover, Daniel. The two of them would have been alone, exploring the most secluded and private lakeside coves on a midsummer's day. It must have been on one of these excursions, Rebecca surmised, that they dismounted and, in a place mossy and cool, allowed the heat of passion to consume them.

As predicted, Eloise and Charlotte's company grew

tiresome well before New York. At the city, Mrs. Bright saw them safely boarded on another steamship, this one intended to take a route for ports along the Connecticut shore before crossing to Long Island.

The steamship made its way up the East River and everyone gathered on deck to enjoy the close of a summer's day. Their enjoyment was short-lived, for once plying the waters of Long Island Sound the weather grew more threatening with each successive landfall. By suppertime, everyone was driven below decks and the meal was canceled. Few had any appetite in any case.

With the passengers confined to their quarters, there was little else to do but retire. Rebecca lay in her berth. Hours passed before she drifted off. Her rest was fitful and occupied by a peculiar dream. In it, Almira sat on a divan, sewing. The room wherein she sat was unremarkable except for a series of stenciled Grecian urns painted along the walls. On the chair across from her a man was seated. From his appearance — unkempt hair and shabby clothing — Rebecca took him to be a common laborer. His patterned shirt, without a cravat of any sort and open at the neck, was entirely inappropriate in the company of a lady, as were his worn and faded blue trousers. Certainly, he was no gentleman. Rebecca saw him writing on yellow paper. She tried to read what was written but her sleep was interrupted by the shrieks and prayers of other ladies.

Opening her eyes, she looked around. The vessel was pitching and yawing in a driving wind and pelting rain. Its hull shuddered and the paddlewheels were alternately submerged or exposed, causing its engine to whine or growl correspondingly.

So they passed the night. It was not until shortly after

sunrise, as their ship approached the easternmost tip of Long Island, that the storm subsided, making way for a fresh, sunlit day. Passengers filtered on deck, staring at each other with bleary and exhausted faces. All, that is, except Phebe. She greeted the morning with a cheerful, *"Bonjour."*

Chapter 16

September 1972

Awakened by a ringing phone, David looked at his illuminated alarm clock. It was nearly 3a.m.

"David, it's me," said a very familiar voice.

"Angela?" he asked. "Are you okay?"

"I don't know. I don't think so. I'm not sure."

David peered over his shoulder into the dark where the phlebotomist still slept. He decided to step into the bathroom and pull on the cord to shut the door behind him.

"What's going on?"

"Listen, this might sound weird, but can you come and get me? I can't stay here anymore."

"What's the matter?"

"I don't know. I just have to get away from here. I'm kind of freaking out, and I just don't know who else to call."

There was a rapping at the door. David pressed his

knuckles into his forehead. Of all the nights for Gail to sleep over, it had to be tonight. He placed his hand over the mouthpiece. "I'll be out in a second," he said over his shoulder.

"David, is there someone there with you?"

"No. Well, yes, a friend."

"I'm sorry. This was a bad idea," Angela said through the phone.

"No, no, it's not a bad idea. Listen, I'll be down as soon as I can. Give me a couple of hours to get things together here, okay?"

"Are you sure? I feel like I'm really causing a problem."

"You're not."

His announcement that the phlebotomist needed to go back to her place in Dannemora—tonight, yes, right now—left the woman in a snit. She slammed the car door on his apologies as the sun rose.

Ugh, nurses… It was just as well.

Following Angela's phone directions, David drove into Brooklyn, and then turned down a side street off Knickerbocker Avenue. It wasn't a great neighborhood, with run-down buildings and clusters of teenagers loitering on the corners—up to no good. The white Karmann Ghia looked too conspicuous as he locked it and stepped away.

At Angela's door, David hesitated before knocking. The background sound of an arguing couple from down the hall and a crying baby from somewhere else, left him hoping that he'd somehow gotten the address wrong.

"Who is it?" The voice sounded confrontational, but it was hers alright.

"It's me—David."

Two deadbolts turned, then the slide of a chain latch.

"God," he said when he saw the plastic cowl taped across the bridge of Angela's nose. "What the hell happened to you?"

She waved him in and immediately relocked the door. "They had to re-break my nose to straighten it."

"Are you okay?"

Angela shrugged. She already had a windbreaker on, and two bags packed. "Can we just go?"

"Sure." He picked up her bags and took a quick look around. The place looked gloomy with its buckling linoleum, woodwork hidden under countless layers of paint, a steam radiator, and in one corner fourteen volumes of *The Motorcar Girls*.

"I know," she said, reading his face. "It's a dump."

In minutes they were in the Ghia and out of Brooklyn on the Cross-Bronx Expressway.

"Shit." Angela frantically rummaged through her purse. "I'm out of cigarettes."

He pulled off the highway near Yonkers. She handed him ten dollars and asked David to buy her a carton of Virginia Slims. Even as he told her he would be right back she was slapping down the door locks.

He came back with the cigarettes and two cold cans of soda.

"What took you so long?" Angela said, tearing open the first carton.

"Here's your change."

"Keep it." She struck a match. "You'll need money for gas." Her trembling fingers fumbled with the pull-tab on the can as she tried to smoke the cigarette at the same time.

"Let me get that for you," he said.

"Sure, thanks."

They got back on the highway and Angela cracked the window on her side. She leaned her head against it and went quiet, smoking, sipping soda, with the plastic nose guard taped across her face.

Somewhere past Riverdale he noticed her wipe the back of her hand across her eye.

"What's the matter?"

"Nothing. Everything."

"Do you want me to pull over?"

"No, let's keep going."

About ten miles further, she'd fallen asleep. He pulled the burning cigarette from between her fingers.

David rose early to check on Angela in the spare bedroom. She was out. For a few seconds, he regarded her in that deepest sleep. It hurt to look at the bruises across the bridge of her nose, but she looked peaceful and calm.

Who was Angela anyway? A girl he met in a bar. One who could keep him up all night, but also liked reciting passages from her current favorite book. He loved that as much as the sex—maybe more. Maybe he could kiss her forehead without waking her up, if he was very, very careful.

In the kitchen, David made a pot of coffee and started scanning advertisements. Three cups and four newspapers later Angela wobbled past him, mumbling a "good morning."

Through the background sound of a flushing toilet and shower, he threw some frozen waffles in the toaster and started a fresh pot of coffee.

Later, at the table, Angela was in her bathrobe with fingers intertwined around her coffee mug. "God, I don't even remember us getting in last night."

"I'm not surprised. You were exhausted, strung out."

"Hey, David," she said, "thanks for coming and getting me yesterday."

"Don't mention it."

"But there's no, you know, expectations. We're just friends, right?"

"Right. And no, no expectations. It's nice to be around you again, but I'm kind of alarmed at how shook up you seemed when I got you."

"Yeah. Everything started to close in on me, like it used to years ago. I was going mental."

"Well, don't do that. Take a breather. Unpack your stuff. Get some rest. Take as long as you need."

Angela yawned. "I think I might even go back to bed."

"That sounds like a good idea. In the meantime, I have to take care of some things in the carriage house. If you need me, I'm out there."

Early in the afternoon, she found David bent over an antique contraption with lots of gears and cranks, cleaning it with a toothbrush and gasoline.

"Did you get some sleep? You look better," he said.

"I did. I must have slept another two hours." She stepped closer and pointed. "What's that you're working on? It looks like a coffee mill."

"You're right. I picked this up at an estate sale last week. It's got an 1868 patent date. Probably used in a general store. There was all kinds of crud in it, but once it's cleaned, it ought to be fine."

"What's it worth?"

"Hard to say. It would go nicely in the right bar or restaurant, as a showpiece. I don't have much in it, so we'll see what happens."

Back inside the house, Angela looked around. Whole sections of the building were refurbished. It looked like all the broken and cracked windows were fixed, and the crumbling plaster had been replaced with new panels of drywall.

David ran his hands across the white surface. "These walls…all along here…the plaster had to be ripped out."

It was obvious David took pride in the improvements with the way he tried to explain every step and every detail.

"Anyhow, then I had to sheetrock it all. Gary down the road helped me. You remember him—he showed me how to spackle and run wiring. I'm kind of proud of how it came out."

"You should be. This looks really good, I mean it. What a difference."

"Thanks. It's nice to hear you say that. I worked my rear-end off in here over the summer, but it kind of kept my head together. Anyway, I agree, it is looking much better."

He took her upstairs where it became clear that except for the Quiet Room, which had a couple of small pieces of furniture added, he hadn't done much on that floor.

"What can I say," he said. "This is all costing a lot more in time and money than I expected."

Chapter 17

June 1842

"Papa!" cried the Gardiner sisters in unison as he descended the piazza steps.

He enfolded them both in his arms. They kissed his cheeks and directed their father's attention to Rebecca.

"Papa," said Phebe, "may I present Mademoiselle Carvalho of Charleston."

Rebecca took his measure. Tall and of a slim build, but handsome, with deep brown eyes and graying hair. His clothing was that of a thorough aristocrat—silk and broadcloth, with a black neck-stock concealing all but the collar tips and ruff of his shirt.

Mr. Gardiner enclosed her proffered hand in both of his. "Miss Carvalho, welcome to Abbey Manor. My daughters tell me you are to be our guest this summer, which pleases me greatly. Consider this your home while you're with us. I insist."

"Isaac," Mr. Gardiner said to the bronze-skinned

young man who'd driven the carriage in from the boathouse, "See that everyone's baggage is taken to their rooms."

They were joined by a small child in pantalettes. Mr. Gardiner reached down and took her hand.

"Fanny," he said, "I want you to meet Miss Carvalho. She attends the academy with your sisters and will be our guest this summer."

Fanny held up her doll by the neck. "Hello. This is Abbigail. We are pleased to meet you."

"Fanny, Abbigail, the pleasure is all mine, and please do call me Rebecca."

Though only two stories tall, Abbey Manor's imposing, stately building with massive, fortress-like chimneys was made to appear larger by its dormered windows along the mansard roof.

Inside, Abbey Manor was cool and dark. Rebecca was given a quick orientation of the ground floor, which included a kitchen, the drawing room, Mr. Gardiner's office, and Grandma L'Hommedieu's bedroom. Upstairs was a similar floor plan. Isaac placed her trunks in a bedroom up there, toward the back of the house.

"This was our governess's room when she lived with us," said Phebe.

"Miss Lynch, is that right?"

"Yes," Phebe said.

"She guided us through our *ingénue*. That is already five years since. She went on to teach in Philadelphia, but now lives in Providence."

"Was the instruction there to her standard?" Rebecca asked.

"Though one ought not to speak ill," said Mary, answering the question, "her letters to us suggested that the standard of education was inferior to our academy."

"Don't you remember," Phebe added, "one of her students thought The Reformation took place in the thirteenth century. Unimaginable."

"The Doyle girls will get you anything you need," said Phebe as she and her sister left the room.

Alone, Rebecca stepped up to her leather trunk and crouched before it. She had bought this one with her father just before coming to Albany. Unlocking it with a tiny key, she lifted the heavy brass latch.

The upper portion of her trunk was made up as a personal cabinet, held in place with two metal slides, each fitted with tooled leather tabs. A portrait of a young maiden dressed in the fashion of chivalry, Rebecca supposed, adorned the front panel. She had flowers in her hair and ones that overflowed from the basket on her elbow. From the one in her hand, she breathed its summery fragrance. It was all done with a lot of pale blue and pink.

Looking at her trunk and all its contents ignited homesickness in Rebecca. She longed to hear someone speak in a southern accent. Yankees didn't understand how important elocution was. If they were more attentive to this, they wouldn't so often sound nasal and harsh. *Yes, a well delivered southern accent would be as music just about now, but particularly if spoken by someone from Charleston.*

Rebecca unhooked her dress and stepped out of it. Since the hem had gotten a bit wet on the steamboat, she was relieved to find no sign of a stain. She turned the dress inside out, folded it carefully, and placed it in the trunk.

At the dressing table Rebecca picked up the pitcher and poured some water into a bowl. She wetted a small towel, applied some soap, and scrubbed the day from her hands and face. After wringing out the cloth, she rinsed it, added more soap and water, and washed her face again, before continuing on to her neck and bare shoulders. It was refreshing to get rid of the soot of the steamboat. With her third application, she washed under her arms and swiped with rosewater.

She was toweling dry when a tap came to the door. It was one of the chambermaids.

"I'm sorry to disturb you, miss," she said with a distinct, if not quite identifiable brogue. "Miss Mary instructed me to bring you this bowl of fruit."

"Thank you kindly. You may place it on that table by the bed."

"Very good, miss," said the maid. She volunteered to return with a fresh pitcher and bowl.

"Not just yet, please," Rebecca said. "I'd like to nap a little bit."

"Of course, miss. I'll bring it later." She curtseyed and turned to leave but Rebecca stopped her.

"There is one thing before you go—your help to loosen my stays would be very welcome."

"Certainly, miss."

As she would have done with Tildie, Rebecca sat on the edge of the mattress and presented her back. As the laces were loosened, she sighed with relief and flexed her shoulders.

Then, without being asked, the maid knelt at her feet, unlaced her shoes and pulled them off. Rebecca was touched. It was a level of attention which Tildie had grown neglectful of in recent months.

"Thank you. I'm afraid I've forgotten your name."

"Bridget, miss. And my sister is Maureen."

"Thank you, Bridget."

"If there's nothing else, miss, I'll leave you to your nap."

Once more alone, Rebecca sat motionless in contemplation. Bridget and Maureen. Irish names. But whether Irish, English, or Scottish, one couldn't always tell one from another. Then there were the humorless Dutch, of which in Albany there were many. Whatever they were, these gentiles all had pasty complexions and, in her opinion, poor appreciation of food.

Being tired, these thoughts soured her mood. She climbed onto the bed and lay down. For the first time in a long time, she missed her family. For all she knew there wasn't a synagogue or another Jew between here and Charleston.

Thank goodness the Gardiners were so accepting, and they had some colored servants too, which made her feel at home. In fact, she had already noticed there were quite a few colored people on Shelter Island, perhaps every fourth person or more. Tildie would have felt at home here too. Pity she didn't come along.

Chapter 18

September 1972

It wasn't until the next day that Angela seemed anything like herself. Really, it was a bit like having a psychiatric patient in the house. David watched her closely, taking note of neurotic behaviors like smoking, scratching, and facial tension.

He always needed something at the hardware store, so they took a trip into Willsboro. In the evening, he fired up the hibachi. She prepared a salad.

"What are you reading these days?" she asked while wiping off the table. "You're always reading something."

Once assured Angela wouldn't laugh, he told her. "A book called Facts in Mesmerism—With Reasons for a Dispassionate Inquiry Into It. It was written by a guy named Chauncy Townshend, published in 1840."

"Sometimes I think you have a rolodex in your brain. But really, it does sound cool. Isn't Mesmerism an early term for hypnosis?"

"Exactly. I found it in a collection of similar books on the top shelf of the bookcase—all the way at the back. Apparently, the guy who owned this place had an interest in Mesmerism, Spiritualism, that sort of thing."

Afterwards they took cups of coffee to the living room. Unlike much of the house, it was very functional—nothing antique, just comfortable and sturdy furniture.

Scanning her surroundings, Angela said, "I never thought I'd be glad to see this place again. But it is sort of nice to be here."

"Well, don't get carried away."

"C'mon, you know what I mean. This house is still spooky at night, but it's a lot better than it used to be."

"Are you saying that this place could grow on you?"

"I guess, sort of. Maybe. I don't know." Angela sank into his beat-up sofa. "Look. Do you remember us talking once? I had this idea that this place would make a great psychotherapy getaway, remember? Sort of a country inn for mentally ill people."

"A country inn for the mentally ill. That's great. You have a way of making it sound so inviting."

"No, really. You know it would," she said, insisting. "Being here is kind of like that for me right now. I can feel myself relaxing. Ever since the attack, my shit's been wound so tight it's not even funny. I get freaked out over everything."

"I hate to sound clinical," David said, "but what else?"

"Well, a lot of nights I can't sleep, and I'm probably smoking too much. More than I used to anyway. I swear, sometimes I think I'm having a nervous breakdown. What do you think?"

"The nervous part, sure. But a breakdown? No, you'd have to be borderline psychotic, or having delusions, hysterical, something on that scale." He was downplaying things. She might well have been on the verge of a breakdown but telling her that wouldn't have been therapeutically advisable. "What's going on for you is pretty normal. It's what they call a neurotic reaction to trauma."

"Yeah. Well, I don't like it."

"Then you can stay here until you feel better."

"Thanks. I appreciate the crash pad, but this house is still haunted by your lady friend, right?"

David folded his arms and leaned against the wall. "Technically, yes, but not entirely. And to be honest, she's not alone."

"What do you mean, not alone?"

"I mean that there's a place on the lake where she and her lover sometimes appear at night. You've been there before with me."

"So let me get this straight—there are two ghosts?" Angela drew a pair of fingers and counted on the tips of each in turn. "Jesus, David, now this place is even more haunted."

"Yes," he said. "But the difference is that she rarely appears in the house anymore. Only once or twice all year. I don't know if you're aware of this, but she used to appear almost every night."

"Okay." Angela swung her feet to the floor and threw up her hands in a gesture of surrender. "I need a cigarette. Have you seen my cigarettes? In fact, do you have any pot?"

David came away from the wall. "I think you left a little when you were here in February. But, in my opinion, this stuff tends to induce paranoid ideation. For a person in an anxious state, such as yourself, it could be antagonistic."

"Thank you, Doctor Freud. Don't get high much, do you?"

"You know it's not my thing."

"Well," she said, "it is mine. Tonight anyway."

He went to his desk and opened a drawer. "You're in luck," he said, taking out a black plastic film canister and a pack of rolling papers.

"Super. Have you got some matches?"

In the kitchen there were matches in the junk drawer, and since he kept a bottle of slivovitz in the freezer, he came back with a shot of his favorite alcohol too.

Cold slivovitz both burns and cools the throat. He liked that. Angela meanwhile sprinkled some marijuana into the folded paper, licked the gummed edge with the tip of her tongue, and rolled it all up into a tight white cylinder of surprisingly uniform circumference. She fan-tailed one end, put a match to the other, and the joint glowed orange as she sucked in the smoke.

"Here," she said, chin tucked in to keep it down while she held the joint out to him.

"Sure, why not," he said, though the hit he took was more for show, a gesture of solidarity.

"So, tell me about that skull head on your desk," she said with a nod in that direction.

"It's not a skull head, it's a Phrenology bust. I bought out an estate last summer. The head came from this guy's grandfather, who was a doctor way before the Civil War."

"Cool."

Her answer sounded disinterested, but David knew her better than that.

"You're right, it's very, very cool." David brought the Phrenology bust over and placed it on the coffee table, then sat beside her. "Essentially, Phrenology is an early nineteenth century science — well, pseudo-science. They believed that you could read a person's character by the bumps on their head. Their personality, intelligence, you name it."

Angela looked on, turned away and blew out smoke. Her eyes were already bloodshot and heavy lidded. "And what are these numbers written all over the top?"

Her question appealed to the pedagogic part of David's nature. "I'm glad you asked." He held up one index finger. "See, they believed that each of these areas corresponded to a particular emotion or function." He rotated the ceramic bust and pointed. "For example, this one here, number five, behind the ear, was labeled as 'combativeness.' A raised area or bump in the contour of the skull at this point indicated aggressivity or, in a more benign form, assertiveness. If the skull showed no prominence at all in area five, it would suggest a person was timid or even cowardly."

"What about this one?" She tapped an area with the point of her fingernail.

"Number four. That's adhesiveness. In other words, how sociable a person is. What we'd today call affiliation needs."

Angela rubbed a pair of fingertips across this region on David's head. "I knew it. You've got a divot there. You're deficient in that quality. No question about it, there's something to this Phrenology thing."

"Hey, I don't think that's fair. You're using the knowledge I've given you against me."

Angela laughed. They'd done this routine before. David sipped his slivovitz, trying to conceal the extent of the smile spreading across his face. How much he had missed her snarky attitude and the competitive banter it generated.

"Actually," he said, resuming his discourse, "even though Phrenology is discredited, it wasn't a completely crackpot idea. I mean, the recognition that certain functions are localized in particular parts of the brain is true. They just misattributed qualities of character to these areas, as opposed to say, motor functions, vision, stuff like that. And, of course, the thought that these qualities of character were reflected in the subtle bumps on the scalp was dead wrong."

"Well, I still think your skull head is cool."

Chapter 19

June 1842

After everyone had taken their naps, the sisters gave Rebecca a tour of the surrounding properties. Abbey Manor wasn't devoted to any one crop such as rice or cotton, but she could see it was still a plantation, with extensive orchards of peach and cherry trees, flocks of sheep, and large vegetable gardens.

Rebecca commented on the cherry pickers.

"They arrive every year at this time," Phebe said. "A whole clan of them from Connecticut, carrying their ladders and baskets with them."

But most impressive to Rebecca were the gardens of flowers and a charming, if mysterious, maze of boxwood hedges.

At 6:30, the Gardiner family assembled for their supper. Father Samuel took his place at the head of the table, and Grandma L'Hommedieu sat at the opposite end, with the sisters and Rebecca on either side.

One of the house girls served out portions, a blessing was said, and the meal began. Pleasant, but inconsequential conversation was made until interrupted by Grandma.

"Phebe tells me you are an Israelite."

The sisters froze but Rebecca took it in stride. "Yes, ma'am."

"And do not your people have a peculiar diet?"

"Some do, yes. But my family are reformed Jews. We are much less restrictive."

"Grandma." Phebe hurried to interject. "Rebecca is from Charleston. She tells me it is a lovely city."

"Are there many others of your persuasion in Charleston, more...Spaniards?"

"We Carvalhos' are Portuguese, ma'am. But yes, perhaps a few thousand."

"Indeed." The aged matriarch grumbled to herself.

"And we are thoroughly delighted to have you here as our guest this season at Abbey Manor," said Mr. Gardiner. His cheerful tone seemed determined to lighten the atmosphere. "You know, I've represented some fine gentlemen from South Carolina over the years. Did you know that your own Senator Calhoun has purchased a subscription to Mary's first book of poetry?"

"Papa, please," said Mary. "Rebecca may not find this of interest."

"No, I'm quite proud. Miss Carvalho, you didn't know that my daughter is having her first volume of poetry published?"

"Mary," Rebecca said, shaking her head, "we all knew you were a poet, but you never told me you were already a published authoress."

"I'm not really, not yet at least. But it is true that the

senator has purchased a subscription. I suspect Papa held him prisoner until he relented."

"Poppycock. It's true, Calhoun is a close acquaintance, but he also recognizes your talent."

"Really, Papa."

"What is the title of your new book?" Rebecca asked.

"I hope it doesn't offend modesty, but the title is, 'A Collection from the Prose and Poetical Writings of Mary L. Gardiner.'"

"The title is too short," said Grandma. "You should change it."

It being a delightful summer evening, the family afterwards gathered on the piazza where the girls were served lemonade. A small crystal glass of port wine was brought for Grandma, and a cigar and brandy for Mr. Gardiner. Casual chatter about relatives and local Shelter Islanders followed. Finding it difficult to participate, Rebecca asked Fanny if they might be joined by Abbigail.

The youngest member of the family sprang to her feet and scrambled up the staircase. Mr. Gardiner chuckled.

"I think you've just made a friend for life," he said.

Moments later, Fanny crashed through the door with her doll. "Abbigail says it was very nice of you to invite her. She's pleased to join us."

Rebecca took one of the tiny wooden hands between her fingers, noticing the articulated digits. The degree of Abbigail's details was impressive. A face finely painted, with wide-open blue eyes, rouged cheeks, and sweet red lips. Black human hair crowned her head, on which a fashionable cardboard bonnet was affixed. Her dress was made with all the attention required of full-sized clothing, complete with a matching pelisse and three petticoats.

"Papa brought her home to me from New York."

"Your Papa must love you very much," said Rebecca in a motherly way, propping the doll on her knee. "For Abbigail is surely the prettiest dolly I've ever seen."

"Abbigail's mommy is dead," said Fanny.

The girl's remark caused Rebecca to pause for a moment. "That must make her very sad."

Fanny shrugged. "Grandma says her mommy is in heaven now."

"Then it must be so," said Rebecca and kissed the girl's forehead.

In the background, birds called from the trees. Searching for the source, Rebecca noticed a nearby bed of shrubbery in blossom.

"Fanny, would you and Abbigail take me to see the flowers?" She stood and held out her hand. The girl took it and led her across the lawn to a hedge of rose bushes.

"My, my, aren't these beautiful?" Rebecca said. "Did you know my own daddy in Charleston keeps a garden of roses, every sort you can imagine, but this variety I don't think he has."

"Your papa grows roses?"

"He does. It is quite a passion with him."

Taking one in her hand, she stroked its petals. The gesture ignited the longing she felt for her vanished friend. Usually, Almira seemed far, far away, but at this moment she felt very near.

"Rebecca," said Fanny, interrupting her reverie, "who is that lady?"

"Who? What lady?"

Fanny held her doll tight to her chest and pointed.

"There. On that bench."

Rebecca directed her attention to the ornamental bench toward which the child was pointing. "I don't see anyone."

"She's sitting on the bench and watching us. Don't you see her?" Fanny turned her head up to Rebecca, searching for an explanation. When she looked back, she gasped. "Now she's gone. Who was she?"

"Fanny," said Rebecca, her heart racing. "What did the lady look like?"

"She was very pretty. She had dark hair like yours and Mary's."

"And what else?"

"She was wearing a pretty orange necklace."

Rebecca felt faint. *That was indeed her.* Dark hair and a coral necklace could only be Almira. Yes, she was near, hovering close in spirit form. If that were so, it could only mean one thing. *She is gone, deceased, dead.* Rebecca held the child tight until her tremors subsided.

It was some while before she suggested they go back to the house, where everyone was absorbed in their own amusements. Mr. Gardiner had his newspaper, and Grandma L'Hommedieu her Bible. Phebe had begun a new embroidery project, and Mary was lost in a poem. Rebecca sat with Fanny and Abbigail.

The summer evening shadows grew longer and gave way to twilight.

"Fanny," said Grandma. She grasped her cane. "Help me up and come with me. I wish you to read from the Bible while I prepare to retire. Goodnight, Miss Carvalho, girls, Gardiner."

After they had gone inside, Mr. Gardiner folded his newspaper and turned to Rebecca. "My late wife's mother is a highly opinionated woman, but don't let her frighten you. On the contrary, she likes you."

Mary and Phebe laughed. "She does. We can tell, even if you can't."

Chapter 20

September 1972

After breakfast David said, "Angie, last week Gary asked me to help him run some wiring in his basement. I hate to leave you alone, but I'm kind of obligated. It should only take two or three hours. You'll be alright, won't you?"

Of course, but once he was gone the building seemed very, very empty. This was Angela's first time alone at the house. It wasn't spooky, like after sundown, but still left her uneasy. A shower would help, and with David gone, it wouldn't be a problem if she used too much hot water.

When the water started running cold, she got out. Time spent examining her nose in the mirror showed the bruises were almost gone. A little make-up would cover most of them, so she applied foundation and powder, tweezed her eyebrows, and put on some shadow and eyeliner. Inspecting her work, she felt much better.

Dressed, Angela went into what David always called "the office," with its rows of built-in bookcases. She selected one volume titled 'Greek Revival: The Neoclassical Movement in Early American Architecture,' but the dry text and the big house with its silent, empty rooms wasn't conducive to concentration, so she put it back to find something lighter.

She began leafing through a stack of magazines in one corner. A few outdated copies of 'Time,' another more substantial magazine titled 'Antiques,' two issues of 'The Journal of Abnormal Psychology,' and, at the very bottom, a copy of 'Playboy.'

Here was a chance to indulge her curiosity unobserved. Angela flipped through the magazine, seeing images of successful men and beautiful young models, ads for cigarettes, expensive cars, and Dewar's Scotch, all promoting a hip lifestyle.

Nude, blonde, and busty, the centerfold smiled with porcelain-white teeth. So this was the competition. Something stirred inside her—jealousy, envy, and maybe even attraction.

Folding the playmate away, Angela was about to return the magazine to the shelf when she noticed typed pages inserted near the back cover. She took them out and read.

"Client: Almira V. Hamilton. DOB: November 16th, 1822."

These were his typed clinical experiences. He would object to her seeing this, but it was too late now, so she eased down on the sofa and continued. The typewritten pages told the story. The first encounters with an apparent ghost. His efforts to prove Almira did exist, and his need to satisfy himself that she wasn't all in his imagination.

The parts about David's changing clinical strategy were especially interesting. If she understood correctly, it evolved from conventional psychology to separation from God as the true cause of his client's suffering.

The story was a revelation. It called to mind her and David's deli conversation back in July. At the time she didn't appreciate his comments, but now, having read this paper, they made a lot more sense.

Final page — Diagnosis
Axis I Disorders:
Reactive Attachment Disorder.
Adjustment Disorder with Dissociative Features.
Axis II Disorders:
Spiritual Estrangement.

Laying the report on the cushion beside her, Angela tried to assimilate the psychological jargon. True, now she had expanded knowledge about David's psychotherapy with the ghost, and maybe David himself, more than he'd ever been willing to tell her. Yet somehow all these facts served to obscure what had previously seemed straightforward, comprehendible, and contained. Across the room, the Phrenology bust gazed back at her. Look at us, it seemed to say, aren't we a pair?

Maybe getting some fresh air would help. She grabbed her cigarettes and pulled on a windbreaker. "Gone for a walk by the lake," read the note she left on the kitchen table.

The lane brought her to a familiar clovered rise where she and David used to share picnics. Angela lit a cigarette and sat. Chin in hand, she looked out over the lake. Except for the drone of a distant outboard motor far out of sight, there wasn't the least sign of human activity.

In the past, this stillness would have been annoying to her, but not today. Nicotine and the rhythmic inhaling and exhaling of smoke settled her nerves.

She thought about David Weis. Who was he really? A psychologist? An antique dealer? A guy with no real religion, no family he seemed to care about, no friends he ever mentioned. A loner who always left her with the impression of chasing or being chased by something.

Whatever or whoever he was, he was irresistible. Not so much in a physical way, because he wasn't that handsome, but he had this driven quality. Even on his morose days, it was magnetic.

Her thoughts drifted back to that psychotherapy report. Almira Hamilton, David's ghost patient, didn't sound like a very happy person. These days, Angela didn't feel like a happy person either. The ghost's guilt, remorse, and anger over her mother seemed all too familiar.

The report was exactly what she would have expected David to write—an organized and comprehensive document—complete with whited-out, retyped corrections. Yet there was something missing, and intuition told her the omission was deliberate. The absent element became clear as day—there was no mention of infatuation with his client.

What was the attraction for him? Obviously it wasn't sex. Ironically, Angela had always thought that was the thing that kept him bound to her—her trump card, her guarantee, her secret weapon.

No, not sex, but something else. David liked fixing things, restoring things. Maybe Almira's attraction was that she was vulnerable, psychologically wounded, and needed to be fixed. But what did that say about her? Was she just another broken doll to him?

By now her cigarette had burned to the filter so she cuffed the butt, remembering how David made a face when she tossed one to the ground the last time they were there.

The sharp call of a bird drew her attention to an adjacent wooded lot. Angela was no Campfire Girl, but she did recognize it as a crow. The bird called again, this time more insistently. She stood and walked toward the trees. At her approach it cawed even more, its feathers shining blue-black amidst the foliage. Bobbing its head from side to side, the bird jumped to branches deeper within the trees.

She took a few steps further. Now at the edge of the wood, it was clear that a well-prepared trail led deeper into this little forest. Her curiosity captivated, she waited for her eyes to adjust before proceeding ahead. The crow called again.

A few yards further, Angela found herself standing at the edge of a small, enchanted clearing. A cathedral of green with a foliage canopy stood open at one end to Lake Champlain and the Vermont countryside beyond. At the opposite end was a tiny collection of gravestones surrounded by an iron fence. Perched atop the tallest was the crow, grooming its ruffled feathers. Another crow swooped in from the direction of the lake and joined it. Side by side, the birds looked at her, their black eyes gleaming with intelligence. They cooed and trilled to each other, low and affectionate, human-like.

Fascinated, Angela couldn't help but come closer and stand at the iron railing around the graves. The crows hopped from one stone to the other. One of them leaned forward, tail pointed upwards, and tapped its beak along the inscription on each tombstone.

It was the Hamilton family—parents, George and Gloriana, the three young children who passed within days of each other, and there, at the end, was David's patient, Almira.

Angela's eyes flashed back and forth between headstones. Comparing dates of births and deaths, she ran through a series of mental mathematics resulting in a sudden blow to the pit of her stomach. At the time of Gloriana Hamilton's death, Almira had been the same age Angela was when her own mother died, almost to the day.

A flood of repressed memories burst into her consciousness. The smell of disinfectants, the steady beep of medical apparatus. Hearing the words "inoperable and cancer." The sight of her mother's body withering away, skin hanging loose, eyes sunken and then vacant. She cried for three days, and then there was nothing, not even sadness.

She heard her brother's voice asking through his tears, "Why don't you ever cry about Mom anymore?"

"Because Mom's dead, that's why," she said at the time, her tone harsh. "She left us both, and crying won't bring her back so just shut up."

Angela hadn't thought about these things for a long time—years. Where was her brother now? In an army hospital somewhere in Vietnam. Her head swam so she laced her fingers through the iron fence for support.

The crows suddenly took flight, startling her.

Chapter 21

July 1842

On Sunday afternoon, the Gardiners went to church. Well attired, the father, Samuel, wore a tall silk stovepipe. The three daughters all wore lawn dresses, with new bonnets and gloves.

Grandma L'Hommedieu stayed at home. Her rheumatism was flaring up again. Rebecca volunteered to stay too. She would have felt out of place at a Christian church, even if a welcome guest.

The Gardiners stepped into an old-fashioned barouche driven by Isaac. At the last moment, Fanny thrust the doll into Rebecca's arms. Abbigail wanted to stay at home with Rebecca. The carriage went down the drive, flanked by cherry trees, as the doll waved goodbye.

"Grandmother L'Hommedieu," said Rebecca, tapping on the door at the end of the hallway.

"Who is it, who's there?"

"It's Rebecca. May I come in?"

After several seconds of silence, the old woman granted permission. Rebecca stepped into an austere, sparsely furnished room.

"I'm here to read with you from the Bible."

Grandma cocked her head. "You are? But you're an Israelite."

"I am, but our first book of Moses is, I think, the same as the Christian Old Testament. Wouldn't it be nice on this Sabbath if we read from it together?"

"Is that so?" Grandma said, sounding surprised. "That seems odd, but since it is the Bible, I don't see what harm could come of it."

"I should enjoy the chance to worship together, but do bring that chair closer, that I might better hear you," Grandma said, gesturing to the Bible on the table by her bed. Her thin hand had prominent blue veins, with almost translucent skin and was sprinkled with a few dark spots.

Rebecca took the Bible in hand. It was very old—older even than Grandma. "Where would you like me to begin?"

"Anywhere, child. It is all God's word."

And so Rebecca opened the book to no particular page and began reading. "This is the book of Exodus," she said, "the twenty-first chapter."

Grandma nodded, as if recognizing an old friend.

Rebecca cleared her throat and began to read. "'If he were married, then his wife shall go out with him. If his master has given him a wife, and she has borne him sons or daughters; the wife and her children shall be her master's, and he shall go out by himself. And if the servant shall plainly say, 'I love my master, my wife, and my children, I will not go out free:' then his master shall bring him unto the judges, he shall also bring him to the door, or unto the door post, and his master shall bore his ear through with an awl, and he shall serve him forever.'"

Grandma held up her hand. "Might I say this is a beautiful passage. Don't you agree?"

"I do agree," said Rebecca.

"Why?" Grandma asked.

"For a man to choose his family over freedom, he must love them very, very much."

Pleased, Grandma shifted in her bed and rapped on the wall. One of the maids appeared in the doorway. "I want a pot of tea with two cups," Grandma told the servant. "Cream and sugar the way I like it and bring us some pie too."

Rebecca resumed reading. A few minutes later Bridget brought in a tray of tea and apple pie. Obviously, Grandma had a sweet tooth.

She held out her hand to Rebecca. "Now give it to me, I shall read." Taking the Bible, she began. "If he take him another wife, her food, her raiment, and her duty of marriage shall he not diminish. And if he do not these three unto her, then shall she go out free without money."

Grandma took a noisy slurp of tea, a bite of pie, and passed the Bible back to Rebecca.

"These stories from the days of Moses are so old-fashioned," said Rebecca, wanting to distract herself from the last passage.

"So it may seem," said Grandma, "but all the situations of life are given here — if not in literal truth than in kind."

Yes, she was right. These were all the troubles of life, and so many of them were at play in Rebecca's life — gentiles and Jews, masters and slaves.

Grandma reached out for Rebecca's hand. "You look troubled, child. Are those tears I see in your eyes?"

Rebecca looked up. Someone at last could see her desperation. "I wish I had a grandmother like you," she said. "My grandmothers are both gone, and I'm so far from home."

"Then, child, I shall be your grandmother whilst you are here at Abbey Manor."

Rebecca squeezed the old lady's hand in both of hers and kissed it, though gnarled and bony. She wiped her eyes without letting go.

From that day forward, Grandma L'Hommedieu refused to eat anything which she believed would offend the rules of Jewish diet, a subject on which, in her own mind, she'd become quite an overnight authority.

Nearly dark, the last flare of daylight disappeared behind the western treetops and the mourning dove's sad call was replaced by the night song of the whippoorwill. Though the rest of the household had gone to bed, the three academy girls stayed on the porch, talking about the latest fashionable silhouette, Mary's not-so-secret admirer—Professor Horsford, and their academy classes.

"Rebecca, have you not a beau?" asked Mary.

Phebe jumped in. "Yes, wasn't Mr. Meade, the daguerreotyper, very taken with you?"

"I cannot say. Perhaps he was, but in any case, he is not of my background."

The sisters expressed in the most discreet way their sympathy for Rebecca's *situation*.

"Don't be sorry." Rebecca's thoughts flew back to Mr. Meade. His fawning manners had been no more appealing to her than the odor of his rancid hair oil. "I'm sure when I return to Charleston, Mother and Daddy will have a parade of suitors arranged for my inspection."

A cool, damp breeze began playing among the trees and across the piazza. Mary volunteered to prepare a pot of tea. When she left, Phebe got up and took the seat closer to her friend.

"I have an idea," she said. "Mary and I have been reading about Animal Magnetism. Its powers generate in the mesmerized a kind of supernatural vision. They call it 'clairvoyance'. Magnetism might be a way to find out where Almira is. What do you think?"

"In truth," said Rebecca. "I have begun to doubt Almira is among the living."

"What do you mean?"

"I haven't told you this, but the week before last I was at the hedge of roses with Fanny. She saw a figure — an apparition — sitting on the bench. It was only for a moment and then vanished. Fanny described Almira perfectly, right down to her coral necklace."

Phebe grew animated. "This is so stimulating. I fear I cannot bear to hear more."

"Cannot bear to hear what, dear sister?" said Mary, placing a tray with cups and a teapot on a nearby table.

"Mary, Rebecca and I have an idea."

As Rebecca looked on, Phebe explained. "While you were away last fall, there was a girl who lived with us at Mrs. Bright's. Her name was Almira Hamilton. She was a sweet girl, but very spirited. She and a very nice young Irish gentleman were terribly in love and, well…" Phebe hesitated.

"What your sister's trying to tell you is that she got in trouble. Only a few of us girls knew about it."

"Phebe," said Mary, "is this the girl you told me about,

the one who eloped?"

"That is her, yes."

"My Daddy in Charleston was going to underwrite a studio for them to make their miniatures, except they never arrived. They disappeared. I've been just worried to death about her, and now I know that the worst has taken place."

"What makes you think that?"

Rebecca related what happened with Fanny among the flowers. "It can only mean one thing," she said.

"But," said Phebe, "we cannot reject the chance she is communicating through her magnetic essence, yet still living."

Mary explained the idea. "Phebe may be right. All the leading authorities agree that the power of mesmerism transcends the boundaries of the physical world."

"Y'all mean that if one of us were..." Rebecca's voice stalled in search of the correct term.

"Magnetized?" Phebe said.

"Yes, if magnetized, one of us might be able to contact Almira, whether or not she yet lives?"

Chapter 22

September 1972

"**Tell me about her.** Who exactly was she?"

"Well," David said, "her name was Almira Hamilton. She was born in 1822. The daguerreotype of her that you're holding was probably taken in 1841. She died late that year, in December, as you know from her tombstone and from that memorial on the wall."

Angela glanced over her shoulder at the framed memorial on the wall, then stared hard at the daguerreotype. "She looks a little frightened if you ask me," she said without looking up. "What else do you know about her?"

"I know she attended the Albany Female Academy in the fall of that same year. Records there show tuition payments and a list of her classes, but it doesn't look like she ever graduated. It was a pretty exclusive girls' school at the time, sort of the Vassar of its day." David reached for the Wedgewood plate propped up on the mantel. "In fact, this is the school as it appeared at the time."

She handed back the daguerreotype and accepted the plate in return. "This school can't still be open?"

"Actually, it is. Sort of. They've moved, and they've changed their name to the Albany Academy for Girls, but yeah, it's the same institution. As a matter of fact, the old building is still standing, barely."

She looked up. "You've seen it?"

"I have. What a downer that was. It's condemned, and the columns are gone, but in its day it was known as the height of Greek revival architecture."

Angela smiled. "It's nice to see your fetish for the Neoclassical movement hasn't weakened."

"Are you making fun of me?"

"I wouldn't do that." Teasing, she poked him on the arm. "C'mon, show me more. This is interesting."

"Alright. In 1840 she was living here with her father and mother, and a house maid. According to her, this room and the little one adjacent were hers, which I think is why she only appears here and nowhere else in the house."

Angela returned the plate to the mantel and scanned the room.

"Okay, Mr. Professor, how does this all turn into a haunted house? There must be something that got it all started."

"Be patient, I'm getting there." He leaned against the fireplace. "Almira's mother died when she was about seventeen, then her father remarried a few months later."

"He didn't waste any time, did he?"

"That's exactly how she felt about it." David filled her in on the essentials of Almira and Daniel's story. Her questions encouraged his teacher mode, a role that suited him well. He removed a red leather book from the mantel. "In fact, this is an autograph book from her time there. I found it in her trunk."

They sat together on the daybed. She browsed through the blue, yellow, pink, and green pages, reading inscriptions here and there. "Hey, David, some of these girls were from out on Long Island. See, Hempstead, Sag Harbor…"

"Yep. Shelter Island too," David pointed to Phebe Gardiner's autograph.

"So, what happened?"

"Well, it's hard to say for sure, but basically she got pregnant by a hired man named Daniel. The two of them had this harebrained plan to elope by crossing Lake Champlain. They thought it was frozen but—" David stopped, still finding it difficult to put her death into words.

"But what?"

"They fell through the ice. He probably drowned right then and there."

"And what happened to her?"

"From what she told me it sounds like she died of exposure on the ice. She's kind of unclear about the details, but that's the indication anyway."

"My God, that's horrible, but it's kind of painfully romantic too."

"I know," he said. "It would make a great novel."

"It would. Somebody ought to write it."

"Yeah, but not me," David said. "I'm not a love story kind of guy."

Angela cocked her head. "You just don't like to think of yourself in those terms."

"No, that's what you want to believe, but you're wrong. Listen, I want to explain some things about me that are important for you to understand. For example— you've always thought it was a mistake for me to get out of psychology, but I can see now that my time as a psychotherapist was selfish. It was intended to give me the illusion of genuine interpersonal relationships by substituting some highly structured facsimile. The whole thing was dishonest at some fundamental level."

Angela looked like she wanted to comment but he gestured for her to hold her thought.

"There's more," he said. "I know myself well enough. I'm a single-minded guy. When I'm locked onto something, I don't like to be distracted from it by anyone or anything. Everything else becomes trivial and unimportant. That's not always good. I also keep people at arm's length. You've probably noticed that already."

"Sure I've noticed it. Anyone who knows you has, but why?"

"Well, I do it out of fear, and I disguise that fear as self-reliance—a belief that I can only count on myself. It's a defense strategy, and, except for the fact that it feels lonely sometimes, it usually works."

"David, what is it?" Angela reached out and took his hands in hers. "What are you so afraid of? What's wrong with you?"

"I don't even know."

"Couldn't you try to be more…open?"

He pulled his hands free. "No, I don't think you get it," he said, boring his index finger down into the cushion. "See, I'm not good at love relationships. I'm good at the obsessive part. The sex part, I excel at it. But the rest of it—the selfless part, the opening up and being vulnerable part, not so much. I have to work at it. It doesn't come naturally like it does for other people."

She reached out to him again. "But I would help you."

"Sure," David said, "you say that now, and I don't doubt you would, but you'll get sick of it. You'll lose your patience with me. Even if I don't fight it—and I can guarantee there's a part of me that will—a big part, but even if there wasn't, even then it won't come easy, because it's not natural for me. Not in the way that you want it to be."

"What way is that?"

"You know...kids, in-laws, holidays, baby talk."

Angela stared at him. He stared right back.

"You're looking at me like I'm some sort of freak," he said.

"Well, aren't you?"

"No, I'm not. I'm not a freak. It's who I am. I think the world is full of misery. Why would anyone bring an innocent baby into this cesspool?"

"That's just rhetoric," she said, waving him off. "You know that. Bringing children into the world is what we're put on earth to do. It's what God wants. It's his way of giving the world another chance. All this other stuff you're saying, it's all narcissistic double-talk."

She had him dead to rights. It was double-talk, it was narcissistic, and there wasn't any clear path to intellectually outmaneuver what she said. To one side sat Almira's trunk. Past Angela's shoulder was the window where the empty klismos chair stood. He then looked from his hands to Angela's body, her breasts, her waist, her belly. David came down from the daybed, kneeled before her and, with arms around her hips, buried his face in her lap. He would have crawled inside her womb if he could, just crawl inside and stay there.

"Poor man," Angela whispered, rubbing his temple with her fingertips. "You want to play your whole life, pursue what interests you, but that's not the way it is. God wants us to have children because every generation is a new chance to get it right."

Chapter 23

July 1842

Following a winding lane, Isaac drove the buggy that bounced its passengers just enough to delight them, until he brought their glee to a stop at a knoll overlooking the sea.

A servant girl, Isaac, and Fanny jumped to the ground, but the older girls waited until their chauffeur silently proffered his hand. Rebecca held her flat straw hat steady in the wind and looked about at the rolling countryside, the flock of sheep, and the unlimited ocean on which the tall masts of several sailing ships were in view.

"My word," she said, drawing in a deep, expansive breath. "Isn't this the loveliest place?"

"*Oui oui, tres magnifique,*" said Phebe.

Rebecca's turn to step down offered her a chance to look at Isaac closely for the first time. She guessed him to be about her age with a dark complexion and darker eyes. His black, very straight hair suggested to her a lineage of mixed blood.

Once he unloaded the picnic basket, the maid arranged its contents and a set of cushions upon a blanket. Mary, meanwhile, took charge of the kite, giving directions to Fanny. "Do exercise care, Sissy, the kite is delicate." Fanny nodded and the two started off toward the most open portion of the meadow.

All the while, that same steady, refreshing sea breeze blew in salt air from the east. Rebecca breathed in more, delighted to be away from Albany's coal smoke and incessant industry.

"Our instructress, Miss Lynch, first introduced us to the delight of having a proper tea party in nature," said Phebe. "It remains a regular habit of ours whenever the weather allows for it."

"Miss Phebe," said Isaac as he stepped up, "tide's out— If you ladies don't need nothing else, I'll go clamming."

Phebe nodded her assent and took Rebecca's arm, and the two strolled together across the meadow.

"Phebe, I had no idea. It's like you and Mary have a fairy tale kingdom all to your very selves."

"Yes, Shelter Island is lovely, though it can be terribly lonely too. Our ancestors, the Sylvesters, once owned it all. Phebe swept her gloved hand along the horizon and pointed to the southeast. "There you can see Gardiner's Island. As you may have guessed, they are our cousins." Phebe looked in the direction of her sisters, who were already some distance off, running now along the crest of the hill, leghorn hats thrown back on their shoulders, pulling the kite behind. Finally, catching the wind it became airborne. "It is good to see them frolic so— especially Mary."

Having returned to the picnic blanket, Phebe and

Rebecca settled themselves. The servant girl was soon pouring lemonade into pink luster cups printed with comic cartoons, the handles of which were only large enough to admit the thumb and forefinger.

Phebe held hers up. A man being pitched head over heels by a bull, with the motto, 'Effects of Teasing' written beneath.

"This is my favorite," she said. "Isn't it funny?"

"It surely is." Rebecca laughed and looked at her own. A costermonger pulling his cart and crying, 'Carrots and turnips ho!'

The pair heard Fanny's voice carried by the wind. Phebe took out her current embroidery project, a nearly finished petit point watch pocket. "Do you like it?" she said, holding it out for Rebecca to inspect. "It is to be a birthday gift for Mary."

"Why, it's just the prettiest thing."

"Yes, I thought so too. I saw the pattern in the Ladies' Book."

Pressing the small pouch to her bodice, Phebe demonstrated the arrangement. "See, she can pin it to her bosom and keep her new watch secure within."

As her friend threaded a needle and began stitching, Rebecca closed her eyes and inhaled deeply. The breeze smelled of seaweed, salt, and a hint of fish. The same fragrance she remembered from the coast of South Carolina, but now South Carolina seemed very far away.

Rebecca opened her eyes. The landscape had an isolated and forlorn beauty. In the distance, Mary Gardiner stood with her back to the wind, skirt and petticoats flapping about her legs, her attention fixed on the kite at the end of the tether. Phebe nodded in her sister's direction.

"When our mother passed it was horrible for us all, of course, but I think especially so for Mary. She wept for weeks—fell into an intractable depression of mind."

Rebecca sipped lemonade. "But," she said, putting down the teacup, "I trust she is now quite recovered?"

"I think not. You know my sister's thoughtful nature. From that day when our mother was taken from us, it was made only more so. That is when she began her constant writing of poems and stories, but they are all of them rather sad, don't you think?"

Rebecca kept her comment neutral but inwardly felt what Phebe said explained much. Glancing at Mary again, she wondered what thoughts were in her mind. There was certainly a sadness about her. Almira had it too—motherless daughters that they both were—though Almira kept hers concealed. Mary, by contrast, displayed hers to dramatic effect.

"And you?" Rebecca asked, redirecting her attention.

"I?" Phebe said. "I see no point in entertaining emotions which provoke sorrow. No, I devote myself to schoolwork. And for recreation, I have my sewing."

"Pardon me. I didn't mean to—"

"Intrude? Not the least," Phebe said, sounding cheerful. "I consider myself a scholar. I'm not like other girls who are always going on about their latest beaus and which gentleman fancies them. You know how it is."

"I surely do."

"Mary, on the other hand, is the dreamer of the family and always has been. She lives in her world of poetry and ideals, with her head in the clouds—very much, I should say, like the kite she is flying today."

Phebe's words repeated in Rebecca's mind. Picturesque Mary, standing in the wind, lost in her own inner world.

In the other direction, out on the tidal basin, Rebecca saw Fanny standing in water past her ankles, skirts and pantalets hitched up to her knees. The youngest sister, evidently now bored with kites, had joined Isaac digging for clams in the muck of the tidal pool with her bare feet. A flock of seagulls cried and hovered above them.

"And Fanny?" Rebecca asked. "What about her?"

"Fanny is still much a child. Mary serves as her mother now, which is all well in my opinion, since Grandma is growing infirm, and Mary is herself soothed by playing that role."

Phebe drew a skein of yellow silk from her basket, threaded a new needle, and resumed working. Minutes passed. Rebecca's thoughts drifted to Tildie back in Albany. What was she doing now? Some chore for Mrs. Bright or visiting with Jack DeGroot? The question of what Tildie did in her own time was occupying her mind more than ever.

"I'm glad you could be with us this season," said Phebe, apropos of nothing. "You are a lively companion. I like the company of persons who have active minds, open to all ideas. I think Professor Horsford is that way too."

"I agree," said Rebecca. "He is firm but just, and most excessively dignified."

Though the sisters observed the utmost discretion, the drama of Professor Horsford and Mary Gardiner was an open secret at the Albany Female Academy. The story was too romantic for any healthy girl to resist. Today however, Rebecca's interest was distracted.

"Phebe," she said, "tell me about Isaac. He is a servant of your family, is that right?"

"Yes, of course."

"But is he, how shall I say, a bondsman?"

"If you mean a slave? No. There hasn't been slavery in New York since, well, since before I was born anyway."

Phebe's matter-of-fact attitude was a relief to Rebecca, who'd learned to be cautious about the least reference to the subject among northerners.

By this time Mary had drawn in her kite and was walking back to the picnic, hand in hand with Fanny.

Inconspicuously, Phebe returned the watch pocket to her basket and closed the lid. "Sissy, I hope you have thoroughly washed your feet."

"Fanny's feet are quite clean," Mary assured her sister as she reached the blanket and threw herself down upon an unoccupied cushion. Her voice sounded a bit breathless, and her face was flushed with exertion. Drawn to her radiance, Rebecca inwardly acknowledged the desire to kiss her cheek.

"I so love flying the kite," Mary said, facing the open sky. "You should both have tried it. If you had, you'd feel as exhilarated as I do."

All seated on cushions now, they were served lemonade and sandwiches cut into dainty triangles.

Mary took a small notebook from her pocket, and having licked the tip of a pencil, began writing. Every so often she would pause, twist a ringlet around one finger, and then resume jotting down her thoughts.

All this, Rebecca watched closely. In truth, she wished they were alone, that, like her notebook, she could be held by Mary and have her undivided attention.

Phebe chided her sister. "Mary, thou art quite ignoring our guest. You must either share thy writing with us or leave it for later."

"Please, don't feel obliged to stop. I'm not one itty bit

bothered."

Mary lifted her face from the page. "I don't mind. It's the idea for a new poem. The inspiration came to me whilst flying the kite."

"Very well then. Out with it," said Phebe, demanding in mock indignation.

"Alright. This is from a poem I call, 'My Native Isle.'" Assuming a posture reminiscent of standing in class to recite, Mary straightened her back and spoke.

> But when against the tide of years
> This heart has ceased to beat,
> Where the green weeping-willows bend
> I fain would go to rest.
> Where waters chant, and winds may sweep
> Above my peaceful breast.

"My," said Rebecca. "It's beautiful, yet sad too."

"But don't you think beauty is inherently sad," said Mary. "And sadness inherently beautiful."

Chapter 24

September 1972

"David, is that Chinese place still in business?"

"You mean Triple A? Sure. In fact, there's a rumor they were expecting us tonight."

"Super." Angela jumped to her feet. "I'll get ready."

She marched out from the spare bedroom a few minutes later. Overdressed, in a New York City kind of way, with make-up, lashes, and an embroidered peasant blouse with enormous sleeves, belted at the waist. She also wore one of those new maxi skirts and knee-high lace-up boots with oversized heels. A citified, hippy-chic outfit, but Angela had the brio to pull it off.

"Wow, those are some serious boots. Are we going to dinner in a combat zone?"

"What? You don't like them?" she said, looking down from her shoulder at one lifted heel. "I got these on sale."

"No, they're very nice."

On the way to Plattsburgh Angela seemed a little hypo, as they used to say. Her flamboyant outfit, her running commentary about everything—people at work, these new digital watches (she didn't like them), the Hunter S. Thompson book (he should read it), and her stalled dissertation on Poe (she had new ideas she was dying to tell him about).

The current ambiguity of their relationship felt awkward, but exciting too, kind of like a first date.

Angela suggested they go get a drink when they were done eating.

"It's on me," she said with grandiosity. "I owe you one."

"What's this place next door, Sonic Booms? A dance club?"

David tried to discourage the inquiry. "I don't know. Judging from the name, I think it caters to the Air Force crowd."

He was lying because he'd been there before, plenty of times. The first time was during the summer, after eating Chinese food in his car. Driven by loneliness, that's how he met the phlebotomist, who was at the bar, drinking alone. And that's the way it was until Angela called him to come get her in Brooklyn. But Angela was firing off questions about the club. She wasn't letting go. Without stirring suspicion, there was no talking her out of it, so in they went.

While ordering drinks Angela surveyed the crowd. "Man, you're right. It looks like most of the guys here are in the army."

A live band started tuning up. Covers of top-40 hits followed. When they launched into "Cry like a Baby," Angela put out her cigarette, sucked what remained of her drink through the tiny straw, and pulled David to his feet.

"Hey," she said, "these guys are pretty good. C'mon, let's go."

Somewhere during their third dance, a young soldier gestured to cut in. David shouted in Angela's ear that he'd get another round and find them a table.

Booms was crowded and it took some effort, but now he could relax, guarding Angela's stool and fresh Screwdriver, nursing his third—no, wait—fourth G&T.

Watching Angela on the dance floor, he reflected on who she was. He should know by now, but with her there was always another page to turn. In the past, girlfriends got annoying after you'd had them three or four times.

Maybe it was because Angela was a librarian, a literature person and most of those others were nurses. The abstract and intangible versus the biological and concrete. Maybe it was her sense of style, or humor, or her working class pragmatism. Whatever it was, he liked it.

When a mood like this hit her, she could go on for hours, wearing dance partners out one by one. He'd seen it on two or three occasions. The night they met was one example, and tonight was shaping up to be another.

Then the phlebotomist appeared. He looked away, but she was already coming over.

"Who's your new friend?" said Gail, perching herself on the empty bar stool.

"C'mon, don't make trouble."

"You're the one making trouble. This is our place. It's off limits, and you know it. You've got some nerve bringing her here."

Angela was already making her way from the dance floor, out of breath, face flushed. Great, David thought, she's in a hypomanic state already. This'll be like mixing ammonia and bleach.

"Hi," said Angela, sizing up the occupant on her stool. "You a friend of David's?"

"Angie this is—"

"Let's just say I'm an old flame," said the phlebotomist, cutting him off. "And you're obviously the new one. Well, you two have a ball. And Dave..." She turned her attention to him. "...if you want to play around, that's okay, just don't do it right in front of me."

"Huh?" Angela said.

"Well, gotta go. It was awfully nice to meet you. Bye-bye, Davey. Talley ho." She disappeared into the crowd.

Angela looked at him. "What was that?"

David shook his head. "Don't mind her," he said, circling his ear with a pointed finger. "She's... you know."

"It's okay. I get it."

It was hard to recapture their carefree spirit, so David and Angela finished their drinks and made to leave. On their way out he saw more trouble looming ahead. The phlebotomist stood by the doorway, drink in hand, chatting it up with the bouncer. He steeled himself for an awkward exit.

"Bye-bye, honey. See you next Tuesday," she said to Angela as they reached the door.

Angela turned on her heel. "What did you say?"

"You heard me."

Before he knew it, the phlebotomist's face was slapped, glass shattered, and a string of curses were spat.

When Gail howled and gripped her shin, the bouncer pushed David and Angela through the door with a warning that he was calling the police.

He pulled her into the night. The two ran to the Ghia and made their getaway. David turned out onto the main drag and gunned the engine. Angela started pumping her fist in the air.

"That felt great," she shouted. "I mean really, really great."

"Oh my God, look at your hand. I think you pulled out some of her hair."

Several strands of blonde hair dangled from between her fingers. Angela held them up like a trophy. "Me heap scalpum white squaw." She gave an Indian war whoop.

They both started laughing and she returned to her moment of glory. "Did you hear the way she screamed when I kicked her?"

"I did. It was unreal, just unreal," David said. "Where did you learn to fight like that?"

"At Catholic school. The nuns taught me."

"Oh, really?"

"You better believe it, so no more laughing at my boots."

A traffic light gave them the chance to take deeper, more controlled breaths, and recover.

"God, it feels good to laugh like that," said David, wiping his eyes. "My stomach hurts." Then he realized Angela was staring at him. How long had she been doing that?

She placed her hand on David's, which was itself resting on the knob of the gearshift between them.

In unspoken accordance, they leaned forward, first brushing their mouths past each other's, until cautiously pressing closed lips together. The scent of alcohol, cigarettes, sweat, and Chinese food was a strange but powerful aphrodisiac. By the time the light turned green, they'd fallen into an open-mouthed kiss, performed with mounting passion, until the driver behind them laid into his horn.

Chapter 25

July 1842

Rebecca awoke to the clap of thunder and spatter of rain. The time had come to learn Almira's fate. Mustering all her courage, she tied her wrapper on and peered into the hallway. A glow of lamplight flared from under Mary and Phebe's bedroom door. They were awake and waiting for her, so she tiptoed across the hall and tapped.

The latch clicked, and the door opened. Rebecca didn't expect to see Mary undressed, wearing her chemise and stockings, with her dark hair let down and braided. Her beauty was like the statues of antiquity — timeless.

"Come in," she said, taking her hand. "We were expecting you."

"Yes, Rebecca, I'm glad you're here," said Phebe from the bed. "Are you ready to try our experiment?"

"Tonight?" Rebecca's voice cracked.

"Yes, tonight, before we lose the romantic advantage of the storm."

Mary climbed back into bed and patted the coverlet. "But do first sit with us for a minute."

Rebecca stepped forward and sat at the foot.

"In preparation, we've been reviewing Townshend's *'Facts in Mesmerism.'* It was a book suggested to us by Miss Lynch," said Mary. "According to her letters, Animal Magnetism transcends the limitations of space. No doubt it could be a way for us to find your missing friend, Almira."

"No doubt," echoed Phebe.

"But what if the worst is true?" said Rebecca. "Can it transcend the limitations of life?"

Phebe, who seemed to be supervising the research, propped herself on her elbows and spoke. "That particular point is not so well established. Some of the experiments conducted by the French suggest it, but others, the British scientist's principle among them, dismiss the idea. As I see it, there is only one way to know for sure."

Thunder rumbled. The three exchanged glances in the lamplight.

"Mary, Phebe, have y'all ever tried this?"

"No, but Miss Lynch has." Mary reached to a nightstand and unfolded a letter written in a nervous hand. "Here, in her most recent missive she tells us, 'I am glad you are interested in Magnetism. I have had one or two subjects and performed some experiments more interesting than anything I ever witnessed.' So you see," Mary said, "all the best and most progressive minds are in agreement."

Rebecca touched her chin. In truth, she felt a little frightened. Conjuring spirits with Tildie hadn't gone well, and that was in Albany—a big city with a lot of people around. She didn't want to imagine what might go wrong with Animal Magnetism in this big dark house, on this very lonely island.

"Now, there's another thing, Rebecca," Phebe said with caution in her tone. "If we do this, we of course cannot tell Fanny anything. She will tell everyone, especially Grandma, and Grandma will say it's the devil's work."

"I won't make a peep," Rebecca promised.

More thunder.

Satisfied that everyone else was asleep, amid squalls of heavy rain and occasional gusts of wind, the girls ascended a narrow staircase to the garret. The sisters led Rebecca to an unoccupied room.

"Now it is for storage, but Phebe and I used this room when we were children," said Mary. She placed her lantern on a trunk. Its flame threw distorted shadows across the low, slanting ceiling and mismatched assembly of furniture. "As you can imagine, it made a cozy playhouse for us on winter days."

Startled by a thunderclap just above their heads, the girls jumped. Lightning flashed through the dormer window. Here on the third floor of Abbey Manor, with the wind roiling and the house creaking around them, they were within the storm not below it.

"Because Mary is a poet, I suggest it be she whom we mesmerize," said Phebe.

Rebecca agreed this was the most prudent approach to take. After all, Mary was the most sensitive. Phebe produced Townshend's book. When she found her spot, one finger went up straight as a cat's tail. "It says here that the person to be mesmerized should be in a relaxed state, seated or reclining." She suggested a nearby elbow chair. Mary agreed and produced a footstool from behind one of the trunks.

"Excellent," Phebe said and gestured for her sister to take up her position. "Now, you should close your eyes and make yourself comfortable."

Mary sat and wiggled in place, until her head lay back and hands rested on the arms of the chair.

Phebe flipped back and forth among the pages which explained the method of inducing somnambulism. "Good. Now I shall apply touch at the appropriate points to establish magnetic communication." She held the tips of Mary's thumbs between her fingers. "The book says that we are magnetically united when the temperature is the same in both of our hands." From behind Mary's chair, she touched three fingertips to each of her sister's temples. Mary's body twitched and shuddered. "The instructions tell us this is to align our magnetic fluids."

She began a series of stroking movements, but all without touching the body. Phebe's hands remained an inch or two removed from the surface and swept down from Mary's shoulders, along her arms to her fingertips. At the terminus, Phebe waved her hand as if shaking off water.

"This is called making passes," Phebe said. She repeated the movements, but this time down the torso and lower extremities.

A flash of lightning revealed Rebecca looking on from an old settee, clutching a handkerchief.

Over the next few minutes three complete passes were made to Mary's body, by which time her breathing had grown deeper. She inhaled heavily, if a bit noisily, then shuddered and went quiet. Her head bent downward.

"I think she is now fully mesmerized," whispered Phebe, taking a seat beside Rebecca. "We'll allow her magnetic halo to unify for a few minutes, and then we can start asking her questions."

"But she seems like she's asleep," said Rebecca. "Will she be able to answer us?"

"Yes. Mesmerists call it a state of sleep waking. Mary will hear our questions and be able to answer, for though her body sleeps, her mind is alert and free of her physical restraints. That is why I think she can answer questions she oughtn't ordinarily know."

"You mean questions about Almira?"

"Precisely. But since it is she and I who are magnetically united, please allow it to be me who asks the questions."

At Rebecca's nod, Phebe rose and approached her sister's recumbent body. "Mary," she said, "can you hear me?"

"Yes."

"Are you asleep?"

"Yes." Her voice sounded monotonous, detached, dissociated.

"We would like to ask you about a friend. Her name is Almira Hamilton. No one knows where she's gone. Can you see her?"

After this question, three or four minutes passed. Mary's breathing quickened. She blew out the air from her lungs and drew in more through her nostrils. "Yes, I see her."

"Can you describe the place where she is?"

"In a room," Mary said without emotion. "Her room, in her home. There are large vases all around her."

Phebe glanced in Rebecca's direction, hoping the odd description might have provided a clue, but Rebecca was equally puzzled.

"Ask where she is," mouthed Rebecca.

"Mary, this room Almira is in—where is it?"

Again, thunder rumbled.

"It is near water."

"Is it in Charleston?"

Mary shook her head. "No. Not Charleston. Somewhere else."

"And what is she doing?"

"Waiting."

In the tension of the moment, Rebecca half rose.

Phebe gestured for her to remain silent. "Mary, is Almira among the living?"

Several seconds passed before she spoke, though it seemed much longer. "I don't know," she said softly. "I only know she waits apart from our physical plane."

Another roll of thunder pealed, this one deeper and much closer, rattling the panes of glass in the dormer. Rebecca was starting to wish that they hadn't dabbled in Mesmerism.

Mary spoke again. This time the sound of her voice had a far-off quality, with a strange intonation, as it might if someone else were speaking through her.

"Help me, please," she pleaded. "Someone please, help me."

Rebecca recognized the voice. "Almira...Mirie, is that you?"

"Becca," the voice begged. "Help me, I'm so cold. I'm freezing. We're freezing."

When she smelled the scent of lavender, Rebecca flew across the room and knelt beside the armchair. "Mirie, where are you?"

Chapter 26

September 1972

"I brought you a cup of coffee," said a cheerful David early the next morning.

"I hope you threw a couple of aspirin in there too."

"No," he said. "But I'll get you some if you like. I'll be right back."

Returning with a fizzing glass of water, he found Angela had put on a bathrobe and was reaching for her hairbrush.

"Hey, forget that," David said. "Drink this. You look pretty hung over."

She swallowed the Alka-Seltzer in one long thirsty gulp, set the glass down, and thanked him.

Sitting on the bed with his own cup of coffee, David took a sip. "That was pretty wild last night."

"You mean us making out at the stop light, or me kicking that girl's ass?"

"Well, both. The whole thing—all of it."

"Maybe we should talk about this," she said, repositioning herself cross-legged on the mattress.

"I know, but it's a little scary. Do you want to go first?"

"Sure, why not." Angela took a drink of her coffee before starting. "Okay. It was wonderful being close with you again, but I don't want things to go back to how they were before."

"Me neither."

"David, I can't do this again. Maybe you're the kind of person who can have sex with me, be in love with someone else, whether they're dead or alive, and get it on with some other girl up here, but I can't. And I can't go around beating people up either. It's a bad habit."

David waved her off. "Don't worry about the girl at the bar. It's over, and it was never anything more than a physical thing anyway," he said, taking internal note of how easy it was to throw Gail overboard. "I don't even know much about her."

"And what about the ghost chick? Is that really over too? I mean, I know you couldn't ever physically cheat with her, but let's face it, you were in love with her in every other way."

"Yeah, there's truth to that," he said, surprising himself with how easy he admitted it. "I still love her in some way, but it's not an erotic love...it's different. She's showing me something profound."

"Profound? Like what?"

"Well...that there is a God, of some kind anyway. I feel like I was blind, and she opened my eyes to the biggest truth of all." Angela didn't say anything, so he went on. "Look, last summer, when we were in that diner you told me you didn't believe in God anymore. Did you mean it?"

Angela rested her chin in her hand. "I don't know." Her tone sounded glum. "Actually, I feel ashamed about having said that. So, the answer is no. I hope not, anyway."

"Things have happened to me and now I'm convinced there's something in control, whether or not I call it God."

"I'm listening," she said, drawing the blankets closer. "Tell me what happened."

"Okay, I haven't said anything about this, but last summer I had a pretty serious suicide attempt. I reached the conclusion that everything was meaningless. Our break-up was a part of it but my condition, if you want to call it that, is a lot older than that."

Angela extended her hand to him. David noticed there were scratches on her arm.

"It was more than an attempt, really, because if it weren't for Almira, I'd be at the bottom of the lake right now. But she saved me, and now she's teaching me why it was wrong for me to try to throw my life away."

"Are you telling me this ghost saved you from drowning? What happened?"

"It's stupid." He exhaled a long breath. "I took a bunch of valiums and swam out into the lake, way out there in the middle. I was tired, and getting sleepy, so I started floating on my back. And just as I started slipping under, I was moved by the beauty of the stars, the mountains, all of it, and I regretted what I'd done. But it was too late."

Angela looked up from his hands. "Then what happened?"

"The next thing I know, I'm on the shore next to my shoes and wallet. It felt like she'd deposited me there. And here I am."

"So, you want to keep meeting with her."

"Angie, it's like Almira's my spiritual mentor. She's giving me an education in what you always found wanting in me — some sort of belief. Please don't ask me to stop. Actually…" He hesitated. "…I'd like you to meet her."

"You're not putting me on?" Angela straightened. "You're serious?"

"Yes, I'm serious. Would you meet her if I could arrange it?" David ran his fingers through his hair. "Look, I don't even know if it's possible. I mean, it's not like just making an appointment, but I think it would be good. Would you be willing?"

"I don't know. I'll have to think about it."

David took her hand. "Look at you, you're all scuffed up." He kissed the scratches on her wrist.

When he looked up, Angela held his eyes for several seconds. "Would you like to keep doing that?"

"Yes."

"Me too," Angela said. "But these are the rules for me — kissing, but no sex. And by no sex, I mean no sex. Just kissing."

"No sex," he repeated, but his lips turned up into smile. "What about —"

"No," she interrupted. "Not that either. Just kissing."

"You're really serious."

"Yes. It's not that I don't want to do more. In fact, right now, sitting here together like this, there's nobody I'll ever want more than you. But only if it means all of you. So, for once, I'm going to try it the old-fashioned way. The other way hasn't exactly worked out well for me."

David scratched his chin, roughed up his mustache with thumb and forefinger, and then smoothed it down again. "And to make everything clear," he said, "we're not dating other people. Or are we?"

Angela opened his hand and turned it over, noticing callouses where David never had any during his days as a psychotherapist. Her fingertips glided across his palm, and when she pressed into it, a familiar desire stirred inside him.

"If it's no one but me," she said. "Then it's no one but you."

David scratched at the back of his head and blew out his cheeks. "It sounds crazy, but all right. Let's try it. We might have to increase the volume of kisses though. You know, to make up for the no-sex-part."

Angela's face blushed then blossomed into a grin. "See, that's what I like about you. You make me smile when I least expect it."

"Really, that's all? Nothing else?"

"No, there's other things. I like the way you kiss."

David leaned into her, and their lips met.

"There's other things too," she said after more kisses. She cupped her hands around his face. "You're smart, you hate sports, and you're thoughtful. Not in a considerate way, though. In fact, sometimes you're pretty selfish. The point is you give a lot of thought to things. I like that."

They kissed once more. Angela passed her lips across his face. "Let's keep the conversation going, baby," she whispered into his ear. "But right now, I need to take a shower."

"Sure. You get cleaned up, and I'll make us some breakfast. I taught myself to make oatmeal—how would that be?"

"Super."

"Will you take me back there?" Angela said from across the kitchen table.

"Where?"

"You know. The little graveyard by the lake."

He breathed in the scent of soap from her shower. She was all scrubbed now. Her skin looked healthy. He supposed *radiant* was the appropriate word. Classic Angela — gray CCNY sweatshirt, long black hair clipped at the nape of her neck, large dark eyes, expressive lips, very light make-up expertly applied. The bruises were gone, and after being reset her nose had a cute tilt it didn't have before. And somehow these new, immutable sexual boundaries had an appeal all their own.

"Sure. We can go back there today if you like."

So, after dumping the dishes in the sink, they dressed for the early autumn chill and, hand in hand, set off for the graveyard beside the clover hill.

"Wait a second," David said before they'd gone more than a few steps. "Maybe we should kiss first."

Chapter 27

August 1842

For the past few weeks Jack DeGroot would call at Mrs. Bright's every Sunday morning and squire Tildie to the Methodist church. If the weather was nice, they would afterwards walk in the park, but nice or not, Matilda and her gentleman always returned to the Temperance House. They would sit by the door, drinking coffee and greet boarders as they came and went.

On this Sabbath afternoon Jack saw one of his favorite boarders approaching. "Emmett," he said, rising to his feet. "I want you to meet my dear Matilda."

The old man held cap to chest and bowed. "I'm Emmett Sandborne, and it's a pleasure to meet you, miss."

Tildie received him demurely.

"Emmett," Jack said, "won't you take a chair, sit down for a minute? Visit with us."

Amid a chorus of creaking bones, old leather, and dry wood, Sandborne went to the elbow chair and sat.

"Tildie," said Jack, "Emmett here knew your mistress's friend Almira and her fellow Dwyer."

Sandborne's attention was instantly captured. "You knew them too?"

"Yes, sir, I did. My mistress—Miss Rebecca—she and Miss Almira were all boarding at Mrs. Bright's."

Jack enlarged the story. "They went to school together at the ladies' academy. Isn't that a coincidence?"

"Jack is right," she said. "I remember Miss Almira and Mr. Daniel too. My mistress, she's awful worried 'cause she never hears a word from them."

"You know that rascal Danny never wrote me from Charleston either, and he promised he would. It's odd." Jack lit his clay pipe with a long straw and asked Tildie if she'd please get them all coffee.

With a rustle of her starched Sunday petticoats, she got up and went to the kitchen.

Sandborne's head swam. If Daniel and Almira were spoken of, it amounted to a lie if he didn't divulge the truth to Jack, and one still greater every time he let the subject pass. The silence he'd held about their forbidden love made their secret rendezvous possible. If not for him the two might be living yet. The thought made his whole body tremble.

Jack reached back and retrieved one of several clay pipes resting on the fireplace mantel. Filling the bowl with tobacco, he broke off the last inch of the stem and offered the pipe to Sandborne, but he didn't take it.

"Emmett," he said, "what's the matter? You look like you've seen a ghost."

"I know the reason you have never received word from Daniel and Almira."

"Very well," Jack offered Sandborne the extra pipe again and this time he took it but didn't move to light it. "How do those children fare?"

"Daniel and Almira were more than just acquaintances of mine. Ever since he was a boy, he and I worked together for Almira's father. We all lived together at her home in Essex County."

Jack listened, pensively sucking on his pipe.

"Yes, before either of them came to Albany, I watched them grow up and fall in love with each other."

Jack nodded in agreement. "Those kids, they were like two peas in a pod."

"They indeed were," said Sandborne. "What a joy to see them together."

"But what has this to do with why they ain't never written?"

"Let me explain," Sandborne said. "I knew all about their intention to marry, go to Charleston, and start a daguerreotype studio. But Mr. Hamilton forbade it. When he took Almira back to Willsborough, Danny followed her. He had a plan for them to run away. He thought they could cross the frozen lake near Willsborough, at Thompson's Point. I warned Daniel it would be dangerous, the ice was too thin to risk, but he wouldn't listen…"

Jack's eyes blinked with anticipation. "Please, Emmett," he stammered, "you don't mean…."

"Yes, what you fear is so. Daniel fell through the ice and was drowned. And Miss Almira, she died out there on the lake. All this I know because I was among those who found her." Sandborne couldn't continue without shedding tears. He wiped them away with a handkerchief but still more came.

"It was my own knife we used to cut her free from

the ice. I helped carry her home. I tell you, she was like a statue."

Jack took the pipe from his mouth as his jaw dropped. "My God."

"I'm sorry. I should have told you long before now, I just couldn't bring myself to do it. Can you forgive me?"

Tildie came into the room carrying a tray of china cups. Her eyes darted from Jack to Sandborne, and back. "Jack, what's wrong?" she said, placing the tray on the table.

"Danny's dead," he mumbled. "Danny and his girl are both gone to Jesus."

"What do you mean? How d'you know this?" Tildie glanced at Sandborne, though in truth she'd known this was the case since the night Rebecca forced her to conjure.

Conjuring wasn't something white folks did, so she let it be. Besides, since Rebecca left for Shelter Island, Tildie lived the life of any white chambermaid. She and Jack went to a white church, they walked arm in arm through the parks and streets of Albany among other white couples, and though he knew she was a Negro slave, and she knew that he knew, they had an unspoken agreement to ignore this troublesome fact until life forced it upon them.

When Jack sat up again, Tildie wiped the tears from his cheek with her fingertips and kissed his bald head. "Poor man. Your heart is broken, ain't it?" She turned to Sandborne. "I had a feeling something bad happened. Miss Almira and her gentleman, the way they just disappeared, and nobody ever hear from them again... Lord, my mistress, she's not gonna like this, but she got to know."

"Then it must be *me* who tells her," Sandborne said.

Chapter 28

October 1972

The wind rustled autumn leaves loose from the trees overhead. Each one predicted an early change from fall to winter.

"It's beautiful here," Angela said, standing by the iron fence surrounding the cluster of lonely graves, "I have to admit it."

"I know," said David. "It really is. I only discovered it late last winter, when we weren't seeing each other. It was all completely overgrown, and the iron fencing needed a lot of work too. Some of the headstones were leaning over, especially that one on the end, but they're all straight now and looking pretty good."

"Do they come out here?"

"Almira and her lover? I don't know that for sure. I kind of think they must though."

"It's so peaceful," she said. "Do you ever come out here yourself?"

"Aside from keeping things weeded, sure. Sometimes I just need to get my head together. This is a good place to do that."

"Hey, there's a little rock on her gravestone." Angela pointed to Almira's marker.

"Yeah, I put it there."

Her puzzled look deserved an explanation.

"It's a Jewish thing," he said. "You put a stone on the grave to signify that someone's been there to pay their respects."

"I thought you didn't practice any religious stuff."

"I don't. It's more of a habit, I suppose. You know, you grow up with these things when you're a kid, and you might think they're gone, but they're not. They're still in you. Sometimes they come to the surface when you least expect them."

She slipped one arm around him and rubbed his shoulder with the other. "I think it's a sweet thing to do."

"Do you?"

"Yeah, I do." She bent, picked up a small rock and, reaching in as far as she could, placed it beside his.

Angela looked through the trees and across the lake. The stone bench was inviting, so she stepped away from the graves and took a seat. Strong breezes ruffled the branches overhead. She took a deep breath to smell the leaves and earth. "You know, it was pretty weird the way those crows seemed to lead me to this place. I mean it was like they knew what they were doing."

"Maybe they did," said David, joining her on the bench.

"The thing is, I was never scared. You'd think I'd be creeped out, but I wasn't. In fact, I felt—I don't know... protected. And all these things I hadn't thought about for years started running through my head."

David took her hand. "I'm just glad you left that note on the table. I would have never thought to look for you here. You had me scared, but here you were, sleeping like a baby."

"If I'd woken up any later, it would have been dark, and I'd have really freaked out."

"Well, all's well that ends well," he said with a peck to her cheek. "What do you say, shall we go back?"

On their way, while holding hands and wading through the first fallen leaves, Angela said, "I hate to say it, but I have to get back to the city."

"I know. I can take you back tomorrow if you want, but you know you can stay as long as you like."

"Thanks, but I was pushing things with the library to take this week off. They weren't crazy about it, believe me. But since it was surgery, they kind of had to give me the time. Hopefully, I'll still have a job when I get home."

He assured her the job was secure.

"So, what happens now?" Angela said, changing the subject. "With us, I mean? There's still some unsettled parts to this."

David nodded. "There are, yes. This is my suggestion — we're boyfriend and girlfriend, we kiss a lot, but we have this agreed-upon boundary where sex is concerned. We visit when we can and take things as they come. If it gets too much for either of us, emotionally or otherwise, we do something different."

"Thanks, baby, I appreciate it. Though I think it's harder on you than me — the rules, I mean."

"Look, I know that you've wanted for a long time to get married. I'm giving it a lot of thought, I really am. But it's only fair to you to say that it's unlikely I'll ever move back to the city. So, I'm thinking about marriage, but I want you to think about whether there's a life for you up here, okay?"

Angela stopped and looked around in all directions, to the barn and to the house beyond it. "I will. I'll give it some serious thought. Maybe peace and quiet is what I really need."

They kissed.

"There's one other thing," she said. "I understand your ghost better now, and really this Almira doesn't sound like a bad person, so...the answer is yes, I do want to meet her."

Chapter 29

August 1842

Late one afternoon, Phebe took Rebecca for a walk into the boxwood maze. Rebecca had seen such hedges before, but never more than a few feet tall. She knew boxwood grew slowly, so judging by their height, perhaps seven feet or more, she estimated these to be ancient.

Absorbed into a deeply shaded, cool, and green world, Phebe and Rebecca strolled through quiet and protected corridors of manicured boxwood, all of it too dense to see through and too tall to see over. As they proceeded, the turn of each corner revealed a new private world, with other plants like flowering alyssum and rose bushes accenting the pathway. Songbirds gathered in the upper reaches and at their feet humble crickets chirped.

After one or two more turns, the maze left Rebecca feeling dwarfed and miniaturized by the unusual scale and proportions. She twirled around and said, "My goodness, this is so enchanting and mysterious."

"Yes." Phebe smiled. "Those are exactly the words — enchanting and mysterious. I knew you would appreciate it as we do. This maze is one of our favorite places at Abbey Manor."

"What a pity Mary has felt indisposed since our experiment." Rebecca stepped back and pressed her leghorn hat to her head, looking up to see the strip of blue sky above. "I do hope she's getting better."

"Don't be concerned. We simply ignited one of Mary's nervous spells," said Phebe. "It will pass in a few days — they always do."

Rebecca nodded in support but didn't comment.

"You think I am a second fiddle to my sister, don't you?" Phebe said, her sudden outburst surprising Rebecca.

Not sure what to say, Rebecca made to politely change the subject, but Phebe stopped her.

"It's all right," she said. "I know it is so. People are captivated by Mary, ladies and gentlemen both. It's a power she exerts even on me, but as with all poets, there are also points where she falls into melancholy, much as did Coleridge and Shelly."

"Or Byron."

"Exactly, Lord Byron too. And at such times, Mary needs feminine support. With our mother gone, and our beloved Miss Lynch as well, it is I on whom that loving duty falls."

"What about your grandma?"

Phebe laughed. "As you may have noticed, our Grandma L'Hommedieu can be a bit prickly. She has little patience for Mary's recurrent episodes."

This wasn't entirely Rebecca's experience, but she thought it better not to dispute Grandma L'Hommedieu's reputation among the Gardiner family.

The two kept walking. They turned to the left, right, then immediately left again. Phebe introduced them to a small alcove furnished with a pair of mossy stone benches, encased by walls of boxwood. Taking a seat, she gestured for Rebecca to do the same.

"When we were children, this maze was our own private world," said Phebe. "We would play-act Mary's stories. On long summer days our papa let us bring a lamb to play with us."

"It's like a fairy world, isn't it?" Running her hand along the cool stone, Rebecca knew she'd been given access to a secret place, a sanctuary. She imagined that Mary and Phebe's habit of addressing each other with archaic pronouns could have begun here, a secret language for a secret place. "Were I a child," she said, "I'd hide here, where no one could find me."

The two sat for a few minutes longer. Rebecca spoke again. "Phebe, what you said earlier, about Mary having a magnetic quality—did you mean like Animal Magnetism?"

"Perhaps," Phebe said after some consideration. "Though, I think it more of a personal allure rather than our shared magnetic substance. Whatever it is, it is something I lack, at least in comparison to my sister." Phebe let her eyes wander over the tall walls of boxwood. "But I'm glad you raised the subject of Magnetism, Rebecca. Our experiment trying to reach Almira was very hard on Mary. I don't think she could well suffer another magnetic session."

Rebecca nodded in agreement. "I don't think so either. Honestly, I do apologize. Trying to contact Almira has been awfully frightening for everyone."

Phebe protested. "No, no, you don't understand. I'm convinced we should continue our investigation of Almira's fate through Animal Magnetism, but I propose that next time, instead of me mesmerizing Mary, you should place me into the mesmerized state."

"Are you serious? You want me to magnetize you?"

"I do."

Given their fascination with Magnetism, it was foolish to think the Gardiner sisters would abandon the quest for an answer through those means. Yet, the course of events left Rebecca reluctant to pursue the question further.

The girls took off their straw hats and fanned themselves. Though the height of the boxwood kept the maze cooler, the air was still close.

"Rebecca," said Phebe, "do you think Almira and her fruit were separated?"

"I cannot say. Everything about our dear friend remains a mystery."

"Perhaps there will be news when we return to Albany," said Phebe. "In the meantime, shall we retire to the manor?"

"Yes, I think it's time for my nap." Rebecca got up and placed her straw hat just so. "I am thoroughly disoriented. How ever don't you become lost?"

"Don't worry." Phebe laughed. "I could find my way through this maze blindfolded." She took Rebecca by the hand. "Come with me, dear friend, I will guide you."

With one surprising turn the spell was broken. Rebecca entered a shaft of sunlight flooding in through the maze entrance. Across the yard, Abbey Manor stood silent and massive, as the eclipsed sun surrounded it with a halo of light.

Chapter 30

October 1972

Once across the line into the Bronx, David noticed that Angela started chain smoking again. He blew past the exit for the bridge to Brooklyn.

"Where are you going?" she said. "You missed the turn off."

"I'm taking you to my place. I don't want you going back to that apartment."

"What do you mean?"

"I mean it's in a slum tenement, and the neighborhood's not safe, so for the time being I want you to stay at my place. I'll sleep on the sofa until you find a new apartment. This doesn't affect our agreement. I promise."

Angela didn't protest. A minute later she said, "Thanks. I was dreading going back there."

At his apartment, David apologized for the stale odor. "I'm sorry this place is such a mess. I don't do a very good job of keeping house, I know."

She looked around, stopping at his set of circular stained-glass windows salvaged from a condemned building propped against the opposite wall, the outermost featuring a portrait of Beethoven. Then she paused at the Art Nouveau birdbath, the walnut shaving mirror with delicate turned brass finials, and boxes of smaller antiques stacked everywhere. He cringed. It all needed a good dusting.

In the kitchenette, Angela checked the refrigerator and gasped. "Jesus, David, everything in here is moldy."

David stepped in from the bedroom. "Okay, there's clean sheets on the mattress and fresh towels in the bathroom." He glanced at the trash can Angela had dragged over to clean out the fridge and winced. "I'll go pick up some groceries, a bottle of wine, and a newspaper."

"That would be super. Why don't you bring back something to eat too? Whatever you feel like."

The next morning, they were up early, circling classified ads for studio apartments in some of Manhattan's safer neighborhoods, and by afternoon they had found a place that looked decent. She didn't have much, but with the Karmann Ghia, moving her things to the new apartment still took several trips.

At 1a.m., punch drunk and tired, they sat on her new floor, surrounded by boxes and eating a pizza. It was decided that he should leave tonight.

"But I hate to leave you in a state of chaos," he said.

Angela bit off a piece of crust. "Don't be," she said, chewing. "I'll get things put away. The thing is I feel pretty safe here. Thanks."

"Okay," David said. "Just to confirm, next time I see

Almira, I'll ask if we can meet with her. Is that right?"

"Could we meet with both of them at the same time?" Angela asked.

"You mean a ghost double date."

"Something like that."

On the way home, David switched off the radio. There wasn't anything on and driving at night was a good time to review the events since Angela's frantic phone call. One minute he's asleep with Phlebotomist Gail, sated and, frankly, worn out. But now Angela's living five minutes by subway from his Manhattan studio, they're an item again, and she wants to meet Almira.

One woman, Angela, wanted him completely— except for sex, the result of some new-found moral objection or some newly emerging hang-up. And Gail, the phlebotomist, who wanted nothing except for sex. Why couldn't the two merge into one woman? A highly intelligent sexual over-achiever.

His mind returned to the whole scene at Sonic Booms...

Man was that crazy. Gail was so aggressive. Maybe she had more emotion for him than she had let on.

Was this a mistake? Did he act hastily, misunderstand something important? He'd callously cast Gail aside for Angela, someone with whom he already had a record of failure. Was it because of the wounded parts that Angela usually kept hidden under layers of attitude? Though it was disturbing to acknowledge that quality was appealing. Gail had that wounded quality too, and over the years there had been others as well.

If he had stuck with Gail maybe she would have opened up more, become more three dimensional. Hadn't they been asleep at his place when Angela called? Maybe they would have shared the Quiet Room instead of some seedy motel. Now there would always be this nagging mystery about their aborted relationship. Thinking about it left him sad. David had an urge to call and talk to Gail, maybe meet her somewhere to apologize, or at least explain, or somehow leave off without feeling sore, but it was too late.

The weather was cold now, so David built a fire in the hearth of the Quiet Room. All afternoon and into the evening David felt mounting anxiety. It was familiar, having appeared and reappeared over the years, sometimes as the harbinger of one of his depressive episodes.

When he was a psychotherapist David would have stopped by Doctor Koenigsberg's office at a time like this. They would talk, maybe about one of the clients or maybe about nothing in particular, and for only a few minutes, but that would have grounded him.

Even after he left psychology and bought the house in Willsboro, it had been enough to know Koenigsberg was down there in the city at his desk, chain smoking with shirt cuffs folded back on his hairy forearms. But now Koenigsberg was gone, and that thought had lost its power.

In recent months, meeting with Almira was something of a substitute, though their conversations more often led to unfamiliar territory rather than back to what was calming.

He positioned the klismos chair before laying down on the daybed. He would wait for her to appear. Maybe tonight.

The clock downstairs struck 4a.m. When David opened his eyes the candles and lamps left unlighted were bright. Almira sat, quietly embroidering Daniel's suspenders.

"Good evening, doctor," she said, setting her needle and placing her work in the sewing basket at her side. "I thought you might like a visit. You've been brooding these few days since."

David sat up and rubbed the grogginess from his face. "I suppose so, yes."

"Won't you tell me what perturbs your mood?"

Almira's presumption of his cooperation was irritating. He didn't like it, but he also knew these were textbook signs of resistance to therapy. Was that how patients saw him — condescending, patronizing, assuming?

"You need not say anything now, doctor, if you are not ready," Almira said. "Was there perhaps some other thing?"

"As a matter of fact, yes. I have a lady friend, the dark-haired woman you have mentioned to me."

"You have been recently together, I think."

"Yes, I suppose you've sensed it. She would like us to meet with you, both of you, if possible. Could we do that?"

"Doctor Weis, this gratifies me. I should be so pleased to take a visit from you and your lady-friend. And though I cannot speak for my husband, I'm sure Mr. Dwyer would as well."

"Thanks," he said. "There is another thing."

"Please tell me, doctor. What is it that weighs so heavily on you?"

Once words were spoken you couldn't turn back so he hesitated, silent and paralyzed. In the end it was Almira who broke the inertia.

"What is it you have to say?"

He looked up, feeling like a child. "I don't know how —" The words caught in his throat. His eyes welled with tears, and he swallowed hard. "I don't know how to…love. I'm no good at it."

"To love is easy, Doctor Weis. It is what God has made us to do."

"Then why is it so hard for me? Why am I so resistant? I don't understand that. I feel like I know how to love all the wrong things — places, ideas, and objects. Myself. But I only love other people as long as there's something in it for me."

Almira leaned forward. "And you fear that if you love another unreservedly, you will lose yourself and cease to be the center of your universe. Is that what you fear?"

David eked out a nod.

"But you never were the center. God is, and always has been. The only way you can have a relationship with Him is by loving others unreservedly."

"Is that what you think I want? A relationship with God?"

"Only you can answer that question, Doctor Weis." Almira stood with her basket hanging from her elbow. "I have to leave you for the present. We will continue this conversation. In the meantime, you have much to think about. When you and your lady wish to visit, we will meet at the clover ledge. You know the place."

"But how will you know when?"

"Trust us, we will know."

"You mean I should have faith."

"Precisely."

Chapter 31

August 1842

The book, *Facts in* Mesmerism, had occupied Rebecca's complete attention since retiring for the evening. After all, if she was going to mesmerize Phebe, she needed to be familiar with the techniques. But not being as well versed in the terminology of Magnetism as the Gardiner girls were, much of what she read seemed difficult to understand. Would she really be able to summon the requisite powers?

The moment the tall clock downstairs began striking midnight someone tapped on her door.

"Rebecca," the voice said. "It's us."

She rose and let the sisters in.

"There is no electrical storm," said Mary once she'd entered the room. "But Papa is away to New York. His strong magnetic presence won't interfere with our experiment."

"Yes, we have the entire floor to ourselves," Phebe

added. "Now, are you ready to be our mesmerizer?"

"I think so. I've been reading all night from Professor Townshend's book."

"*Tres manifique*," said Phebe with enthusiasm.

Mary had a suggestion. "Miss Lynch says the subject should gaze fixedly into a candle. Perhaps this time we ought to do the same."

The setting was arranged. All lights were extinguished, save one — the single candle.

"Oh my," Rebecca said. "Look."

Everyone turned their attention to the window, where a sudden break in the clouds revealed an enormous full moon that bathed the grounds of Abbey Manor, its gardens, and the boxwood maze in moonlight.

"Are we ready?" whispered Mary.

"We are." Phebe took her seat in the most exacting way.

Rebecca returned to her place and closed her eyes, trying to establish a magnetic alignment. Opening them again, she pressed her thumbs to Phebe's palms, as she remembered seeing Phebe do. When she glanced over toward Mary, her face indicated quiet encouragement.

Feeling more confident, Rebecca listened for Phebe's breath to slow and grow deeper. Recalling the next progression, she placed her fingertips to Phebe's temples.

"Imagine you're floating on a pond. A very, very quiet pond," Rebecca said, glad that she had studied so diligently. "You are aligned with the perfect magnetism of the universe. Its power is pouring into you as pure water into an empty vessel."

Phebe sighed and her fingers twitched, which meant it was time to begin making passes. Imagining she was cleansing her halo of everything but their own magnetic unity, she guided her hands over every inch of Phebe's body.

Once complete, Rebecca returned to the head of the chair. She spread her fingertips across Phebe's now-drooping head and, bending over, whispered into her ear. "Phebe, do you hear me?"

There was a barely audible acknowledgement.

"Very good. When you raise your head, open your eyes and stare into the candle. The flame will be as a threshold to wherever I direct your attention. Do you understand?" Rebecca didn't remember reading that she should instruct Phebe with these phrases, but it seemed instinctively correct to do so.

"Open your eyes now."

Phebe did as told, her eyes glassy and unfocused.

"Phebe, direct your thoughts on Almira," Rebecca said in preparation to pose her first question. "Is she and Mr. Dwyer safe?"

Phebe did nothing but breath for a long while. Overcome with suspense, Rebecca and Mary looked to each other for answers but Phebe suddenly spoke.

"I see a man and a woman, arm in arm in the park. The bond of love is strong between them. It surrounds them."

"Tell us more. Take another look into the flame," instructed Rebecca.

"They are sitting in a room. There's an old man with them. He is upset. They are all upset. They are talking about…I don't know."

"Phebe, concentrate on the flame," Rebecca urged. "Look into it. What are they talking about?"

"They are talking about Almira."

Confused, Rebecca pressed her again. "Who are these

people?"

"Your girl, Tildie," Phebe said after a long silence. "She's with her bald gentleman."

Rebecca was taken aback. "Are you sure?"

Phebe nodded her head. "The old man says Almira is gone, forever."

"What else?" Rebecca said, her forehead pressed to Phebe's temple. "What else does he say? What else?"

"She is your sister," said Phebe dispassionately.

"Almira is my sister?" Rebecca drew back, puzzled by the response. "What could you mean?"

"Not Almira. Tildie," Phebe said without emotion. "Tildie is your sister."

"That's impossible." Rebecca stepped away from the chair. "You're mistaken. She's my servant. She's a slave—she's a Negress."

"Yes, and she is your sister as well."

Rebecca raised the back of her hand to her face and, with a dull thud, fainted to the floor.

When she awoke, Mary and Phebe were bent over her prostrate form. From downstairs Grandma L'Hommedieu was slamming her cane against the wall, demanding to know what in heaven's name was going on upstairs.

Phebe ran to the rail on the landing and called down. "Everything is alright, just…*Un le'ger* accident."

The sisters put Rebecca to bed. For a long while they sat on either side of her, cooling her wrists with damp cloths.

"I think we ought not experiment further with Animal Magnetism," Mary said. "The results are too shocking."

Later that night, Rebecca jerked awake.

The clock downstairs chimed 5a.m. She lay there being cognizant of a dream — no, a memory. The memory of the day her father brought Tildie home from Birmingham, telling her he'd bought her to be a lifelong servant and companion. At the time, little Becca thought it a loving act, like bringing home a living doll to look after her. Why was Mother so displeased? No, not only displeased, but furious, distraught? These memories, long forgotten, boiled to the surface, competing for attention.

They had an argument late at night. It must have been several days, maybe a week after Tildie arrived, when Rebecca awakened to hear her parents embroiled in a terrible argument like never before.

"No, she's a sweet child," her father kept repeating.

"A sweet reminder of your faithlessness, your animal lust, that's all she is."

Words of conciliation followed, more intelligible from their tone than by the words themselves. Then her mother's voice again, articulated sharply by the anger in every syllable.

"Don't touch me," she said. "Go back to your dusky mistress — I'm sure she'll please you more."

Chapter 32

October 1972

The mistake was thanking Angela for a delicious supper of spaghetti and meatballs.

"It's rigatoni," she said, instructively. "Spaghetti is a cut of macaroni, like linguini, fusilli, or rigatoni, like we had tonight but it's all macaroni."

"See, I didn't know that," David said. "It makes me wonder what else I don't know."

"Yeah, me too."

They both laughed and agreed she was funny for a girl.

"So, you really want to go through with this?" David asked, returning to their earlier conversation. "It's probably going to be scary if they appear, and there's no guarantee they will. The one thing I can guarantee is that it will be cold and uncomfortable waiting out there tonight, but it's the only way."

"But why outside?"

"I think in order for them both to appear it has to be at a place they went to together in life."

Angela finished gathering plates from the table. The coffee pot started to percolate. It filled the kitchen with its aroma as she poured cups for them both. "I don't understand why it has to be at night though."

"Ghosts don't appear in daylight. Everybody knows that." David took a deep drink from his mug. "Have you got a cigarette? I feel like smoking."

She passed him one. He got a light from hers and took a deep drag.

"You look like some kind of European intellectual with that long cigarette — like Roman Polanski, except maybe a little taller."

"A whole lot taller," he corrected. "And I don't think Roman Polanski has a mustache either, but let's get back to the ghosts. See, I'm getting the hang of this. From what Almira told me, the logical place where they could have been free to be together, be comfortable — even, you know, intimate — was the clover ledge by the lake and maybe that stand of trees with the little graveyard in it. It's where they were able to love each other, so that's why we're naturally drawn to it. I don't mean to sound tacky or trivialize it, but they left good vibes there. And that's where we can find them tonight."

Angela sat poised with her own cigarette. "That makes sense."

David briefly wondered if George and Gloriana Hamilton ever went there together, then refocused his mind. "Here's the plan," he said. "Before it's completely dark, we'll walk up to the clover ledge. We try not to take any modern stuff with us, no electronics, no plastics, nothing. We wait until they materialize. Hopefully, we don't have to wait all night, but my experience is that ghosts are unpredictable."

"Then what happens?"

"Well, if it goes like other times, once it starts, they'll materialize pretty quickly, over the course of several seconds. Try not to react too much—they like things calm. Don't touch anything that materializes with them, like a book for example. But above all, don't touch them. Somehow it messes with their energy."

"Okay. No touching the ghosts. And they won't touch me, right? Anything else?"

David thought for a moment. "When they speak, you might not actually hear voices. It might be more like you're just aware of what they're thinking. You probably won't hear them make other sounds either, like clothes rustling. At least that's the way it is for me."

"Anything else?" she asked.

"No," he said. "That's about it."

"Then let's do it."

Chapter 33

August 1842

The next morning Rebecca felt scattered by the previous night's events, wandering from one thing to the next. What if it were true that she and Tildie were sisters? And why wouldn't it be? Mesmerism was practically beyond refute.

What would that be like, being Tildie's sister? Would it be much like Phebe and Mary were to each other? Rebecca thought not, but who knew? It was all very hard to comprehend.

At one moment she would catch herself imagining how they might have sisterly fun, taking tea together, visiting the dressmaker, going shopping, much as they had so many times before. Then Rebecca would remember they would require a servant to attend them properly on such occasions, and who would that be?

Fantasizing life with a new sister was impossible, knowing what she now knew. Rebecca was called upon to be both mistress and sister to Tildie. But as Grandma had once read to her, one cannot serve two masters.

Regarding Grandma L'Hommedieu, she behaved especially surly at the breakfast table, having been awakened in the night. "Whatever was going on upstairs at such an hour? Why weren't you girls asleep? You have too much time on your hands."

"We're sorry, Grandma," Phebe said. "We were telling ghost stories when I fell out of bed."

"Don't tax my credulity." Grandma scowled back. "I do not believe it, and I do not like it."

Fanny begged to hear the story for herself, but Phebe said, "Never you mind. These are stories for grown up girls, not for children."

The rest of the breakfast conversation was taken up with the evening's party at Charlotte Nicoll's home. According to Phebe, Eloise Hunting would also be there, as would any number of suitable young people from Sag Harbor.

Seeing that Fanny was again excluded, Rebecca promised to play dolls with her later.

After breakfast, the sisters, tired from the previous night's excitements, returned to their room for a nap. Rebecca knew she couldn't sleep. Instead, she exited at the back of the house and strode quickly through the flower gardens, proceeding to the boxwood maze where she might hide and collect herself.

Retracing the route taken by her and Phebe, she turned left, right, left, and then left again. Soon voices—no, just one child's voice playing both parts of a conversation—came from around the corner.

There she was, Fanny, sitting on the bench with her

doll Abbigail, unmindful of being observed.

"Would you like some more pie?"

"Yes please," was her own reply.

Rebecca watched and listened to the child hold a lively conversation for both her and the doll for a few minutes before speaking.

"Fanny," she said, "may I visit with you and Abbigail?"

The girl twisted around, holding her doll by the waist. "Yes, we've been expecting you."

Rebecca took a seat opposite them. "What have the two of you been doing?"

"We're having mulberry pie and tea," said Abagail. "Would you like some?"

"I surely would." Rebecca was glad to find refuge in this make-believe world.

"Abbigail told me you would be joining us." Fanny propped the doll on her knee. "So we saved a piece for you."

For the next while, the three pantomimed all the parts of a tea party, even wiping their lips with imaginary napkins, until Fanny cupped one hand around her mouth and whispered, "I have a secret. Abbigail isn't real. She's a doll."

Later that day, the girls began preparing for the long-awaited visit to the Nicoll home. It was a welcome distraction for Rebecca. Both housemaids and Fanny were called into service. Certain dresses had to be selected and then rejected in favor of others. In the end, Mary chose a pale blue muslin and Phebe an identical one in pink. Rebecca's choice was limited to one of striped watered silk. Accessories were just as important and also took considerable time. With no small amount of trading involved, each finally had their individual ensemble perfected.

Bidding a good evening to Grandma and Fanny, the girls climbed into the barouche with Isaac at the reins.

"Rebecca," Mary said after the carriage had drawn away from Abbey Manor, "You've been such a dear this summer, being so kind to Grandma L'Hommedieu as you have."

"Yes, it's plain that she loves you more than us," said Phebe.

"Grandma is a dear, she really is…" Rebecca's expression turned worried. "Mary, Phebe, please don't reveal anything about what happened last night. It mortifies me to think what might be."

"My dear friend," said Mary, "the effects of ecstasy are imprecise. We can't place our entire faith on what is said under its influence."

Rebecca wrung her hands. "I understand, but please don't try to pretend. Embarrassing as it is, seeing the faces of the servants bear the features of their master isn't unusual in the South. And that such is the case in my own family should be no great surprise."

While Mary stroked her forearm, Phebe patted the other. "It will be *complètement et pour toujours confidentiel.*"

At the Nicoll house, Rebecca counted a dozen carriages and buggies parked outside. Inside, she was introduced to ladies and gentlemen, all well dressed and quite a few of them cousins of Eloise or Charlotte.

They were friendly, but after introductions, Rebecca grew bored with the regional conversation of the guests—oysters and the whaling industry for the men, church, sewing, and children for the ladies. Free to drift about the room, her attention became fixed on the tinkle of musical rainfall of tiny harps and bells playing from across the parlor. Rebecca made her way to a musical box situated on a sideboard table. She stood before it for some seconds, fanning herself and listening to the delicate chimes.

"You like the music box?" said a young man who stepped up beside her. He had sandy hair, gray eyes, and a lavishly embroidered waistcoat, from which dangled a silver chain.

"Surely I do." She smiled. "My daddy has a musical watch which sounds on the quarter hour, but this is so much more…symphonic."

"Might I demonstrate the mechanism to you?"

Rebecca liked his looks. His kind face and easy manner were soothing after what had been a trying day.

"Why yes," she said. "I'd be obliged if you did."

Lifting the top of the box disengaged the mechanism. The music stopped. He turned to her and described how pegs on a brass cylinder provoked the ringing of tiny bells and dampered reeds. One could change the song by inserting different cylinders and winding the box with a key, which he did, as one would wind a mantel clock. When the lid was closed the music resumed.

"And it will continue until the tension of the spring is spent," he said.

"My goodness. All that music from an itty-bitty box," she said.

"You don't sound like you're from around here, miss…?"

"Carvalho," Rebecca said. "It's Portuguese. I'm from Charleston."

"You don't say? All the way from South Carolina."

He bowed slightly. "Well, Miss Carvalho, I'm Tom Cook, and I am from around here. Sag Harbor, and as far as I know I'm not Portuguese."

Rebecca burst into the first spontaneous laughter she'd experienced since coming to Shelter Island, and she made only a weak effort to conceal her amusement behind her fan. "You're a funny man, Mr. Cook."

Cook smiled back. "Do you have many funny men in Charleston?"

"We do, but not enough."

Before she could say more, Eloise stepped between them. "Rebecca, I see you've met Mr. Cook."

"Indeed, I have."

"Tommy, did Miss Carvalho tell you she is from South Carolina and a true Southern Belle? She even brought one of her slaves with her to Albany. Isn't that true, Rebecca?"

Cook's expression hardened. He turned back to Rebecca. "Your family are slave holders?"

"Yes," she said. "Though we normally refer to our people as servants."

"Nonetheless, you keep a girl in bondage?"

"It's not as you might think," Rebecca said, trying to salvage what she knew was already spoiled.

"I'm sure it isn't." Cook's voice had turned cold. "You will excuse me, Miss Carvalho. I hope you enjoy your visit to Shelter Island." A quick bob of his head ended the conversation.

"Oh dear," said Eloise. "I've done something wrong, haven't I?"

Leaving the house was all Rebecca could think of. She slipped discreetly through the back door and into the cool night. From the barn, a fiddler played a lively hornpipe, accompanied by a tambourine. She went closer. People were eating cobbed corn and clams from the shell. This was a barn dance, such as she'd once seen on her cousin's rice plantation, except most of these people were white.

It was cold, though still in August. Rebecca rubbed her bare arms. She hated Eloise for her indiscreet remarks. She hated Yankees, gentiles, Tildie, and everyone.

That night she prepared for bed silently. Deep in thought and knowing what she had to do, Rebecca sat at the writing table, dipped her pen, and composed a long letter.

Chapter 34

October 1972

"And now we wait," said David once they settled themselves on the rock ledge.

Time passed, growing terribly dark until a nearly full moon rose. Huddled together, he wished he had brought a thermos of coffee.

"What was that noise?" whispered Angela.

"That's a Barred Owl. He says, 'Who cooks for you?'"

Her relief seemed short lived, her body soon trembling. "David, really, it's like Halloween out here. We've got a graveyard over there, a full moon, and an owl... What's next, the Wolfman?"

David laughed. "The Wolfman? What a complicated guy. He would have made an interesting patient."

More time passed and David was starting to wonder if she would be able to see this through, but then he noticed what they had been hoping for. He nudged Angela with his elbow.

"Look over there, at the edge of the woods," he said. "They've materialized."

"Oh shit." Angela squeaked and gulped air. "I can see them too."

She clenched her hand within David's. "Don't be afraid, they won't hurt us," he whispered, putting his arm around her shoulders. "Tell me what you see."

"It's two people wearing old-fashioned clothes."

"Right, that's them," said David. "And it looks like they're coming in our direction."

The couple appeared perfectly formed, perfectly solid, and though the night was dark, glowed as if in full sunlight. The effect was otherworldly.

They glided closer, perhaps as near as ten feet. Though only distinct from their knees up, anyone could discern the details. He with his beaver hat freshly brushed and rakishly tilted, claw-hammer coat and silk vest. She held a parasol over her pearl-gray bonnet, and her short-sleeved dress was accented with plaid ribbon.

Though they looked almost comic in their wildly old-fashioned costumes, Almira and Daniel also seemed like any couple, with her arm threaded through his, as ordinary sweethearts might on a Sunday promenade.

"Angela," David said. "This is Miss Almira Hamilton."

"Hamilton was my maiden name, but I am now Mrs. Daniel Dwyer."

"You see, Doctor Weis," said Daniel, "when we awoke after our accident, we were married. We knew it was so from the bands on our fingers."

Now David could see the gleam of matching wedding bands. "Excuse me. Mr. and Mrs. Dwyer, please be introduced to Miss Bellasaro. She is my very special friend."

The Dwyers nodded. "Good afternoon, miss."

At first, Angela's voice faltered, but she mustered up her courage. "It's very nice to meet you both. Please, sit with us."

The Dwyers went to the ledge. Once all four were sitting together, Almira released the catch of her parasol, collapsed its canopy, folded the stem, and placed it on her lap.

"Doctor Weis," Daniel said, "I want to thank you for making it possible for us to be reunited. But for you, I would still be wandering the shores of this lake, searching for my beloved."

Almira snuggled closer to him. "And I would still be forever waiting."

"Excuse me," said Angela. "I can't help but comment that you both look very real for…ghosts."

Daniel and Almira looked at each other and laughed. David laughed too.

"I hope you're not offended."

"Heavens no," said Almira. "You usually appear to us as ghosts too. Isn't that funny."

"Do you see us clearly now?" David asked. "Are you aware of us day to day while we are in the house or out on the property?"

"We are aware of your presence if we want to be," said Daniel. "But it is an effort and very tiring for us, and even more so if we wish to be more than invisible observers."

His voice had the slightest trace of an accent — a touch of Irish brogue perhaps, or maybe Maritime Canadian. David couldn't place it.

"It is much less so during your night," Almira said. "I don't know why."

"What do you mean by our night?" asked David.

"Your night is much as our day," explained Daniel. "For us, at this moment, the sun is shining, and the weather is delightful." He withdrew a watch from the pocket of his waistcoat. "By my reckoning, it is not quite 2p.m., on a perfect afternoon in May."

Almira was distracted and pointed toward the lake. "Danny, look. A schooner passes. Which is she?"

"Might be the General Scott. I can't be sure from here."

David and Angela peered into the night. The lake was visible, but only as a black void. There certainly was no schooner sailing past, at least not in their world. Two distinct streams of time were braided together in the same location.

"It sounds like you're happy," said Angela. "Are you?"

"We are, in our own way," said Daniel. "But it can be a lonely life for us." He placed his hand on Almira's and squeezed. "You see, we are aware, always, of what our lives were meant to be and the children we would have had but for our reckless acts."

With her bonnet removed and head resting on his shoulder, Almira's eyes focused on some far-off idea. Daniel petted her hair.

"And now it is like we've lost the children we never had," she said. "The tragedy binds us to this place. Sometimes it's terribly unhappy for us, more than tongue can tell."

"Do we have your permission, Doctor Weis," Daniel said, "and from you, Miss Angela, to share this place and sometimes be among you?"

"And maybe," said Almira. "We can visit again?"

David looked to Angela. She looked thoughtful rather

than threatened, so he said, "I don't see why not."

At once, Almira's face lit up. "We promise never to intrude on your privacy. Unless you wish it so, you need never see us. In all candor, though, when the two of you are at peace here together, we are drawn to you. We're drawn to your happiness as moths to a flame. I can't put it any other way."

It warmed David to hear this. If the affection he and Angela shared was even apparent to ghosts, it must really be strong.

"Miss Angela," said Almira, "I must confess. One evening Daniel and I were strolling together near the carriage house—we were in our world, you see—but I noticed a light in one of the rooms of the house. I admit we approached the window. We were drawn to it, and that night we could see you both very distinctly."

"I know it was wrong of us to intrude," said Daniel, leaning in, "but the two of you were so happy, so important to each other. It delighted us."

"And," said Almira, "we saw the most curious thing. You, Doctor Weis, were holding a Phrenology head, explaining the principle of the science to your lady."

"You know about Phrenology?"

"Naturally. We studied all the sciences at the academy." Almira yawned and her image went momentarily transparent.

"My wife is very tired now," said Daniel. "We have to go, but it has been a lovely visit for us, and especially to make your acquaintance, Miss Angela."

The Dwyers stood. Daniel replaced his beaver hat and Almira her bonnet, letting the ribbons hang loosely.

"Good afternoon, until we next meet." Almira sprang her parasol. Their forms changed to balls of light that sped into the trees from where they'd come.

Both David and Angela sat silent for a minute, maybe longer. She was the first to speak.

"What a trip! Did that really happen? I mean, they're ghosts, but they seem like such a nice young couple." She grasped David's arm more tightly. "You can tell they're lonely though. I feel sorry for them."

David had to agree. He picked up the lantern and lit it. "C'mon, let's go in. It's cold, and we're tired."

Chapter 35

August 1842

It was late, and everyone was asleep except Rebecca. Now that her departure from Abbey Manor was imminent, thoughts about all that had happened at Shelter Island and what must be resolved once she returned to Albany left her restless. By now, her father would have her first letter, followed by the second and third. She knew that once sent there was no way to stop the cascade of events that would follow. Fresh air might clear her mind. Rebecca went downstairs.

On the piazza, a voice startled her. "Is that you Miss Carvalho? Please, take a chair and join me."

It was Mr. Gardiner, sitting alone in the dark.

"Thank you," Rebecca said, taking a seat. She looked around, but there was nothing to see except some stars. Sitting alone with Mr. Gardiner, and in the dark no less, wasn't what she expected. "Isn't it a beautiful night, sir?"

"It is."

The silence that followed his short response was filled with whip-poor-wills and far-off cicadas. With her eyes adjusting to the darkness, Rebecca could discern Mr. Gardiner's face, if dimly, framed by the white points of his starched collar.

"The summer has flown by with such speed," Rebecca said. "It seems I only just arrived at Shelter Island a few weeks since, and here I'll be leaving on Saturday."

Mr. Gardiner sipped from a tiny glass. From the way it twinkled, she knew it to be crystal.

"I assume you're eager to return to Albany and your studies," he said.

Rebecca shrugged. "In truth, I'm not so sure."

"Is that so? I'm surprised. Why do you have such mixed feelings about returning?"

"Not about the academy," she said. "It's an excellent institution."

"What then?" She struggled to answer but Mr. Gardiner encouraged her again. "Come now. You may be free with me."

His fatherly, reassuring voice made it easier for her to speak.

"Being so far north it is uncomfortable for me to have my girl with me."

"Your servant."

Rebecca noticed and appreciated his choice of words.

"Yes," she said. "In another, more southerly city— Baltimore perhaps, or even Philadelphia, having my girl attend me wouldn't generate a fuss, but in Albany, well, such is very much the case."

"I see."

A cricket began chirping underneath the piazza. Rebecca hesitated to say more, but the need to unburden herself was rising, so she went on. "And then there is the fact that I am a Jew, and for some people that is another reason to exclude me from their society."

"I'm sorry to hear this, Miss Carvalho, though it does not shock me. Nonetheless, I hope you have not felt so among us here at Abbey Manor."

"No, sir. You and your daughters have been nothing but kind to me. Even Grandma."

Mr. Gardiner laughed. "Yes. Grandma's become quite protective of you."

A long silence followed where Mr. Gardiner finished his port and crossed his legs, and Rebecca rested her head in her hand.

"What will you do when you've finished at the academy?"

"I don't think I will," said Rebecca. "I'd like to go to another school. Indeed, I've made up my mind to do so."

"One in the South."

"No," she said, "not precisely. Madame Grelaud's French School in Philadelphia. They're known for having southern students."

"I understand," said Mr. Gardiner.

"They also accept Jews like myself — Roman Catholics too. Since I will be yet a year to graduate, maybe it's not too late for me."

Mr. Gardiner cleared his throat. "And your plans beyond that?"

"Really, I have none. Go back to Charleston I suppose and marry someone suitable to my parents."

"If I may be so bold," Mr. Gardiner said as he played with the empty glass. "You sound equally disenchanted with that prospect as you do with returning to Albany."

Rebecca chuckled. "You're quite perceptive, sir. My

excitement is...subdued."

"May I make a proposal?" said Mr. Gardiner. "Once you are finished at this French school, come back here. Live with us at Abbey Manor. Be a governess to Fanny. She already loves you, as does Grandma L'Hommedieu."

"But what about Mary and Phebe? Wouldn't they want to see to their sister's education themselves?"

"There is a social season in New York," Mr. Gardiner said. "Mary and Phebe are likely to be absent from Shelter Island during much of it, and who knows but that either or both will be engaged or married ere long. Motherless as the poor child is, Fanny needs someone who will stay with her throughout the year."

Cocking her head, Rebecca posed a direct question. "Do you stay year-round, sir, or do you spend the winter in the city?"

"I keep a law practice at Dykeman's offices in New York and make periodic trips to that city, as well as to Philadelphia, Boston, and occasionally Washington, but when not away, I am here."

Though Mr. Gardiner's response seemed rehearsed, seconds passed while she considered the idea. He was right. As things stood now, a more-or-less arranged marriage awaited her in Charleston, but even with all its isolation, there was something stimulating and exciting in the thought of staying with the Gardiners on Shelter Island.

"Take some time," he said. "Give my offer some thought. The room you are in now would be yours."

"Miss Lynch's old room."

"Yes, as a matter of fact, and you could bring your servant too."

Spending time alone with Mary had excited Rebecca's interest all summer, and not having to share her attention with Phebe felt even more luxuriant. They meandered along a low bluff overlooking the beach, Mary's arm entwined in hers. Fanny could be seen ahead, collecting seashells as Phebe walked nearby, the hem of her skirts gathered up in one fist to prevent soiling.

A steady sea breeze was rising with the approach of day's end. Alone with Mary, thoughts of Almira seemed very, very far away. Rebecca said, "Your father has extended me an invitation to serve as Fanny's governess when my education is complete."

"Has he?" said Mary. "I'm not entirely surprised. Papa told us you and he had a delightful conversation last night. He thinks a great deal of you."

"I shouldn't be forward, but he seems lonely."

"He is. Having Miss Lynch with us was a tonic to him. It's a small wonder he should seek to restore the arrangement, and I know the rest of our family would be overjoyed were you to accept. Do you think you will?"

"I'm not sure," Rebecca said. "And please forgive my asking this, but you don't think he entertains further… ambitions, do you?"

Mary tapped her hand. "I should say not. Despite anything Lottie or Eloise may have insinuated about he and Miss Lynch, I can assure you that my papa would never embarrass your virtue."

"I'm sorry, it was wrong of me to even ask the question."

"Please don't apologize. Shelter Island is small, and here gossip finds fertile ground."

"You're so understanding," Rebecca murmured.

Rebecca tilted the stem of her parasol to shield them

from the wind and the setting rays of sunlight but doing so only lent an even more intimate and exciting privacy to their conversation. Provoked by Mary's matchless profile, she felt her heart racing and, overcome by attraction, kissed her perfect lips.

Mary looked downward and blushed, giving a demure smile.

"That was bold of me. I'm sorry," said Rebecca.

"No," Mary said, looking up. "You are as a sister to me and Phebe."

Rebecca felt wounded and exposed, for Mary's words showed she did not comprehend the true intention of her affectionate act. Desperate to move on from so awkward a moment, she composed herself and introduced a new subject. "You must be excited to be so soon again with Professor Horsford."

Mary sighed. "It's such a dilemma. Papa is stubborn in his opposition to our friendship. He will never allow Mr. Horsford to court me. According to him, the professor is a mere academic."

"Mary, let me offer some advice. My daddy will do whatever I ask, I need only work on him long enough. You must learn to do the same."

"You don't know my father." They walked some distance further before Mary resumed her commentary. "Professor Horsford's regard for me, and mine for him, is, I fear, hopeless."

"You mustn't think that."

Mary didn't answer for several seconds. Rebecca had the impression she was deciding what and what not to reveal.

"Maybe because clouds rested so heavily over my early years, I have not looked for happiness on earth as others do. Nor do I expect my span here to be a long one."

"Oh hush," Rebecca admonished. "You oughtn't say such things."

But Mary would not be dissuaded. "It's true. I have had this presentiment all my life. Don't you think it possible some minds are constructed as to catch the shadows of future events?"

"Do you mean through in-born powers of Animal Magnetism?"

"Perhaps," Mary said. "But I think Magnetism has run its course for me. I'm afraid the future itself can alone answer my inquiry."

The two stopped and turned to the west, looking across the bay toward Greenport and the setting sun. Below them, Fanny and her sister still gathered shells just beyond the reach of the surf.

Projecting her usual serenity, Mary said, "I am sorry if my poor mood has incommoded you during your stay with us. Sometimes I am seized by a terrible prostration, and when it comes upon me, I'm powerless to resist its call."

Rebecca brushed her remarks aside as no great deal, but inwardly gained the knowledge that a turbulence lay behind the mask of Mary's perfectly calm persona.

"It must be terrible," she said, trying to sound sympathetic. "Is there no remedy?"

"I fear not." Mary looked out across the water. "There are so many expectations placed upon me, both from without and from within. At times, it is quite oppressive."

Mary glanced in Rebecca's direction with a tear in her eye.

"You poor thing," said Rebecca.

Shifting the conversation, Mary asked, "What will you do about your girl, Tildie?"

"Oh goodness, I've written to my father, telling him I now understand the nature of my relationship to her. Much will depend on his response, which I hope to find waiting for me in Albany.

Mary's hand lighted on Rebecca's shoulder. "I'm sorry Eloise was so indiscreet at the party last week."

"No matter. I've become quite used to it since coming north."

The day of departure arrived. Everyone rose well before dawn. While Isaac carried trunks to the carriage, the Gardiners and their housemaids gathered on the piazza steps. The girls said their goodbyes. Grandma L'Hommedieu reminded Rebecca to read her Old Testament every day. The old woman squeezed her hand and kissed her cheek.

"Bless you child," she said. "And farewell."

Next was Fanny. She threw her arms around Rebecca's waist and pressed her face into her.

"Abbigail will miss you," Fanny mumbled into Rebecca's dress.

Rebecca crouched, kissed her forehead, and asked, "Won't you miss me too?"

Fanny shook her head. "No." She turned and ran upstairs.

Chapter 36

November 1972

A week went by, maybe more. Except for a couple of late-night phone calls, their extraordinary visit with the Dwyers was hardly mentioned. Maybe Angela needed time to assimilate it. He certainly did.

In the meantime, David did a lot of reading, learning that the distinction between Psychology and the paranormal was not so clear in the early nineteen century. This meant that movements like Animal Magnetism and Phrenology were the common progenitors of present-day Psychotherapy, Hypnosis, and the Occult.

Downstairs, while he roughed out a diagram of this idea, he felt the distinct perception that Almira was in the house.

David was right. Entering the quiet Room, he found her standing beside the daybed, gazing intently at her own memorial hanging above it.

"It must be strange to look at your own epitaph."

Almira turned toward him. "Not so much now. The first time you showed it to me, doctor, was quite upsetting, but now I understand it."

"And you can see it well?"

"Yes. It existed in my time—therefore I see it clearly. Those things of your time I see only faintly, if at all." She went to her chair and took her place, reached down and pulled the sewing basket up to her lap. She opened it and started withdrawing the implements of her work—skeins of silk floss, scissors, needles. "It's terribly inconsiderate of me, Doctor Weis, but I've nearly finished Daniel's braces. You won't mind if I embroider whilst we talk, will you?"

"No, please," he said. "I love to watch you sew. It's soothing."

"Soothing or not, it is a lady's constant task, this making up of mementoes." She looked up and smiled at him. "Nonetheless, we take much pride in it." She threaded her first needle. "I wonder, Doctor Weis, were you to see a memorial to your own life, what would you think? How would your epitaph read?"

"That's a good question," he said. It wasn't something he would have asked of himself. He looked over his shoulder at her memorial—weeping willows, a lamb, a woman in a dress appropriate to the early 1830s, and a monument with Almira's dates of birth and death written on it.

David tried to imagine his own name substituted for hers—David Aaron Weis. Born August 22, 1941. Died, who knows when. He would probably make it to the turn of the century, but that seemed a long way off. Anything after 1999 sounded too futuristic to take seriously.

"Quite a few nice antiques were bought and sold," he said. "A few people mildly better off, but probably as many who would remember me with some bitterness, I'm sorry to say."

"You feel you've drawn more from the world than you've given back."

"Maybe."

"Is that disappointing?" she asked.

"Well, sure. I mean, on balance it doesn't amount to much, does it?"

"You can change that," said Almira. "You know how to."

"You're referring to marriage and children."

"No, not necessarily," she said. "Are you?"

"I don't know." He organized his thoughts. Romantic relationships... Sexual ones were one thing, but this business of marriage and children was another altogether. Marriage was a dying institution anyway, right? Hip and sophisticated couples didn't need it anymore. Almira couldn't be expected to understand that. "You and Daniel said that you watched me showing Angela the Phrenology bust."

"Yes. We thought it was amusing."

"You also said it was clear she meant a great deal to me. What did you mean by that?"

"Daniel and I have an enhanced perspective on such things. That you share a great love is obvious to us," she said. "The two of you have a common destiny after all, just as Daniel and mine are one."

She threaded a new needle, this time with blue floss. "My mother was a very accomplished embroiderer. Have I ever told you that? It was difficult to tell the back of her work from the front, it really was."

David sat with his chin in hand. There were few things he loved watching more than this.

"But to return to our conversation, do not forget that in our position, Daniel and I can see destiny's path more clearly. I know now that it is only through serving others that we become happier. We are made better for the act. I was aware of this before, but only vaguely. Now I see it clearly."

Sometimes, though not too often, in his psychotherapist days, there would be sessions that just clicked, just gelled. Even with their roles reversed, this was one of them.

It felt right, the whole gestalt, as Koenigsberg would say, so he hazarded an idea. "One time, we talked about the way I need to keep myself apart from people. I'd like to talk about that again."

Almira cocked her ear. "Do begin. Tell me what is on your mind."

"Okay, this business of me preferring to be apart from people, it's a personality feature I'm aware of. I admit to it. Occasionally it causes me problems, particularly with girlfriends. My question is—is it driven by narcissism, or is the fear of rejection behind it?"

"Which do you think it is?" Almira pulled a strand of silk floss through her work. "You may choose only one."

"Well, then I'd say it's sustained by narcissism."

"And why is this so?"

He was about to answer, but a sudden realization stopped him. "Except it's not so much that I think I'm superior to other people, because I don't think I am. It's more that they're usually a waste of my time."

"Tell me why," she said.

"Because they distract me from my goals."

"Then you suffer the company of others only so long as they serve a purpose."

"I know it sounds awful, but yes." David shifted in his seat. "See, the narcissistic theory comes down to intellectual competition. As long as I feel smarter than most of the people I meet, I feel alright. It's a kind of an adult line of thinking, and a lousy way to relate. It's kind of sick really."

Almira looked up. "Tell me the child's thought."

He bit on his thumbnail. Staying quiet at this point would have been easy but for the rare therapeutic momentum which propelled him forward. "The child's thought involves rejection. Rejection requires other people. It assumes interaction, and if that interaction results in rejection, it hurts."

David stalled, so Almira encouraged him.

"Alright." He took a deep breath. "There's this deeper issue. It's about losing one's own individual identity when you dedicate yourself to another person, as we might in a love relationship, right? It's like the couple becomes a filter between you and yourself. They used to call this an annihilation fear."

"They?"

"Psychologists, psychotherapists."

"If this is a class of scientists," Almira said, "I think these learned men are mistaken. You see, I think this is about marriage, and how marriage is meant to enlarge us. It makes us more than we could ever be alone."

David studied the braces on her lap. For two years he'd watched her embroidering them but never, ever finishing them. Today he felt like those unfinished braces. His own life represented in them as an ongoing, evolving process, and not the completed thing in itself.

"Incidentally, Doctor Weis, how is your lady friend, Miss Angela? Daniel and I so enjoyed our visit with the two of you. When will you favor us with another?"

Chapter 37

August 1842

All the way back to Albany, Rebecca's thoughts were distracted. Unresolved and difficult issues in her life seemed everywhere. The inconclusive results of her investigation into Almira's disappearance. The question of wether to stay at the academy or complete her education in Philadelphia. And what to do about Tildie? That she was her older sister was the only thing which seemed certain.

By the time they reached Mrs. Bright's doorstep everyone was tired. Already cranky, Rebecca's impatience was only stretched further when Tildie was not there to receive her. According to the other housemaid, she was away on an errand for Mrs. Bright, but Rebecca suspected otherwise.

Once the trunks had been carried upstairs, she gathered up the stack of letters on her bureau and collapsed on her bed to sort through them. There were several from her parents and brothers in Charleston, a few others from cousins in South Carolina, and one from Madame Grelaud's in Philadelphia, but nothing from Almira. Though disappointed, she was not surprised. Indeed, Rebecca had given up hope of ever hearing from her friend again.

Slicing open the envelopes, she scanned the letters to see if any were her father's response to her most recent missives. None were. There was, however, a confirmation from Madame Grelaud's that there was yet room for her in their autumn semester.

At the sound of a tap, Rebecca sat up.

"Miss Becca? Mrs. Bright says you're back. Alright if I come in?"

Rebecca got up, unlocked the door, and opened it. Face to face with Tildie for the first time in a long while, it was immediately clear that they were, if not sisters, certainly related. They were the same height, had the same eyes, even the same facial contours. That Tildie was wearing one of Rebecca's old calico dresses only made the similarities more apparent.

She took her by the hand. "My dear Matilda," she said, noticing that, calloused or not, the subtle shapes of their fingers and hands were identical.

"Good to see you, Miss Becca. You had a nice summer at Miss Phebe's plantation?"

"I did. And you? I do hope Mrs. Bright didn't work you too hard."

"No no, Miss Becca, not too hard. I even had time to make you the new petticoat you wanted. Corded, just like these girls up here are wearing."

"That's so sweet of you," Rebecca said. "I feel terrible, I didn't bring you anything. It was thoughtless of me."

She glanced around her room and picked up her parasol from the table. "I did buy a new parasol in New York. Would you like this one?"

"You serious, miss? What do I need a parasol for?"

"I don't know. Perhaps when you go to church on Sundays."

"Well, thank you, miss," she said. "That's kind of you."

The two embraced but the social code forced them apart. The rest of the evening was spent unpacking Rebecca's trunks, talking all the while about the previous two months. Eventually, Rebecca asked, "Tildie, I haven't perchance received a letter from Almira, have I?"

"No, miss."

"And you haven't heard anything about her either? No news whatsoever?"

Matilda seemed to stall before answering. "Don't think so, Miss Becca."

But Phebe's mesmeric revelations at Abbey Manor suggested otherwise. "Not even a word?" Rebecca pressed. "Do try to remember."

"You know what? Mr. Jack, he's got a man living at his place who knew Miss Almira."

Rebecca drew in her breath. "What? You're not fibbing now, are you?"

"No, ma'm. This old man, he says he lived at Miss Almira's house on a big lake."

"Tildie, what else did this old man say?"

"Well, he say Miss Almira run off with Mr. Daniel. But that's all I know."

"Can you arrange for me to meet him?"

"Don't know, miss, but I'll ask Mr. Jack."

"We thank a merciful God for returning us all safely to this home," said Mrs. Bright. "We ask that we enjoy success in our studies. We ask that He grant us the knowledge of a world created by Him, and to serve Him. We ask that He bless this table, and that He look with mercy upon our undeserving souls. In Christ's name, Amen."

"Amen," everyone repeated.

Rose ladled bowls full of oxtail soup from a large tureen on the table.

"Mary, we thought you'd graduated, but you're here with us again," said one of the Skinner twins.

"I am," she said amid the tinkling of spoons against china. "Since Phebe's still a scholar here, I want to take further classes in painting with watercolors, and besides, our alumnae association is having our first meeting next month."

"Will Professor Horsford be there?" asked Miss Platt. "I'm sure it's the sort of thing he'd take an interest in too."

Mrs. Bright gave Suzie Platt a hard look.

"Perhaps he would. I cannot assume anything." Mary offered a fleeting smile. "It would be unladylike for me to so speculate."

Rose collected the soup bowls and replaced them with mutton and carrots.

"Rebecca," Harriet said, "I heard you were leaving us for Philadelphia."

"Who told you this?"

"Charlotte Nichol and Eloise Hunting. They said you were leaving our academy for a school which finds your southern institution acceptable."

Rebecca cursed her casual remarks on the way to Shelter Island. Though two months since, and vague in her memory, her naïve trust had returned to haunt her.

"Yes, Madame Grelaud's French School. But I have not yet made that decision," she said.

"Harriet," said Mrs. Bright, "do not tax my patience with this subject."

"I'm sorry, ma'am. I meant only to encourage her. Mrs. Gralaud's is open to, well, all kinds. Isn't that true, Rebecca?"

Rebecca was too addled to reply. Mary spoke up instead.

"You know Harriet, Madame Grelaud's is very highly regarded. Our own governess, Miss Lynch, herself one of the most accomplished graduates of our academy, instructed girls there after she had taught me and Phebe all she could. Any of us would do well to attend that august institution."

Monday began the commencement of the quarter. When Rebecca went to hang her mantua that morning, Professor Horsford approached and asked if she had a few minutes, during one of the study periods perhaps, to speak privately.

"Now is convenient," Rebecca told him, and within minutes she'd taken a chair by his desk.

"Miss Carvalho," Horsford said, "during your absence I made consultation on your behalf with an attorney regarding your dilemma. According to him, while emancipation of the Negro girl is prohibited in your home state, those laws don't apply outside of South Carolina.

So, there is nothing to prevent your granting Matilda her freedom whilst here in Albany. There is a complication. If you have not yet reached the age of majority, and I assume you have not, that fact would likely render void any action on your part."

"There's another problem, professor," said Rebecca. "Tildie is not mine to emancipate, but my father's. Only he could do this."

"Is it possible he might agree to Tildie's freedom?"

Rebecca's reflex was to reject the idea but then she wasn't sure.

Horsford leaned forward, his mouth pinned closed by the knuckle of his index finger. Rebecca had seen this mannerism of his before, whenever he considered a thorny problem. Then he lowered his hand and said, "This is quite complicated, isn't it?"

"Oh mercy, I think few northerners appreciate how the races are entangled."

"Entangled, perhaps," said Horsford with a forcefulness she'd never heard in his voice before. "But does that euphemism not dodge the great crime? Surely, Miss Carvalho, you are aware of the injustices which slavery imposes? The bondsman has not one of his most essential rights and is all too frequently abused in the most vicious manner."

"Please, professor, must I endure another thrashing for something I didn't create?"

Horsford looked down at his clenched fists. "It was unfair of me to berate you. Forgive me."

Rebecca waved him off, took out a handkerchief and wiped her eyes. "I have of course heard of such things, surely I have, and since coming to Albany over and over again, but not in my family. In my family, we always treat our people with kindness. Our people are all house servants though, and I know harsher discipline occurs on the plantations." Shifting in her chair, she looked around the room and noticed a Phrenology bust and an articulated skeleton. "We do have one old auntie. She cooks for us and does some sewing. My father bought her from someone who whipped her cruelly. I know not what her offense was, but with my own eyes I have seen the stripes across her shoulders."

"Stripes?" said Horsford.

"I'm sorry, professor. Scars from the lash. I am embarrassed to say we in the South commonly refer to them as stripes."

The conversation with Horsford left Rebecca in turmoil. She'd always believed that as long as she treated her servant with kindness, it didn't matter if Tildie was enslaved. Now she wasn't sure.

Rebecca scarcely entered her room when she stopped short. A pair of letters were on her bureau, and both from her father.

Of course she wanted to open and read them at once, but she was not alone. Tildie waited inside to unhook her dress and loosen her stays, as was their habit at the end of the day.

"Miss Becca, what dress you want me to take out for supper?"

"Not just now." Rebecca's stomach already hovered somewhere between dread and anticipation. "Right now I have to lie down for a little while."

Alone, Rebecca flew to her bureau and snatched up the envelopes. Across one was written the words, "Open first."

Chapter 38

November 1972

Rebuilding the main staircase was unplanned and impulsive. Twenty-four hours after starting, David regretted the decision. *What a mess. The central artery of the house is in pieces. Remember, everything costs more and takes longer than expected.*

During a conversation with his neighbor at the mailbox, David admitted he was in over his head.

"Okay," Gary said through his open pickup truck window. "I got some time today. How about I swing by after lunch with a couple of beers and we get you back on track?"

There wasn't anything in rebuilding that Gary didn't already know how to do and wasn't willing to share. They worked all afternoon, David learning all about stringers, risers, and treads. By the end, the boards were cut, the stringers were secured, and the risers were back in place.

Gary grabbed his back and made a big display of groaning. "All right, I'll have that cold beer now."

A few minutes later, can in hand, he walked David through how to install the treads. "But wait until this weekend when I can help you set the spindles and railing. That's a two-man job, Dave, and it's easy to screw it up, so you don't want to try doing it alone. Right now, I've got to get home. I promised the wife I'd be back for supper."

After heating up a can of soup, David returned to the hallway and spooned it straight from the pan into his mouth while walking from point of construction to point of construction, inspecting all the work he and Gary accomplished that day with no small amount of pride. If he worked until one or two in the morning, he could finish the stairs. That would be a tremendous feeling.

He drank coffee and planned his work. Using the back staircase, David brought the stepladder to the upper landing, clamped a powerful grip light to it, and directed all 300 watts straight down on the unfinished staircase. He tuned the radio to a Burlington station and placed it on the floor beside the ladder.

Starting at the bottom, David brushed and wiped the surfaces clean. He applied glue at the appropriate points, as Gary had instructed, and tucked the tread under the next riser. Screws and finishing nails were applied where they would be inconspicuous or soon covered by the spindles.

With a half-focused mind, David glued, tucked, nailed, glued, tucked, nailed. In his dissociated state, he really didn't know how long it had been, but he was not yet halfway to the top.

The other half of his mind thought about the women

in his life. Angela of course, and Almira too, but the phlebotomist as well. He even thought about Tina, and Cheryl Jankowsky. They all had something in common — they desperately wanted to love, and to be loved. So did he, but they went about it like they were blind, crippled people on a sinking ship, flailing, grasping, and pushing away all at the same time.

Part of his mind still managed to listen to the radio. David became aware of a piano being played in a minor key, followed by a raspy electric guitar. A wave of sadness surged through him. He thought he'd been reflecting on all these things dispassionately, but when the lyric 'see the love there that's sleeping' reached his ears, he stopped short. His eyes flooded. He was working in a dark and empty house, on a dark and remote road, climbing a staircase on his hands and knees — rebuilding it one step at a time. Working his way to the top, where the light was.

How does someone unfold their love? He didn't know.

How do people become controlled? He didn't know.

And people being bought and sold, how did that happen? He didn't know that either.

All his education in Psychology felt inadequate. The years he'd spent in school, conducting therapy with patients, or talking in bed with lovers seemed a waste of time. This world, full of distractions, was forever tricking him to chase after the next great antique, the next great meal, the next great orgasm.

David put down his hammer and looked up for an explanation, but with his vision so blurred by emotion, he saw only an indistinct white glare. He bent his head forward and let it all go. All his sorrow for these people, and for himself.

Seconds later the music was gone, replaced by a jingle selling the new Pontiac. Feeling foolish and giddy, he laughed and wiped his nose on his sleeve, then picked up the next tread. Glue, tuck, nail — glue, tuck, nail.

Chapter 39

September 1842

The envelope labeled "Open first" was addressed in her father's bold, artistic hand, as every letter from home had ever been. At the writing table she sliced open the envelope and took the letter out. This one began with regrets that her year in Albany had been disappointing, and she was thrilled to read, "Finishing your education at Madame Grelaud's would be very acceptable to us."

Rebecca squeezed her fist in joy. She turned the page and continued reading...

> "Though you had your heart set on Albany, you have come around to our way of thinking. No matter, for you know that if it will but bring a smile to your face, it will be done if within my power."

Tears flooded Rebecca's large eyes. Surely, of anyone

in her Charleston life, she missed her father above all.

A hard knock came to the door. Before Rebecca could answer, Tildie, very upset, barged in.

"Miss Rebecca, what's this I hear, that you gonna pick us up and take us to Philadelphia? You ain't told me nothing about this. Nothing, not a word."

"I only just this very moment learned it was even possible."

"You're lying. You were telling everyone about it last night at supper. Rose told me."

Still sitting, Rebecca could see the fury in Tildie's eyes as she stood over her and, for the first time, thought she might actually strike.

"Why we can't stay here?"

"Please, Tildie, don't pitch a fit. Madame Grelaud's is a good school. You'll like Philadelphia, I'm sure, and they are accustomed to our kind."

"You mean they accustomed to your kind," she said, her eyes wide with rage. "Ain't nobody accustomed to my kind. You know that. But you don't care 'bout me. I got a life here, but all you care about is you. What am I gonna do you take me to Philadelphia? What am I gonna do?"

Rebecca stood and reached for Tildie's arm, but her servant pushed her away. Tildie sat, buried her face in her apron and wept.

Another tap came on the door. "Miss Carvalho, is everything alright?"

Rebecca got up, opened it a few inches. "Yes, Mrs. Bright. Tildie's just a little upset. Everything is fine."

"Very well then." Mrs. Bright tried to look past her. "You don't think she'll faint again, do you?"

"No, ma'am. She's fine, truly she is. We're having a

little talk."

With the mistress of the house reassured, Rebecca closed the door. Tildie sat across the writing table, staring with unfocused eyes.

"Tell me just why you are so disconsolate," Rebecca said.

"Huh?"

"Why you're so upset? Tell me."

"You're white, Miss Becca. You're free. You won't understand."

"I might."

"Don't think so, miss."

But Rebecca encouraged her again. Tildie swallowed hard and sniffled. Rebecca retrieved a silk handkerchief from her bureau. Tildie blew and wiped her nose.

"I, well, you know I spend a lot of time with Mr. Jack while you was at Shelter Island."

"I suppose so, yes."

"He likes me a lot, Miss Rebecca. I like him too. Makes me think what it might be like if me and him..." Tears welled up in Tildie's eyes. One ran down her cheek. She wiped it away. "Don't ask me to leave him. I ain't gonna do it. Mr. Jack, he calls me his Little Miss Matilda. Nobody called me that before. Nobody ever says, 'thank you. sweetheart' to me, but he does. So please don't ask me to leave him, 'cause I'll run away, I swear it."

Clairvoyant descriptions of Tildie and Jack DeGroot as a loving couple were apparently accurate, and not just a parlor trick. "I had no idea your friendship with Mr. DeGroot was so...advanced. What do you propose we do?"

Tildie poked a finger to her chest. "You asking me? I'm just a slave. I don't have no say."

"Please, don't despair yet. Give me some time to think."

"Thank you, miss." She got up and tucked the silk handkerchief into her pocket. "I'll see this gets laundered."

Alone again, Rebecca went to the miniature of her and Almira displayed on her bureau. Desperate as they seemed at the time, those were simpler days. There was still another letter to read.

Chapter 40

November 1972

David was double parked in front of Angela's new apartment. She skipped down the steps in her peacoat and beret, then threw her bag onto the tiny backseat.

"Hey, something looks different," David said.

"Sure. My hair's crimped. I braided it wet for you last night."

"No, there's something else."

"Really?"

"Yeah, something's changed."

Angela stared dead on, allowing him to inventory her features.

"That's it. You're not plucking your eyebrows. You're letting them grow out, aren't you?"

Angela gathered her hair behind her neck, struck a dramatic pose, turned profile left, then profile right. "What do you think?"

"I like it."

"Yeah, I thought you might. Having penciled eyebrows was starting to make me look old fashioned."

"Well, aren't you?" David teased.

"I'm trying to be."

"Before we pull out into traffic, how about laying one of your old-fashioned kisses on me?"

Angela placed her forearms on his shoulders, laced her fingers behind his neck and, lips apart, gently pressed her mouth to his.

It was the first weekend of November, and David had just agreed to spend Thanksgiving with Angela's parents on Long Island. The whole thing was a big step. This had been the breaking point for them last year, to turn it down again would have been a real relationship buster, so he stifled his misgivings and said yes.

Well out of the city now, they hummed along on the New York State Thruway, still a hundred miles from Albany. A song on the radio sparked an emotional chord reminiscent of what had happened while rebuilding the stairs.

"Who's this?" he said, taking pains to sound nonchalant.

Angela looked up from her glossy magazine. "George Harrison."

"Is he a Jesus freak now? I thought he was some kind of Hare Krishna."

"You like it?"

"Sort of, yeah. It's, you know, uplifting."

She went back to her article. After a few more songs David started fiddling with the tuning knob until he switched the radio off. "Hey, I haven't told you, but the Dwyers would like to visit again."

"They told you this?"

"Almira did. She materialized a few days ago."

Angela put out her cigarette and cranked the window all the way up, making the car's interior much quieter. "So what did you and her talk about?"

"Well," he said, "you know that my sessions with Almira were therapeutic, clinical."

"Primarily," she corrected, "but not exclusively."

"Primarily, yes. But to be honest, since she reappeared, it's more like I'm the one in therapy, not her." David stalled.

"And...?"

"And she's helping me sort things out, talk them through."

"Okay, like what sort of things?"

"Like how I feel about relationships and commitment... and marriage."

"Really?"

"Yes, really."

Bemused by it all, she shook her head. "Boy, life's gotten pretty strange being around you. I mean, think about it, me and you are double dating with ghosts."

"I agree, that's pretty weird."

"What's weirder is that for the first time in my life, I've got a guy I really like, and our relationship isn't contingent on me putting out, which is exactly what makes my relationship with him super sexy. Does this make any sense?"

"Not to me, no, but it wasn't my idea."

"I think you're a slave to your libido."

He laughed.

"The heaters in these VWs stink," said Angela. She loosened the laces on her sneakers and brought her feet up on the seat. "David, you told me that girls' school in Albany was still standing, right?"

"It is, but it's not much to look at nowadays. Who knows, it might even be torn down by now. I don't know."

"Could we drive by it?"

"I guess so, sure. And while we're at it, we could hit Larry Greer's shop. Would you mind?"

In Albany, they parked the Ghia in a multi-storied, concrete garage, then descended a stairwell which smelled of urine and stepped out onto North Pearl Street. David pointed to a pile of rubble diagonal from them. Construction—or rather de-construction—workers in hard hats and heavy gloves were milling around, loading pieces of architectural wreckage into dumpsters while a jackhammer pummeled the last intact pieces of the Albany Female Academy into smaller-sized chunks.

"That's it," David said with a frown. "Or what's left of it."

"It's really sad," Angela said, taking his hand. "That building on the plate was beautiful. What a drag."

The two walked as close to the site as the barricades would allow. A few of the crew were on a cigarette break nearby.

"You guys just knock this building down?" David asked.

"Yeah, day before yesterday."

David pointed to the dumpster. "Alright if I take a piece?"

"Take all you want, just don't go near the pit."

He approached close enough to see the pit that was once the basement now mostly filled with debris. The dumpster didn't have anything interesting, but pieces of glass and brick littered the ground. David kicked them around, then selected a fragment about the size of his shoe. It looked like it came from a cornice or doorway.

He heard wolf whistles over the din of front-end loaders and jackhammers. David looked up to see Angela crossing to the other side of the street. By the time he caught up with her, it was clear she was, for lack of a better clinical term, spooked.

"There's a luncheonette around the corner," he said. "C'mon."

Seated at a window table they placed their orders.

"It sounded like those dopes were giving you a hard time back there."

"It's okay, I'm used to it. Guys are like that sometimes." She went to light a cigarette but realized they had sat in the no-smoking section. "Shit."

"Do you want to move?"

"No. It's okay. I'm alright."

David sensed her defenses going up like drawbridges, so he changed the subject. "Believe it or not, in 1841, Almira lived in a boarding house somewhere on this exact street. You'd never know it—all the old buildings are gone."

Angela looked through the window. It was hard to imagine academy girls in their bonnets and old-fashioned dresses, walking back and forth from their proud Grecian temple dedicated to learning.

Lunch platters were placed on the table. After a few bites, David pulled several napkins from the dispenser, wetted them in his glass of water, and began cleaning the piece of masonry he'd picked up. Fluted lines revealed a Neoclassical aesthetic, recognizable even on this tiny bit of the building.

"You can see here how this was once painted to simulate marble."

Angela took a look from behind her sandwich. "Jeez, it's really too bad. That whole building was broken into little pieces. Gone the way of all flesh. Isn't that the expression?"

"Hey, what's happening," David said amidst the jingle of sleigh bells.

Larry Greer sprang from his swivel chair, all potbelly and gray ponytail. "You tell me," he said, cheerfully.

"Not too much. Angela and I are heading back up to Willsboro. Thought we would stop by. You remember Angela."

"Sure, I do." He extended a big paw. "You're one of Davie's wild psychiatric nurses, right?"

"Knock it off, Larry."

"I'm just kidding around," Larry said. "You know me."

"It's okay," said Angela, and she meant it. "Just remember—I'm the librarian."

"Hey, Larry," said David. "You remember that girls' school we talked about, the female academy?"

"Sure."

"We just came from there. It's all knocked down."

"Yeah." Angela inserted herself into the conversation once more. "Would you believe it—we've actually got a piece of it in the car."

"She's telling the truth." David nodded.

Greer shook his head in disgust. "That's too bad. This city looks less like Albany every day."

David and Larry settled into antique dealer jargon—

full of inside references. Angela wandered off to browse.

The shop's main showroom displayed an eclectic variety of fine arts and furniture, ranging from nineteenth century primitives to a pair of Egyptian revival ashtrays. She noticed an Art Nouveau centerpiece of three nymphs in diaphanous gowns posed to support a fruit bowl. The sort of thing David liked. Angela looked for him over her shoulder, back toward the counter. It was too late. He and Larry were in a deep huddle. From the sound of things, he was trying to sell the coffee mill she'd watched him clean with a toothbrush. She didn't want to interrupt, so she went back to browsing.

The back room was full of bookcases. This was her territory. A quick scan indicated a few thousand books and several hundred magazines, maybe more. Over a dozen cartons of miscellaneous ephemera. She walked her fingers along the spines of the shelved books, like she'd seen in the television ad for the Yellow Pages. Every so often she would pull one out, open it, then put it back in place. They were in no particular order. Librarians hated that. How long would it take to impose the Dewey Decimal system on this chaos.

Wading into the stacks, Angela's attention was captured by a girl's autograph book. Her name: Norma. Class: 1912. Favorite expression: "Oh, you kid!" Her favorite mode of conveyance: motor car. Favorite candy: peppermint.

The memento was quaint and charming, in no small part because she wished her teenage years had been more like Norma's. The yearbook was a keeper. She placed it to one side, to be picked up on the way out.

On the next shelf an atlas lay flat on its side. Years working at the library had taught her to check under large format books such as this for smaller items hidden beneath. There was indeed something—a paper-bound booklet. What was printed on the cover screamed treasure.

Angela marched out from the back room clutching the booklet as if it were a trophy. At the counter David and Larry were still making deals. She cleared her throat.

"Hey, I found something you'd be interested in. Are you ready?"

"Ready for what? What did you find?"

Angela held up her discovery and read aloud, "Report on Phrenological Classifications, Adopted by the Albany Phrenological Society, September 3, 1840."

"Let me see that." David plucked the booklet from her hands. Scanning the cover, he read the rest of the title: "By E. N. Horsford, Professor of Natural Philosophy and Mathematics at the Albany Female Academy." Larry, why didn't you tell me you had this?"

"Hey, I forgot all about it. If I remember right, it came from the same estate as that Wedgewood plate you bought last year."

David leafed through the report. "What do you need for this?"

Larry waved him off. "Forget it, you've already got too big a tab with me."

Business being concluded, David and Angela prepared to leave.

"Davey," Greer said as they said their goodbyes, "she's good luck. You ought to bring her around more often."

"I will—"

"And Honey," Greer added, "you're a whole lot prettier than any of those psychiatric nurses."

"You never give up, do you?" Angela complained, though it was all in good fun.

"I'll mail you some Polaroids of this coffee mill," David said in closing. "It would look great in the right place, and who knows, maybe we can both make some money."

Greer raised a clenched fist. "Right on, brother. And about that other thing—trust your Uncle Larry, you're making the right decision."

Now behind the wheel, Angela had gotten them somewhere past Saratoga when she slapped her forehead. "Shit."

David pulled his face up from the Phrenology report.

"I found this cute little autograph book at Larry's shop," she said. "It was from 1912. I put it aside and forgot it when I found your report."

"Don't worry," David said, his voice suggesting his attention was elsewhere. "I have to send him some photos. I'll put in a note for you. He'll save it, and I can pick it up for you next time I'm there."

"Thanks." She noticed he was already reimmersed in his reading. David's powers of concentration were enviable, so much so that if she wanted his attention sometimes it was necessary to hit him over the head. "So...what does that report say?"

"From what I'm reading here, Horsford's comparing the different systems of Phrenology being used around 1840."

She tilted her head. "And Horsford is important because he had something to do with the daguerreotype of Almira?"

"Right," David said. "He was a partner in the

229

Daguerreotype studio where it was taken — probably the senior partner."

"And you think he took Almira's portrait."

"Maybe. Possibly. My impression is that he didn't actually expose all the daguerreotypes himself. Some were probably done by his partner, a guy named Cushman. And as it turns out, Cushman died early on from mercury poisoning."

Angela was intrigued. "Mercury — why mercury?"

"It was part of the process to develop daguerreotypes. Handling it was a real problem, and a lot of the early daguerreotype photographers died because of it."

"Alright," she said, now genuinely engaged. "What else do you know about this Horsford guy?"

"I'm glad you asked. Believe it or not he invented baking powder."

"C'mon. Really?"

"Yeah, and I can tell you he married one of his students, a girl named Mary Gardiner. She died a short time later, and then he married her younger sister, Phebe."

Angela lifted one of her newly grown eyebrows. "What else?"

"Phebe Gardiner was a friend of Almira's. I know that from her autograph book." David tapped the dashboard. "See, they both lived at Mrs. Bright's boarding house on Maiden Lane."

"And Maiden Lane is the little street where we had lunch."

"Right. Exactly." David would have rung a counter bell if he had one. She saw him shift in his seat, turning toward her as much as was possible within the confines of the Karmann Ghia. "But wait. Guess where Mary and Phebe Gardiner were from."

"I don't know. Surprise me."

"Shelter Island."

A bit ruefully, Angela thought of feet with painted toenails half buried in warm sand. "No kidding, the same Shelter Island we were supposed to spend a weekend at last summer?"

"There's only one, and I promise, we still will." David went back to reading the Phrenology report. She stole a few long glances his way. Her boyfriend needed a shave, and he could be a pain in the ass sometimes, but he was really smart. You could never tell what he would come up with from week to week. A lifetime with him would be hard to predict.

Chapter 41

September 1842

"Having familiarized all of you with the principles of Phrenology, I ask that we darken the auditorium so that I might better display the specific regions of the faculties," Combe said.

A murmur went through the crowd as the gas lighting was turned down.

"The *Lanterna Magica*," said Phebe, leaning in toward her sister and Rebecca. "It's so exciting."

Though most of the audience were not strangers to the magic lantern, its use in conjunction with educational lectures was still novel.

At the back of the room Professor Horsford ignited the oxy-hydro lamp inside the apparatus, then adjusted its flame for maximum luminosity.

Combe stepped from behind the podium and, in his Scottish brogue, said, "The good professor will introduce the first image please."

Horsford inserted a glass slide. Its image was immediately projected to a white canvas screen positioned beside Combe's podium. Experienced with lenses from his work with daguerreotypes, Horsford brought into focus a profile view of the bare head, lightly colored, and with specific regions demarked and numbered.

"Phantasmagoric," Mary whispered.

With an extended pointer, Combe directed the audience to several regions, identifying the facets of character displayed within each. "Here adhesiveness, here inquisitiveness, here cautiousness, here, behind the ear, combativeness, and here secretiveness."

A nod from Combe signaled Horsford to withdraw the slide and replace it with another, this time an anterior view, followed by the posterior and superior, as the famous phrenologist continued his lecture.

At the conclusion, Horsford extinguished the magic lantern, and the gas lights were brought back up amid a smattering of applause.

"Though some of you may have questions of your own, to anyone who has given the subject the attention it deserves, the scientific foundation of Phrenology is self-evident," said Combe. "Notwithstanding, I will gladly answer any questions."

One person observed that Phrenology seemed capable of predicting the capacities of any adult individual, but, they asked, could the science be applied to newborn babies and young children?

"Most definitely," Combe said. "Indeed, you will be interested to learn that Her Majesty, Queen Victoria, and Prince Albert have engaged me to make phrenological examinations of their children."

A ripple of awe swept through the audience. One man

at the back of the room shouted, "Rule Britannia!"

"Quite," said Combe, sounding self-satisfied. "As we can see, the science is not only accepted but relied upon amongst society's most advanced, most progressive elements."

Phebe raised her hand. "Professor Combe, my sister and I have been studying recent volumes on Mesmerism. Do you perceive a relationship between Phrenology and the principles of that science? In other words, is there reason to rename the field as Phreno-mesmerism or Mesmer-phrenology?"

With a twitch of disapproval on his long face, Combe glanced downward at the watch in his vest pocket and cleared his throat. "Young lady, that the power of Animal Magnetism informs the faculties of all organs, and most especially the brain, is true. However, I am reluctant to grant Mesmerism a status beyond that of a glorified parlor trick."

"Truly," Phebe said with some surprise. "We have ourselves experimented with mesmeric states, and the results were most impressive. Indeed, *au-delà de réfuter*, I should say."

Combe frowned again. He didn't like challenges to his interpretation, especially by Americans, and in French no less. He placed a chair before the projection screen. "Young lady, perhaps you would be so good as to step up here, that I might demonstrate my answer to your question."

Phebe rose. A few people twisted in their seats and others turned their heads, clearly all were curious to see which lamb was being led to the slaughter. She strode up the center aisle where minutes before the lantern had cast its beam.

Combe instructed his subject to be seated. "Now, my dear, please do relax whilst I offer this satisfaction of your questions." The tips of his long and boney fingers were pressed to either side of Phebe's head. "Ah, just as I suspected. Your areas indicative of aptitudes for the sciences are pronounced, as is your inquisitiveness — although, as we would expect, correspondingly less so than for a male of your stature."

Phebe rolled her eyes back to try and see as well as feel the locations Combe was assessing.

"Please do hold steady, miss," he said, shifting his hands. "There. I feel definite prominence in the regions associated with impulsivity. This can result in faulty interpretation of the more complicated sciences. I would thus entreat you to exercise more discrimination in separating the chalk from the cheese, as we say in Scotland."

Phebe was dismissed, and Combe began his closing statement all before she'd even reached her seat. For Phebe, it was a disappointing finish to the lecture, and all the more so since her questions were, if precocious, entirely sincere.

Rebecca watched Horsford approach them as the crowd left.

In a whispered voice, he apologized to Phebe for the rough handling she'd received. "Do not feel wounded, Miss Gardiner. Mr. Combe is a giant in his field."

"The man is a brute." Bristling, Phebe jerked her chin. "*Il se prend pour qui.*"

Mary soothed her with a motherly pat on the arm. "Dear sister, thy heart will yet heal." Turning to Horsford, she redirected the conversation. "And you, professor, we were all so very proud of your skill in manipulation of the lanterna. Indeed, your contribution made for the pinnacle of the lecture."

For the first time, Rebecca saw Horsford break his solemn dignity and reveal a boyish smile.

"That's very kind of you, but the manipulation of light and focal length is quite simple really, easily mastered." He turned to Rebecca and said with the slightest bow, "It was my pleasure to see you too, Miss Carvalho. I fear I've neglected you. Can you forgive me?"

"Thank you, sir, I thought the lecture was just so very informative."

Outside, a persistent rain fell. After hailing a closed carriage from the academy's portico, Horsford helped the girls in. First Rebecca, then Phebe. Mary was last. The sequence was no mere chance but rather an understanding among the party, allowing him the opportunity to show her special attention.

Once the doors were closed and the carriage pulled away, Phebe said, "Did he ask you?"

"To escort me to watercolors?" asked Mary. "Yes."

Rebecca noticed that Mary wore a fetching smile, so different from her usual serious nature. She was beaming really, and Rebecca thought it quite becoming. It seemed the dour Professor Horsford and the melancholy Miss Gardiner could induce smiles in one another.

"I have more faith in Animal Magnetism than I do Phrenology," Phebe said. "Anyone could draw regions on the head. We, on the other hand, have personally experienced the power of Magnetism."

While they all agreed, Mary touched a fingertip to Rebecca's knee. "Our friend, you've been so quiet this evening. Didn't you find Doctor Combe's lecture stimulating?"

"Even if he was insufferably pompous," interjected Phebe as she laid her head on Mary's shoulder.

"Please, y'all don't mind me," Rebecca said. "The truth is that I've received news from home—some of it exciting, and some of it quite disconcerting."

"Do tell us," the sisters said.

"Firstly, my parents have consented that I continue my education at Madame Grelaud's. I begin there the first of next month."

"Rebecca, we'll miss you terribly," Mary said.

"Will you promise to be our correspondent?" Phebe asked as she resumed an upright posture. "Will you promise to visit us again at Shelter Island? Please say you will."

Rebecca agreed. "But there is more. I also received a confidential letter from my father revealing that, as we discovered when Phebe was mesmerized, Tildie is indeed my half-sister."

The gloved hands of both Gardiner girls went to their chins.

"I know," Rebecca said. "It's quite a shock to learn. The news is, well, I surely don't know what it is, except that to conceal this fact from her seems a betrayal in itself." Rebecca turned her head, parted the curtain, and looked out on Albany's streets. Gas lights cast a yellow glow on her face at even intervals. "Apparently she and this fellow DeGroot are in love. Tildie made it plain to me they want a life together, a married life. It breaks my heart to think I'll have to separate them."

Phebe straightened and made a quick analysis. "But any union between Tildie and her gentleman is impossible anyway. She is your servant, bonded to you, and thus cannot legally marry."

"And," Mary said, "are not marriages between the races prohibited?"

"I think not everywhere in the north," said Rebecca from behind her handkerchief. "Especially since Tildie is but one-fourth caste. But she would still have to be freed, and since she's my father's property, I'm powerless to take independent action. Honestly, I don't know what to do, I don't."

"It's quite simple," Phebe said. "You have to convince your father to emancipate her at once."

"Dear sister," Mary said with caution in her tone, "thy innocent heart is true, and to beseech in the service of love is noble, but I fear your idea is a trifle naïve."

"The truth," Rebecca said, "is that I already have, and at length, and in more than one letter. I thought surely I would have received his answer by now."

"Emancipated or not, the only honorable choice is to inform Tildie of the facts." Mary looked to her sister. "Phebe, dost thou not agree?"

"Without doubt. It is the only course suitable to a lady."

Chapter 42

November 1972

Sex changes everything. David kept reminding himself of that as he mulled over the previous night. They'd stayed up late, drinking wine and talking. Talking led to necking, and necking led to him thinking he could seduce her. In the end, she would not be seduced. Though frustrated, maybe it was for the best. They would have broken their agreement and might not be walking this lane together in the carefree light of day.

It was a rare opportunity, this agreement. Seldom could couples go back to the pre-sex make-out stage, with clear rules that removed a lot of the pressure sex imposed. Somehow, they had done it (no thanks to him), and still their relationship was loaded with exciting sexual tension. Hadn't Angela pointed that out the day before, on the way to Albany? How did she put it? Ah, yes…super sexy. They'd been given another chance, and since this no-sex-rule was Angela's idea all along, he felt inclined to follow her judgement.

The late morning weather was unusually mild for November as they kicked their way through fallen leaves, talking about nothing in particular.

"God, it's peaceful out here," she said after breathing in the autumn air.

"It is. Hey, you don't mind if we go out to the Hamilton graves, do you? Just to make sure everything looks good before winter sets in?"

Hand in hand, they walked the countryside bordering Lake Champlain. Across the hills in Vermont, the leaves were all down. The normally forest-green ridges were gray, brown, with deep green swatches of coniferous trees streaking the landscape.

She took out a pack of cigarettes, made to take one, but then put it back in her coat. "You know, those construction guys in Albany, they really freaked me out."

David squeezed her hand a little tighter.

"It's okay," she said, tossing it off like it was no big deal. "I'm over it now. It's just that's what happened the night I got jumped. Those two muggers started off by whistling at me too."

"So, when the guys on the demolition crew did the same thing, it stimulated your trauma reaction."

"That's not how I would have put it, but sure, if you say so."

He wished he hadn't given in to the let-me-show-you-what-a-big-shot-psychologist-I-am impulse. It was insensitive, and he knew better. At least Angela didn't take umbrage and finished her idea.

"The thing is, I thought by now I'd be over all this."

"Give yourself some time, Angie," he said. "Because it may take time."

Crows called from the stand of trees nearby.

"Yeah, I suppose so."

"But you feel all right now?"

Angela looked over, pulled him closer and smiled. "I feel fine."

They took the path into the woods where the Hamiltons were buried. Some debris had fallen inside the iron fence surrounding the tombstones. David opened the gate and stepped through to gather branches and pull a few weeds.

"Have you noticed we have company?" she said.

Crows had shadowed them all the way from the house, past the clover ledge and into the woods, jumping from branch to branch, calling back and forth to each other.

"If you're talking about our fine feathered friends, yes."

"You're going to think I'm crazy," she said, "but I think it's the same ones that lured me back here last summer."

In truth, he too felt the supernatural was near, but David didn't want to alarm her, so he glibly said, "Why not? They say crows are among the most intelligent of all birds, and nothing about this place surprises me anymore." He slapped the dirt off his hands. "Thanks, I feel better."

"Hey, Weis," she said. "Didn't you forget something?"

"Thanks for reminding me." He placed a little rock on Almira's tombstone.

Once out of the woods, they were buffeted by gusts of wind blowing up the valley that raised white-capped waves on the lake, a warning that the last breath of Indian Summer was about to end.

Angela exhaled. "You know, I'm not as set against living here as I used to be. I have to admit, I'm calmer here, and there's a slower pace to things. It helps settle my nerves."

"Really? You mean that?"

"I do. I think I could live here. There's not a lot going on jobwise, but it's beautiful, and it's peaceful. Besides, this place means a lot to you. That's obvious. It's good for you."

"Not all the time," he said. "It gets lonely here, and if I get in a black mood, well, that's not good. I need someone to share this place with, the way it's meant to be enjoyed."

Just past the barn, abreast with the carriage house and at the edge of the yard, he stopped. "I don't mean to creep you out but look at that upstairs window."

Angela gasped. "Holy cow! Those crows — they're sitting on the window ledge. They're tapping on the glass."

"You know what window that is, don't you?" David said.

"No."

"It's the Quiet Room."

Angela poured evaporated milk into their coffee and placed the mugs on the table.

"Baby," she said, sitting down, "the point I'm making is that those are the same crows that led me to the graves in the first place. I know it, and so do you." While they both stirred their coffee she went on. "And with all the windows in this house, why would two crows sit and tap at the window that just so happens to open into your Quiet Room? It's like they were saying, hey, we'll meet you here tonight."

David took a drink. "It makes sense to me. So you're saying you'd like to try meeting with them?"

"Right."

"Tonight, in the Quiet Room."

"Right," she said again. "And here's why. David, I've come right out and told you I would be willing to live here. But we both know I'd be giving up a lot—everything I've worked for—like grad school, I'd be throwing it all away."

"Maybe not."

"Maybe not," she conceded. "But probably."

"So what do you propose?"

"I'd like to ask them if there's anything we can do to, you know, help move them along, or at least diminish the ghost presence around here."

At first David didn't answer. He felt himself getting defensive. Angela was asking him to choose between a future with her and his access to another world. On the other hand, wasn't Angela offering another world too? Marriage, family, children?

"Okay, in theory I'm with you, but this isn't a precise science. I mean, they probably feel every bit as entitled to be here as we do."

"Sure, I get that." She stood. "Do you want another cup of coffee?"

"If you're having more, why not."

Angela took their mugs to the counter, refilled them, then added milk and sugar. "I think what I'm really saying is that these ghosts take up a lot of our attention. If we stay together, I don't want to see our lives become their lives. I want us to have a life of our own." She brought the mugs back.

David thanked her and said, "I understand. I really

do. But it's kind of like ending therapy with a client. You don't just terminate."

"Don't worry," she said. "I'll let you take the lead."

What she was saying was right of course, but his journey of self-discovery under Almira's tutelage wasn't quite finished.

"Thanks. Now if we're going to wait for them to appear, the first thing is to light a fire. That room is like a freezer, and we may be in there all night."

By midnight the Quiet Room was warmed, and once the candles and lamps were lit, the scent of hot cocoa in antique luster cups completed a domestic setting of days long gone by.

Stacked on the mantle, one upon the other, was Almira's autograph book, Horsford's treatise on Phrenology, *Facts in Mesmerism*, and *The Young Lady's Friend*. Angela had read some of The Friend last year. Indeed, it was this very book which had first undermined her faith in the assumptions of modern relationships.

Having selected their reading material, the couple settled on the daybed. He settled at one end, while she reclined on the single roll-arm, her legs comfortably stretched across his lap.

Angela chuckled to herself.

"What's so funny?" he asked.

"Listen to this," she said to him, and began reading.

> "Very giddy girls will sometimes so far forget themselves as to ridicule personal defects: they will speak like a stammerer, or listen like the deaf, or imitate the awkward movements of the near-sighted or the lame.

Nothing can be more inhuman. No expression of disapprobation is too strong for you to use on your young companions whenever they fall into this fault. It is not sufficient that you do not share in it, you should express your utter abhorrence of the practice."

"I guess human nature hasn't changed very much," David said.

"I guess not."

David got up and raked the coals in the hearth to an even glowing bed.

"I hope we're not going to be stood up," said Angela, refilling their cups of cocoa. "But even if they don't appear, this is still a nice way to pass the night. Kind of romantic."

She was right, it was romantic. How many hours over the years had they spent in parallel reading, or reading to each other? It was hard to say, but those hours were among the happiest of recent memory.

He returned back to Horsford's report on Phrenology. The deeper he got, the easier it was to see connections between the consensus in Phrenology with, say, Maslow's Hierarchy, Trait Theory, or even Freud's Id, Ego, and Superego System of Personality.

With a legal pad placed across Angela's legs, he took out a pencil and started drawing triangles, boxes, concentric circles, and labeling them. Next, he drew arrows to indicate relationships between these concepts and the principles of Phrenology.

David read Horsford some more, then studied his diagram again. How did Animal Magnetism fit in with all this? His impulse was to rise and retrieve 'Townshend's

Facts,' except that he noticed the peculiar glow which always preceded Almira's appearance. Angela was dozing, so he shook her by the knees.

"Hey, wake up."

"Huh? What's going on?"

"Wake up. I think we're going to have company."

She scanned the brighter room. A wood fire blazed now where only a bank of glowing coals was heaped up. Angela sat up and patted her hair.

"Do I look alright?"

"You look fine. Now listen, do you see those bright spots over there?"

David and Angela stood.

Two orbs of light floated by the window, near the ceiling. They circled the perimeter of the room and came to a stop where they started. Over the following seconds, Daniel and Almira's forms became outlined. The manifestation started with their faces, spreading first in substance and depth through the torso and limbs. The process seemed to be harder for Daniel, who sometimes faded in and out or exhibited the stop action phenomena David associated with strobe lights.

David, of course, had seen Almira come to life on dozens of occasions, so he wasn't frightened, and really never had been. Instead, having questioned whether Daniel would even be able to materialize someplace where he'd been unfamiliar in life, David's interest was scientific. Daniel's struggle to grasp the physical plane now was confirming David's theory.

Angela meanwhile witnessed all this with a mixture of astonishment and fear on her face, for ghosts were still new to her. She clung to David's arm, watching wide-eyed from behind his shoulder.

The Dwyers, unlike their previous May promenade, were this time attired appropriately for an indoor gathering—no hats, bonnets, or parasols. Almira wore a silk dress with short sleeves, and white fingerless mitts. By her side in black broadcloth, with a richly embroidered silk vest, stood Daniel.

"Good evening," David said with a little bow.

The Dwyers nodded and bowed in return. "We were hoping you might receive us tonight," said Almira.

Daniel remained quiet.

"Please forgive my husband. It is difficult for us to be where we are strangers." She turned to him. "Darling, these were my chambers in our time. Doctor Weis has restored this room to its appearance just as I remember it, excepting, of course, my memorial."

Daniel pointed to the window. In a voice which sounded garbled, like a man speaking underwater, he said, "I do remember being outdoors, looking up to see you watching from that very window."

Angela, who'd recovered some courage and composure, gestured to the daybed. "Please, won't you have a seat?"

Silently the couple positioned themselves. Almira noticed the book lying beside her on the cushion and picked it up, or rather a transparent facsimile of it. "Has one of you been reading this?"

"I have," said Angela. "I hope you don't mind."

"Goodness no, not the least bit. It was a gift from my mother. Don't you think it's a touching gift?"

"It is. I wish I had had a copy when I was a teenager. My mother passed away when I was just sixteen. I felt kind of lost for a while after that."

"My dear friend." Almira sighed. "We share that tragedy in common. And but for my husband's love, I should have never known happiness again."

Daniel took her hand. "My wife flatters me," he said in a voice now undistorted. "It is she who brought me all the happiness I've known."

It was striking, how affectionate they were together, leaning into each other, arms and fingers intertwined. Most people had a conception of Victorians as staid and uptight. David knew this, and looking at early photographs, it was easy to understand why. But here he could see the proof that it was otherwise. These were flesh and blood human beings, once at least, and maybe still, with beating hearts and thinking minds brimming over with the full spectrum of thought and emotion.

"But you're together and happy now," David said. "Aren't you?"

"Yes, but it's not all the lark you might think. You have complete lives, whilst we are forever at this place and time." Daniel's form flickered, so Almira finished his answer.

"For while we are blessed to have each other, and every meaningless trifle we might desire, we're also left to ruminate our mistakes, separated from God's family."

"For how long?" David asked.

"We don't know," said Almira. "It may be a thousand years, but until the spirits of our children are fulfilled, we have made the choice to remain here with them." She drew a handkerchief from her pocket and brought it to her cheek.

Daniel wrapped his arm around her shoulder and kissed her temple. "It was our contract with God, you see. We would spend an eternity here until our children are born or we have atoned in God's eyes."

"You mean that you've chosen to be here?" Angela said. "I don't understand why."

"Why don't you tell them," said Daniel, gently nudging his wife.

Almira looked up from her handkerchief. "Because I, we, couldn't leave our children to suffer death without being first born. Can't you see how horrible that would be?"

"We begged God," Daniel said. "We pledged to him that we would never leave them. We asked it to be so but that we could give them the life they were denied. We would stay here by the lake, at this place for a thousand years, and so make good for our selfish acts."

"Isn't there anything we can do to help you?" Angela said.

Almira's adoring eyes turned from her husband to them. "There is something, yes, but we daren't speak the words."

David felt like a psychotherapist again. "Why not?"

"Really," Angela said. "If there is anything we can do, we want to know."

Almira looked to her husband for a sign of permission.

"Dear-heart, please," he said. "What you're thinking is too much to ask of anyone."

She shrugged him off. "No, I must. God has sent them to us that we might satisfy our destiny. Can't you see that?" Almira redirected her attention back to Angela and David. "There is something."

"What?" David and Angela asked in unison.

"Marry and have our children, hatch our little birdies."

Startled, no, really shocked, David glanced at Angela,

wondering if she was the future mother of his children to be, and reached for her hand.

"Mirie, please," Daniel said.

She held his hands down. "Darling, they are living. They can have the children we lost, the children we can't have. They would be restored, and we would be released."

"Is that true, Mr. Dwyer?" Angela said. "Is that what would happen?"

Daniel's image went momentarily transparent. When he regained solidarity, he nodded solemnly. "Yes. That is our understanding."

"We would ask only this. That we might visit with them sometimes." Almira tried to go on but had to hide her tears in Daniel's shoulder.

He stroked her hair. "You have our word it would only be at night, for a moment or two when all of you have gone to bed. If we might just see them sleeping peacefully, or watch them play but once, that's all we ask."

Almira lifted her head. Her face was tear-streaked and her eyes red, but she smiled with hope. "And only until they are grown. For as they grow in body and spirit, so will we fade away."

There was a minute of silence.

"I don't know what to say," Angela mumbled.

David was speechless too.

"Forgive me," Almira said. "I knew it was too much to ask"

"No, don't say that." Angela wiped away tears of her own. "It's just, Almira, I want to help you. I'd have your children, I really would, but I want children of my own too. Would they be yours or ours?"

Optimism flashed across Almira's face, but it was Daniel who answered. "The first two children would have the fulfilled souls of our unborn twins, but you and Doctor Weis would be the only parents they would ever know."

"And what if we had more children?" David said from the edge of his seat.

"Once our babies are born, our duty is complete."

Almira squeezed her husband's hand. "Doctor Weis, Miss Angela, if only you would entertain our request, we would be forever in your debt. Whatever your decision be, if this is beyond you, we understand. Our request will never intrude upon you again."

David and Angela saw their forms flicker and begin to fade, and then they were gone. Vanished.

After an indistinct period of time went by, Angela turned to David who was still spaced-out.

"Wow," she said. "I didn't expect that."

"Me neither."

"And I'm so tired too. I've got to go to bed. I can't even talk about this right now. I feel, what do you guys call it, dissociated? Is that right?"

"Yeah," said David. "Interaction with ghosts is draining. I always feel exhausted after these things too." He got up and extended his hand. "Angela, let's go to bed — together." She made to say something, but David motioned for her to hear him out. "C'mon. Just to sleep and hold each other through the night. I mean it. We can talk about all this some other time."

Chapter 43

September 1842

"So, your gentleman wishes to speak to me?"

"Yes. Jack says he'll come by after supper tomorrow. He can help you meet this old man who knew Miss Almira."

It was hard to believe the truth might yet be revealed. Rebecca had given up hope, but there might be an answer after all. "Tildie," she said, "thank you for arranging this. As I think you know, it means a great deal to me."

"I know it does, Miss Becca." Tildie began unhooking her mistress's dress. "Did you enjoy that magic lantern show?"

"The lanterna magica? Yes, it was very nice." Rebecca looked at her hands. They were trembling. The time had come. In light of her recent conversation with Mary and Phebe, she could not in good conscience conceal their true relationship any longer. *It must be done,* she told herself, over and over. But just saying the words would set in motion a cascade of events most unpredictable, except that life would never be the same. That was the one certain thing.

And what was more, for the first time ever, Rebecca was uncertain about the morality of servitude. Yet all this paled in comparison to the paramount issue — the father she thought she knew so well had been lying. His lifetime of deception was disturbing. How long would he, could he, have kept this secret? Mother knew, that was obvious now, but there must be others as well. Other sisters? How could she have been so naïve, so blind?

After discovering so many years of falsehood, her father seemed a stranger. Yet, as the hours stretched into the last few days, another idea had taken hold. She was coming to see him as a passionate man, in much the same way that she herself was. She could empathize with him as, like her, he had insatiable longings and wantings to possess and be possessed.

Rebecca put on her nightdress. She went to her bed, sat, and patted the mattress. "Tildie, sit here beside me. There is something else which I must tell you."

"Yes, miss. What you need?"

"I don't need anything." Rebecca hesitated. "I don't quite know how to say this, but I shall try."

"What is it, miss Becca?" Tildie said, growing impatient.

"We're sisters," Rebecca blurted out.

Tildie gasped. "What're you saying?"

"Well, half-sisters to be exact."

"What do you mean, miss? You pulling Tildie's leg."

"No," Rebecca said, calmly. "It's true."

Tildie stood. "How long you've known this?"

"A few weeks, I suppose. The idea has been a growing

suspicion of mine since last winter, but only during the summer did it become clear, and now I am certain."

"I dun understand."

"I'll try to explain." Rebecca leaned forward and took Tildie's hand, beseeching her to sit back down. "This past summer, while I was at Shelter Island, the Gardiner sisters and I experimented with Animal Magnetism." Tildie's expression changed from puzzled to suspicious, but Rebecca went on. "Anyway, while in the throes of an ecstatic state—"

"You been playing with spells, haven't you? Miss Phebe and her sister, Miss Mary, those girls got some kind of witchcraft about them. I've heard the way they talk to each other, theeing and thying. They casting spells if you ask me, and I told you Jesus don't like it when we play with the devil."

Again, she made to rise, but Rebecca held her hand firm to the mattress. "No, no. It's nothing like that at all." Another approach had to be taken, so Rebecca breathed in deep and tried again. "Tildie, how old are you?"

"'Bout twenty-one, maybe twenty-two."

"And what do you remember of your life before you came to us in Charleston?

"Me and my momma was living with the master and his family. My momma looked after their things."

"And what do you know about your father?"

"Don't know anything, miss—only he was a white man."

"Do you remember my father from before you came to Charleston?"

"Of course I do, miss. Him and the master was good friends."

"Well, I've discovered that your father is my father as

well. That makes us sisters. Half-sisters anyway."

"Miss Rebecca, you sure 'bout this?"

"Yes, Tildie, I'm absolutely sure. I wrote to my— our father asking him directly, and he confirmed my suspicion in writing."

"He wrote this to you? Let me see it."

"I'm sorry," said Rebecca. "I don't have the letter. On his instruction, I burned it. You probably couldn't read it anyway."

"I read a little." Tildie corrected.

"So you do."

It sounded patronizing, and that wasn't what Rebecca intended. "Tildie, I'm sorry, but as peculiar as it may seem, we are sisters. That is the nut and the shell of it."

The two sat face to face, utterly quiet, studying each other's features for traces of the father they had in common. Rebecca broke the silence.

"Perhaps it would be best if you simply called me Rebecca from this point forward, at least when we're alone."

"Dunno I can do that. Seems mighty strange."

"So it does, but I am discovering that life is itself strange, and this is what it has today offered us."

"Miss Becca," Tildie said, "this mean I'm not a slave?"

"No, you're still a bonded servant."

"And I still black?"

"Yes, you're still black. One-fourth at least."

"And you still going to take me with you to Philadelphia."

"I don't know," said Rebecca, rubbing her temple and brow. "I'm trying to...to do something. Arrange somehow that perhaps you can stay here for at least a while longer. It's very difficult." She gestured to the outside world with a sweep of her hand. "Tildie, the thing is this. You could run away, but you'd only do that to be with Mr. DeGroot, and since you and he are, as they say, known, you could be easily found and taken back south."

"By slave catchers," Tildie said softly.

"Up here, as things are now, probably not. But even if you and Jack were married, it wouldn't carry the weight of the law, and my father or his estate could always make claim to you and to your children."

"Your daddy would do that to me?"

"Our daddy," Rebecca said. "But yes, he might. He would be within his rights to do so."

The following day Rebecca and Phebe were in her room studying French. A knock sounded at the door.

"Miss Becca, there's someone at the back steps to see you."

"Excuse me, Phebe. I've got to attend to this." Rebecca got up, already knowing who it was and why they were there.

Following Tildie downstairs, she was led through the kitchen—a room she'd only been in a few times before—to the rear entrance. They stepped out on the back porch.

"Good afternoon, miss." The man took off his hat, exposing a bald head. "I'm Jack DeGroot. We've met before."

"I remember, sir. It is about a year since."

"Yes, that's right. Tildie tells me you want to know what happened to your friend, Miss Almira."

"Surely," said Rebecca in a soft voice, hoping Mrs. Bright wouldn't detect their conversation.

"Well there's an old gentleman boarding with me.

His name is Sandborne, and he knows what happened. He saw it himself, with his own eyes. He can tell you all you wish to know. He's willing to meet with you at the park of the capitol building on Sunday afternoon, if that would be suitable."

DeGroot's wording suggested this Sandborne witnessed an actual event. Someone inside called for Tildie, who excused herself and left as Rebecca resumed the conversation. "Sunday afternoon is fine, sir. Shall Tildie bring me at about 3p.m.?"

"That will be perfect."

"Will I likely see you there as well?" asked Rebecca.

"Yes, miss. Me and Tildie, we try to spend what time we can together."

"Thank you, Mr. DeGroot."

DeGroot handled his hat and made to speak some more, but his voice seemed to catch with emotion. He cleared his throat.

"You know, miss," he finally said. "I would buy her freedom if I could. But no one will lend me money— not in these times. Being separated is just breaking our hearts."

"Believe me, sir, my hands are tied. Though I have entreated my father to emancipate Tildie, there is nothing I can do outside his wishes."

"I understand. But if only you could help us stay together so we can marry, I'll do anything, I swear. I'm desperate." Jack hid his face in his hands. His shoulders heaved. He sobbed, and for a moment bellowed like a wounded bull, then caught himself. "Please, miss," he said through sniffles. "I'll take care of her. I promise."

Rebecca felt her own tears coming, but knew she had to maintain her poise. "You both have my sympathies," she finally said. "But this is beyond my influence."

DeGroot made a slight bow and wiped tears from his cheeks, then returned his hat to his bald head. "God bless you, miss. Please tell Matilda I couldn't stay, that I had to get back."

Chapter 44

November 1972

The day before Thanksgiving, David drove down to his studio in the city, called Angela and arranged to pick her up in the morning.

"You're sure about this?" she said toward the end of their conversation.

"I'm sure."

"Alright, super. I'll see you at ten."

He wasn't sure, not one hundred percent anyway. David hung his hand from the phone receiver for a few seconds. Spending half the day driving through a wasteland of suburbia to eat with a bunch of strangers, stay there overnight and use their shower in the morning sounded unappealing, but maybe it was necessary. Married people did that, or so he'd been told, and wasn't that the real purpose, getting a sample of married life?

Coveting his remaining solitude, David went over to the hi-fi, selected a new Deutsche Gramophone recording of Beethoven's 7th symphony, poured a slivovitz, and settled on the portion of the sofa that wasn't buried under books.

By the time the allegretto started, he was more relaxed. He loved this movement, the way the tension and emotion built and built and then tumbled down to start all over again. Could Beethoven have possibly wrung out another drop of agony? No, he thought not. Beethoven had it right.

It got to him, the minor key, but they always did. Beethoven's perfect interweaving of sadness and beauty spoke to David's romantic belief in life as essentially meaningless, but on an epic scale.

The music revived his recent conversations with Almira, how he'd been articulating his need to keep himself apart and alone, yet the kettle drums corrected him. He was part of humanity, like it or not.

The brooding face of Beethoven in stained glass sat across the floor from him. What a mind. David raised his shot glass to a musical genius going deaf.

Some suggested Beethoven was manic-depressive on top of going deaf, but yet he still kept creating. In this second movement he set the listener up to agree that nihilism was the only reasonable belief in this lousy world. Then, with the plucking of a few strings, he showed that you were misinformed. Brilliant. The lesson to come away with is to not take yourself too seriously.

David got up. He raised the phonograph needle from the turntable and placed it back down in the groove to hear the movement again.

In the morning, the two proceeded eastward, further and further out on Long Island. On the way, Angela tutored him on how to handle her relatives.

"I'm warning you, they're loud. And if you don't dive in and interrupt them, you'll never get a word in edgewise."

Here and there as they drove, David noticed old farmhouses and taverns. He'd see one standing alone like some speck of the past which hadn't been washed away in a deluge of tract houses and strip malls. Long Island must have been a beautiful, pastoral place in the 1800s when William Sidney Mount was painting scenes of everyday life here, but so much of it was paved over now.

"How long have your father and his wife lived out here?"

"Almost two years," she said. "I've only ever come out here a few times. I took the train. It was a pain in the ass."

Angela drew a scrap of paper from her coat pocket and checked her directions. Minutes later they were parked in front of a ranch house with cedar shingles, identical to a dozen or more on quarter acre lots along a freshly laid, asphalt street. Except for an occasional oak standing lonely in a backyard, there wasn't a tree more than seven feet tall in the immediate area. The land had been bulldozed clean, erased, then carpeted with pavement and cookie-cutter houses.

Angela's family was every bit as ethnic as David was afraid they would be. He'd been warned. Yes, they were loud, but they were friendly, mostly.

Mr. Bellasaro was a sturdy built kind of guy with muscular forearms, around one of which he wore a wristwatch on an expandable band. From behind his gregarious exterior, he looked David over with a wary eye. Astonishingly pregnant, her stepmother was barely able to get up from the sofa.

David took inventory of the rest of the family...

Uncle number one seemed to like him, as did both her aunts. Uncle number two didn't like anybody, and the spinster aunt was bland and untraveled. An array of pubescent cousins with seemingly identical first names rounded out the holiday crowd.

Through the warm glow of wine David observed this extended family, all of them comically lacking in self-consciousness, talking over each other, gesturing with their hands or groaning as they pushed back from the table.

As for the table, the turkey was overcooked and received cursory attention, but the sausage and peppers and aunt number two's tray of lasagna more than made up for it. The wine flowed red and freely from the gallon at the head of the table, where Angela's father held court.

"Weis," he said, topping off David's half empty glass. "What kind of an Italian name is that?"

Angela rolled her eyes. "Dad, please don't start."

"Hey, it's a simple question."

David nudged her knee. "My parents were born in extreme northern Italy."

"No kidding, where?"

"Austria."

The joke was a defensive maneuver, showing off his knowledge of geography and intellectual agility to relieve his anxiety, but as a style of social interaction it was less than ideal.

Uncle number one and her old man laughed, while uncle number two started cracking walnuts.

"My daughter tells me you're a psychiatrist who's in

the antiques business. Is that right?"

"I deal in antiques, but I don't do psychology anymore."

Angela's father didn't respond. David felt the heat being turned up. This guy was no dope, so a more detailed explanation was unavoidable. "The truth is I needed a change of career, and since my family owns a few apartment buildings in the city, it was possible for me to make that change."

"A change of career," repeated Angela's father. "I can understand that."

After the main course was finished, Thanksgiving ended with espresso coffee, fortified with anisette and a razor thin lemon slice. There was a box of Italian pastries too, and later on a game of Michigan Rummy.

It was fun, he had to be honest. And by the time most of the family left, he felt good about them. Angela, her stepmother, and one aunt were finishing up in the kitchen. Talking to women was easier so he offered to help but got sent away.

"Well, I guess it's just us guys."

Bellasaro looked up from his easy chair, wine in hand. "What?"

It felt like he'd disturbed someone in a deep reverie, so David apologized.

"I start to think about the old days," Bellasaro said. "Anyway, it's late. Are you tired? You must be tired. Come with me."

Her father led David down a carpeted hallway. Along the way they passed a pair of high school graduation portraits. Angela's picture was in black and white, her hair in a flip, wearing cat eyeglasses. Her younger brother's high school portrait had him in color, sporting a nascent mustache of which only a teenager could be proud. They passed Angela's room. At the end of the hallway there was another bedroom. Angela's father switched on the light, revealing David's coat and overnight bag already placed on the bed. He looked around at the hockey stick and the posters on the walls.

"This was supposed to be my son's room. Now he's in a hospital in Japan. They tell me he might be in a wheelchair for the rest of his life."

"I'm sorry."

"Thanks. It breaks my heart. I'd have rather seen him be a draft dodger in Canada than be the last guy wounded in Vietnam. Christ, the poor kid didn't last two weeks. At least his mother wasn't around to see this happen, God rest her soul."

The sound of Angela's laughter came from the kitchen. The old guy tilted his head to the noise.

"She takes after my late wife, always busy, ambitious, always on the go, until she got sick. For a couple of years, I kept hoping Angie would move back home. We even set up a bedroom for her, but she didn't want to move out to the island. Besides, she got her heart set on this college thing. I tried to talk some sense into her, but once my daughter makes up her mind, you can forget about it."

"Angela's a strong-minded girl," David said, choosing his words carefully.

He put his hand on David's shoulder. "You're a psychiatrist, maybe you can talk to her."

Should David remind him he wasn't a psychiatrist, and what did he expect him to do? Persuade her to quit school, become a kindergarten teacher or a secretary with a typewriter? She wouldn't go for that. David didn't know what to say, so he didn't say anything.

Her father picked up his story. "She had a hard time for a few years after her mother died. It was tough on the kid — tough on all of us. Maybe I didn't help. I was...." His voice trailed off, then he refocused. "I'll tell you something...you're the first guy my daughter has ever brought home. So be good to her, okay? That's all I care about. I don't care what part of northern Italy your family doesn't come from, or that you have long hair like some kind of a hippy. Just be good to her."

Chapter 45

September 1842

"**That old man sitting** with Jack," Tildie said, tilting her head, "that's Mr. Sandborne."

As Rebecca approached with her sister, the men stood and doffed their caps. Next to the portly DeGroot, Sandborne looked slight of frame and thin. He wore his long gray hair tied back with a ribbon in the style of the previous century. Most of all, there was an air of sadness about him. It showed in every line of his face and every weathered feature, but especially in his pale blue eyes.

"Miss Carvalho," said Jack with a gesture. "This here's Emmet Sandborne. He can talk with you about your friend."

Sandborne brought his cap to his chest. "Very pleased to meet you, miss."

"By your leave," said Jack, "me and Matilda, we're going to walk a while and come back."

"They look very happy, don't they?" Rebecca said,

watching them stroll off.

"Aye, ma'am, they do."

Rebecca and the old gentleman took seats on the bench, and she opened the conversation.

"Mr. Sandborne, you knew Almira Hamilton?"

"Oh yes. I lived with the Hamiltons from when she was but a little baby. Oh, how well do I remember those days. And you, miss—you knew Almira as well?"

"She and I were classmates and lived at the same boarding house. We grew very close. I came to love her as a sister and friend."

"I understand."

"Mr. DeGroot tells me you knew Daniel Dwyer as well."

"I did," he said. "Me and Danny lived and worked together on the Hamilton's property. Wasn't he a skinny lad when Mr. Hamilton brought him home from Burlington? I well remember the day. They gave him a suit of clothes and fed him, and he lived there with us until Miss Almira was sent to the academy."

"He wanted to separate them, you know, but Danny followed her here to Albany, which I suppose is when you came to know them."

All the things Almira had told her were being confirmed. It left her hoping she might still be alive.

Loosening the drawstring of her purse, Rebecca retrieved the miniature of her and Almira together. She held it out to Sandborne. "I think you'd like to see this."

Cradling the case in his calloused hand, Sandborne slipped the tiny brass latches and opened it. The old fellow's jaw dropped, as if he suddenly saw Almira standing before him. He glanced toward Rebecca, then back at the daguerreotype. "It is like she lives again."

"We had this portrait made just a few days before her father took her away," Rebecca said.

The old man didn't respond, but his hand shook. Rebecca realized he was struggling to control his grief and looked away. In the distance, Tildie and Jack were arm in arm.

Sandborne's blue eyes squeezed shut. He pulled a handkerchief from inside his jacket, raised it to his face and wept. "Pardon me, miss," he said after wiping his eyes and blowing his nose. "I loved her like my own daughter, and to suddenly see her face again, well, you may understand if I am overcome."

"Mr. Sandborne," Rebecca said, "please, where is Almira?"

The old gentleman closed the cover as if it was the lid of a coffin and gave it back to Rebecca.

"I warn you it is a tragic tale."

"Please, sir, don't spare me. What has happened to Almira? I just have to know."

"Then I will tell you the rest," said Sandborne. "When Mr. Hamilton returned from Albany with his daughter, I knew Danny would follow, and he did. He made his way back. He told me all about his plan to take her away with him across the lake and marry in Vermont. He said they would continue on to Boston and take a steamboat to South Carolina."

"Yes," Rebecca said. "They were to go to Charleston."

"You knew about this?"

"Of course," she said, unable to hide the impatience from her voice. "My father was going to underwrite Daniel's miniature gallery."

"Did you know more?"

"That she was with child, yes."

"Very well…" Mr. Sandborne rubbed a hand over his eyes. "The night they were to leave, I placed a taper in the window. It was a signal to Almira that she should meet Danny at midnight." Sandborne went quiet, pressing his lips together for a moment. "I don't know if I can go on." His voice sounded unsteady. "But I'll try." The old man fixed his eyes at the ground before him and took a deep breath. "Though the lake was frozen, the previous day was unusually warm. I warned Danny that it might not be safe. I begged him to stay until the weather turned cold again, but he refused, we had a terrible argument. He said Mr. Hamilton could send her away at any moment to have their baby secretly, which was true, and then he might never find her and his child again. When he bade me farewell, I wept to see him go. In the morning, Mr. Hamilton came running to the carriage house. He was shouting that Almira had disappeared and that we must get up a search party to find her. The poor gentleman was beside himself with worry, yet I couldn't say a word lest I betray them. I deceived him and all the other neighbor men who helped us search. I prayed Danny and Mirie made it across safely and were perhaps already married.

When we finally found the tracks of Danny's horse, we followed them to the lake. I knew something had gone wrong for we could see a figure out there on the ice. Mr. Hamilton went mad with anxiety for his daughter. He ran to her, not caring if he should break through the ice. For while it had turned terribly cold overnight, we all knew it might still be thin."

"Mr. Sandborne, what did you find?"

He turned his weary eyes to Rebecca. "It was her, Almira," he said in a raspy voice. "She was kneeling on the ice beside where Daniel and the horse had fallen through. There was no sign of Daniel. The break was already frozen over again. She must have fallen in too for her clothes were turned to ice. A thin veil of drift-snow surrounded her. She looked so peaceful, so beautiful. Poor Mr. Hamilton, he wept and cried out. He raved. He tore at his hair. It took three strong men to pull him away.

I tell you it was a horrible thing to see. Her body was frozen to the ice. She was like glass. Indeed, we men had to chip her loose. With my own jackknife I cut her cape away so that we might free her corpse."

Rebecca broke into tears. "My dear Mirie, I'm so very, very sorry."

"Please, miss, don't cry," Sandborne said. "Only I could have prevented it, for only I knew the truth. Yet I said nothing, and now I carry that burden everywhere I go." The old gentleman withdrew a small gold cross from his waistcoat pocket. "I found this on the ice not far from where she lay. There were beads scattered all about her too. I recognized them. They were from a papist chain Danny used when he said his prayers. He was a Roman Catholic. Did you know that?"

Too upset to answer, Rebecca only nodded. The parting clouds bathed the park in a warming bright sun, but she had no reason to stay longer, there was nothing left to know.

Chapter 46

November 24, 1972

They were up and out early with instructions. David shouldn't be a stranger, and Angela would get a phone call as soon as her stepmother went into labor.

On their way out of the housing development David said, "You never told me your old man was a cop."

"He's not—not really."

"Okay, but a police detective turned insurance investigator is pretty close."

In the light of day, David could see more family resemblance, and now he knew where she got her habit of presenting a tough exterior.

"Don't get me wrong," he said. "I like him. He's straightforward."

"Good. He's a decent guy, my dad, and I'm sorry if he got sentimental on you last night. That's what happens when he has too much wine."

David dismissed it.

"And thanks for doing this, by the way. It wasn't so bad, was it?"

"No, it wasn't bad at all."

David reflected on the last twenty-four hours, identifying points where he had set himself apart as a protective measure, and sometimes hidden behind a shield of intellectual rhetoric. He wasn't at his best, no, but he would get better at it.

"Hey," said Angela, "who was that artist you told me about, the one from Long Island with the paintings? Remember? You wanted to see them."

"William Sidney Mount?"

"That's the guy. While we're out here, we ought to go check it out."

David's whole face lit up at the idea. "Angie, you're a genius. I think we're not that far from Stony Brook where the museum is."

He pulled into a gas station and retrieved a road atlas from under his seat. "Yes, Stony Brook was pretty much the next town over. David saw a phone booth. "I'm going to call to see if they're even open."

He hated phone booths. This one was like all the others — filthy with litter, cigarette butts, and obscene graffiti. Handling the receiver made him cringe as he dropped a dime in the slot.

"Operator, I'd like to place a station-to-station call to the Suffolk Museum in Stony Brook, New York."

"Deposit seventy cents please."

Realizing he only had another thirty cents in his pockets, David leaned out of the booth and called to the car. "Angie, do you have any change?"

She started rummaging through her enormous handbag and brought a handful of loose coins.

"I'm sorry, sir," said the operator a few minutes later. "There's no answer at that number."

It was a big letdown. Seeing the Mount paintings was something he'd wanted to do for a long time, and this would have been a great opportunity.

"What a bummer," Angela said when he told her the line was dead.

He started the car and put it in gear. "Yeah, well, some other time I guess."

While headed for the Long Island Expressway, David's thoughts drifted back to Mount. Maybe one day soon he would be able to view the largest collection of his paintings in the country. Mount and Almira were contemporaries, and his scenes of everyday life could have used hers as a model. He wasn't sure if paintings could make one homesick for a past which was never his, but his feelings toward them could only be described in those terms.

Near the Expressway, Angela spoke up. "David, from where we are now, how far are we from Shelter Island?"

He considered the geography of their location. "I don't know, maybe seven-five miles. Certainly, less than a hundred miles anyway."

"How long would it take us to drive there?"

"We'd have to take a short ferry to the island, but it shouldn't take more than a couple of hours at most."

He looked at her, and she looked at him.

"Let's go," they said together.

David yanked the steering wheel, made a U-turn and headed east.

Traffic on the Montauk Highway along Long Island's southern fork could be bumper to bumper during the tourist season, but not on this gloomy day in late

November. In truth, the landscape was bleak. This whole southern shore of Long Island was flat, composed of potato fields and second growth scrub-pine.

David noticed Angela was absorbed in thought.

"What are you thinking about? Your Poe dissertation?"

"Sort of, yes," she said. "I was thinking about Almira and her lover. Their whole story. It has a kind of gothic quality to it, don't you think?"

"You mean the young muse frozen in death at the moment of her most perfect beauty?"

"Exactly. It's all like a story by Poe. Horsford, with his doomed, idealized wife, the interest in Mesmerism, and Phrenology. And there's the whole mercury poisoning part, that has a kind of grotesque Poe flavor to it too." Angela pulled up her handbag, recovered a spiral notebook and read aloud. "'I could not love, except where Death is mingling his with beauty's breath.'"

"That's Poe, isn't it?"

"Yes, Poe, exactly. From one of his earlier poems."

She went on in this vein the rest of the way, pointing out the parallels between Almira and the female leads in Poe's poetry. She did have a degree in American literature after all.

With Peconic Bay to the north and the Atlantic Ocean to the east and south, the ferry landing at North Haven had the scent of the ocean everywhere, and the sounds too—lapping water, seagulls, dinging masts, and buoys. Indeed, no location along either fork of Long Island was more than a few miles from a large body of saltwater at any point.

They had already driven on board the ferry and were waiting for it to depart. The temperature was warmer here than at her father's place in Smithtown, so they got out and leaned against the fender. An unbroken ceiling of clouds hung overhead, but the horizon was bright.

"David, what was this place like in Almira's time?" Angela asked.

He gave it some thought. "I think the biggest difference is that at that time this area had a very active whaling industry. There would have been dozens of tall-masted ships in Sag Harbor, Greenport, and other places around here. I mean a real forest of them. Supposedly a lot of the Sag Harbor fleet became derelict vessels in San Francisco Bay."

She threw a puzzled glance his way.

"The crews abandoned their ships out there for the California gold rush," he said.

Angela pinched his cheek. "You're so smart."

He moved away from the car and looked around.

"Hey," David said. "Let's take the top down. It's mild enough, and I doubt we'll be driving fast anyway once we're on the island."

Once they finished pulling back the top, Angela got in the driver's seat. David took a final glance at the road atlas. He guessed Shelter Island to be five or six miles across, but it was difficult to say. Its irregular shoreline had dozens of coves and inlets describing its perimeter.

She put the convertible in gear, and they were on their way. Following what looked like a coastal road, Angela smiled through its curves and twists. She downshifted to second gear, taking a curve and then up-shifted again. Along the way, David pointed out Long Island's north fork or Inner Peconic Bay, at other times they were far enough inland to be out of sight of water.

They drove by some stately late-Victorian houses,

large rambling Queen Anne affairs. She liked them but David thought they were architecturally overwrought. Most of the homes looked like summer cottages, closed up for the winter. If what the ferry attendant told them was true, the population of the island exploded during the summer months.

"Beaches?" the attendant had said in response to their question. "There's three or four of them open to the public, but at this time of year, it doesn't much matter. There's plenty of spots where you can pull off the road and walk out to the shoreline."

After a few miles, they decided to button up the rag top. For while the sky grew brighter, it was also growing windy and colder — too cold for joyriding in a convertible. Angela turned down a sandy lane. A beach access road, private and secluded. Before long it dead-ended, and the tires rolled to a crunchy stop.

Together, they reached back and restored the roof. Wind whistled through the gaps in the convertible top until it was clamped down.

"Let's take a walk along the beach."

She shook her head. "Can't we warm up a little first? I'm really cold." Angela turned her head upward toward the wind which blew around them and took out one of her long cigarettes.

David considered the setting. It was intimate and private. This could be a good time. "Angela, there's something we should discuss."

That night in the Quiet Room Almira and Daniel placed a request at their feet which had profound ramifications. There were so many things to think about. In truth, he knew both of them needed time to consider it separately before tackling the question together.

She twisted around in her bucket seat.

"That was quite a visit we had from the ghosts, wasn't it."

"I know," she said. "It's hard to find words to describe it all. Sitting down with ghosts, them asking us to have their children..."

"You told them you would," he said. "Did you mean it?"

"I did say that, didn't I?" Angela took a drag on her cigarette. It wasn't calming, so she ground it into the ashtray. "But it's kind of moot unless we're married. Remember? That was a big deal to them, but we should want that for ourselves anyway."

David looked across at her, finding it hard to read her face. With temples pounding, he smoothed his mustache again and checked his pocket. Moments of hesitation. Maybe it was only seconds, but when one is too many that's all it takes. He looked down at her hand, small, pale, curled into a fist and nearly concealed within her coat sleeve. He reached for it. She pulled away.

"I've got to go," she said, her words tinged with panic.

"No, wait." David leaned over to stop her but with the seat pulled forward, and with the steering wheel between them it was impossible. The door slammed in his face. She moved briskly across the dead turf, almost running.

"Shit." David got out and chased after her, down a wooden boardwalk to the beach. It looked like the tide was out. She was already yards ahead of him, walking along the high-water mark. He wondered if their relationship had run out of road and would end here on the shore of Shelter Island.

"Hey," he said, trotting up beside her. He tried to slip

his hand under her arm.

"Leave me alone." She kept walking with her hands plunged deep into the pockets of her oversized peacoat.

Wasn't this ironic? Here they were together and finally walking the beaches of Shelter Island, but at the end of something and not the beginning.

"Angela, please. I have an idea. It might sound crazy."

She stopped.

"Almira said that she and Daniel could be stuck in their ghost state for a thousand years, until they atoned, or their children were born."

"I'm fed up with your stupid ghosts." Angela rolled her eyes and resumed walking. "I'm interested in our living life, not this dead-person dream world of yours."

"No, please." He took hold of her arm. "Hear me out."

She stopped again. "All right, I'm listening."

"She asked us to have their children for them."

"So, what are you suggesting?" Her voice sounded guarded.

"I'm suggesting we have those children, but not for them. I'm suggesting we have them for us."

Angela turned to him. "Are you serious?"

"I'm serious."

"We'd have to be married though."

"Yes, of course, I know that," he said.

"David." Her tone sounded like a warning, that she meant every syllable of what she was about to say. "Don't mess with me. I take this shit seriously, so if you want to step on that path then we have to walk it to the end— together. There's no bailing out when things get rough."

The tide was coming in. Waves were lapping nearer and nearer. The kicked-up wind blew streaks of her long black hair across her face.

She pulled them aside and fixed her deep brown eyes on his. "You snore, and you've got some peculiar habits, but I think the bumps on your head fit the bumps on mine."

"Like in Phrenology," he said.

Angela snorted and resisted the urge to smile. "That's right."

David wanted to reach for her but running fingertips along the sleeve of her coat was as close as he dared.

"You know I'm not on the pill anymore. If we get married, we're going to have babies—theirs, yes, but ours too. So, if you want me, you have to be prepared to take all of me, not just the fun parts."

He looked past her shoulder and out to sea, past Gardiner's Island, beyond which began the open Atlantic. Getting married might be like putting out to sea in a lifeboat for two, with all the uncertainties of unknown shores and the vagaries of weather, but always safe as long as the boat was sound and neither of them tipped it over. A boat for two in a sea of sharks. They had to stay afloat and survive or sink. Either way it would be a shared fate. The cloud cover was breaking. It was time to set sail.

"I'm willing to be everything to you. I'll make you my queen."

"If I make you my king," she said.

"That's the idea, yes."

Angela was oddly non-responsive.

"No. Let me try this again." Starting over, David got down on one knee. "Angela, will you marry me? I mean it. Right now. Become my wife."

She blinked back at him. "Forever and ever?"

"Forever and ever."

An offshore wake disturbed a gang of seagulls loitering nearb. It splashed far enough in to leave them surrounded by a swirling inch of ice-cold saltwater. David didn't stand up. Whatever would get wet was wet already.

"You mean it?"

He didn't answer her question. Instead, he reached into his pocket. "Let me see your hand."

She pulled her left hand out of her pea coat and held it out.

"Angela, I bought this as an engagement ring, but let's skip that stage. I'd like you to accept it as your wedding band."

Another wave swept the beach a few feet away.

"If you like it, let's find a Justice of the Peace."

"Right now?"

"Right now, today, this afternoon."

"Then the answer isn't that I like it—the answer is I love it."

Chapter 47

September 14th, 1842

The mood at Mrs. Bright's grew more somber over the fortnight before Rebecca's departure. Naturally she couldn't keep herself from reviewing the course of events, and often had second thoughts. Rebecca's obsession with learning of Almira's fate had led to Occult practices. Conjuring and Magnetism were both harrowing but discovering Tildie and she were sisters was the unanticipated and far more significant result.

If only she had gone to school in Philadelphia, as her parents had wanted her to in the first place. Now her selfish caprice was harming innocent lovers.

Yet in the end, Rebecca knew that even if she stayed in Albany for now, she would soon leave. By then the bonds of love between Tildie and her gentleman would have only grown stronger. No, she reasoned, marriages were arrangements, and Tildie needed to acknowledge this fact. Better to mow down her love now while the shoots were still tender.

Tildie meanwhile kept to herself, saying little to her mistress. Feeling more and more resentful as each day passed, she scurried off at every chance to be with Jack, the one she loved, or would hide, crying in her attic room.

Aware of all that took place under her roof, Mrs. Bright relaxed her ordinarily inflexible policies surrounding male visitors to her home. From the back door Jack was allowed access to the kitchen, where he would sit the whole evening, peeling potatoes or reading from the newspaper, while Tildie baked, prepared meals, or put up jam.

Evenings in the drawing room were uneasy. The older girls knew enough to stay away from certain subjects, but the younger ones, such as the Skinner twins, knew too little to avoid asking embarrassing questions.

"Why are you leaving for Philadelphia?"

"Why did we see Matilda crying? Don't you like living with us?"

On the final night, Harriett sat in the drawing room giving piano lessons to Betty Wheeler, while Rebecca visited with the Gardiners in their rooms, sharing a last cup of tea before her morning departure.

There had been no word received from her father, and now it was too late to hope for a last-minute communication. The belief that he would emancipate Tildie, even after having acknowledged paternity, was surely a childish notion all along.

"I don't suppose you'll miss Harriet Ames very much," Phebe said.

"No, I don't suppose so. In any event, one week hence I'll be in Philadelphia, beyond the reach of her ill-bred remarks."

"Miss Lynch did always tell us Albany was — Mary, how did she put it?"

"More Dutch than decent."

"Yes," Phebe said. "More Dutch than decent. Isn't that funny?"

"Please," Rebecca said. "I'm proud of my association with The Albany Female Academy, but Madame Grelaud's is familiar with girls of my background."

"Dear friend," Mary said. "There's no need to explain. We understand these things."

Phebe put her work aside and got up. "Shall I have us served another cup of tea?"

While her sister was gone for a fresh kettle, Mary said, "Phebe and I will accompany you to the landing when you leave tomorrow."

"Goodness, that's hardly necessary."

"No, we insist," said Mary.

"Apparently, Mr. DeGroot and that old gentleman Sandborne will be here with a carriage at noon."

By the time Phebe returned, the piano was quiet. A ticking clock could be heard while they sipped from their luster cups.

Rebecca broke the silence with a detached observation. "We made a gallant effort to do what we could for Tildie, didn't we? But it seems the sands have run through the hourglass."

Neither of the Gardiner sisters challenged the thought.

"I do thank you both most kindly though," Rebecca said. "Marriage is every woman's wish. Perhaps someday Tildie's hopes can still be realized. For now, I'm afraid I've failed her, and sharing with her the knowledge that we are related makes our association all the more uncomfortable."

Jack stayed especially late that night.

"Mrs. Bright," said Rose in her shawl and slippers, "Jack DeGroot's still out there, sitting on the back steps with Tildie. You want me to run him off?"

"No Rose. Leave them alone. When I retire to bed, I'll ask him to leave."

That night Rebecca had a dream so vivid it seemed to her like real life. In it she was walking a lane nearby to a lakeshore. The countryside was mountainous, so she thought it must be someplace up north. Ahead she saw Almira and Daniel a short distance off.

Suddenly, she was with them—all three holding hands together, relaxing on a carpet of the lushest green clover imaginable.

Playing among them were two newly born lambs. Rebecca ran her fingers through their curly wool, thinking they were just the prettiest, most precious things. One of them made to suckle from her fingertip.

"Mirie," Rebecca said, "I thought you and Daniel were perished, but you're not. You're alive and together."

"Yes, we are together." Daniel cuddled Almira closer. "Isn't it wonderful?"

"For how long?" Rebecca asked.

"Perhaps a thousand years," Almira said. "We do not know, but we shall wait here until our children can join us."

"And you're happy?"

"We are," said Daniel. "As happy as those who wait can be."

Chapter 48

December 6th, 1972

It was a lot to think about. Having a wife and someday children would be different. There would be less solitude, less solemnity, more distractions, but it might not be so lonely either. Maybe that sense of life's purposelessness wouldn't sneak up on him so easily. Besides, he still had the Quiet Room. He could escape there if he started to feel overwhelmed.

This fear that he would be subsumed within someone else was constant. With other girls he could always keep his distance. By compartmentalizing his life, it was easy to stay out of their reach, but nowadays that was not so much the case. Being without Angela, being apart from her, left him feeling incomplete and, if not diminished, certainly short of his potential.

She was strong, with a complete personality — not just, as she put it, "the fun part." He liked the way she could relate to him as an equal. Above all he could talk to her — this was key.

Those observations she made on their way to Shelter Island, the ones about how Almira's life had parallels in Poe's writings. That deep rap about Poe's obsession with death as the ultimate interruption of female beauty's transitory nature was a great conversation. She was intellectual, insightful, and articulate — and that was precisely what made her so tremendously attractive.

Across from him, on the other side of his desk, sat the Phrenology bust. Beside it, and serving as a paper weight, the fragment of cornice from the female academy. He touched the spot on his head which corresponded with adhesiveness. There really was a slight depression there, suggestive of undeveloped affiliative propensity. Maybe she was right.

The carriage of David's typewriter jolted back to life. He must have absentmindedly pressed the return key. He'd been sitting there with the hum of the machine, thinking and staring at the blank sheet of paper curled around the platen for half an hour.

The light from his fluorescent desk lamp reflected harshly off the paper. That was familiar. What wasn't familiar — the wedding ring on his hand.

For the last few nights, he'd been waiting, and now David could sense she was very near. In the dark hallway he could already perceive the glow of her lamps and candles shining from around the door's edges like the auras seen in Kirlian photography.

He rapped gently on the door. "Mrs. Dwyer, it's me, Doctor Weis. I was hoping we could visit." David tripped the latch and pushed the door open several inches.

Sitting upright, Almira wore a dress he'd seen her

in before, a gray with a green design. An open book lay on her lap, and on the floor beside her was the sewing basket. She looked up at him from her reading and smiled. "Good evening, Doctor Weis. I see you've been reading the sciences."

"You're referring to Professor Horsford's report on Phrenology?"

"Yes, it's very interesting. Have I ever told you I knew him?"

"I don't think so, no."

"Well I did. Not personally, of course, but he was one of our professors at the academy."

Almira closed the booklet, crossed the room, and placed the report on the mantel. Its transparent image snapped perfectly into the physical copy as she drew her hand away.

Back at her seat, Almira reached into the sewing basket at her side and brought out Daniel's braces, the never ending, never finished braces, and resumed embroidering.

David sat on the daybed and looked around. Almira's trunk rested in the corner. She sat on the klismos chair. The overmantel mirror still never showed her reflection, and of course the stenciled Grecian urns draped with swags of greenery still covered the walls. Being immersed in her world again felt good. The rhythmic needlework soothed him. He could easily have lingered for a long while, basking in Almira's presence.

She drew a needle through her work. "Judging by your expression when you entered, it looks as if you have some news for me. Do tell me it is so."

Almira's voice reminded him of the purpose of his visit. "As a matter of fact, I do have something very important to tell you." David held out his left hand and pointed with his right. "Do you see? It's a wedding ring."

Almira rested her needle. She leaned forward and inspected the wedding band. "Indeed, it is." She smiled. "These few days since, Daniel and I have been so happy for you and your lady, and proud too."

David was confused. "It sounds like you knew already. How?"

Threading a length of blue floss, Almira smiled. "We who have crossed are more sensitive. At first, I thought it must be hope informing me, and only when you returned from your journey did I know for certain that you and Miss Angela were joined in matrimony."

"Well, it happened kind of suddenly," David said. "We had a civil ceremony on Shelter Island last week. A justice of the peace thing. It was all pretty spontaneous. In fact, so far you're the only person who knows." The words tumbled out of him, making him breathless. David felt like a boy again, presenting his mother with a fist of dandelions. "I guess we'll have some kind of interdenominational church ceremony in the spring. I don't really know, the details are up to Angela, but I'm really into it, and I think it's a good idea."

"You've been so reluctant to take a wife, doctor. It would seem that you've had a change of heart. Is that true?"

"You could say that, yes." He found Almira's comment uncanny. He'd spent so much of the day contemplating that very idea. "See, I thought I could do it all alone. Build a complete life alone, but I can't, and I'm not sure I even want to. Until now, I always saw admitting to this fact as a weakness, but I don't see it that way anymore. I'm going to try another approach."

Almira wiped a tear from the corner of her eye.

"You're crying," he said. "I thought you would be happy."

"I am, yes, but this also means we will no longer be visiting. Our conversations have come to an end." Almira made as if to speak again but stopped herself.

A series of emotions played across her face. David recognized affection, friendship, love, and a touch of sadness.

"Doctor Weis," she said. "Knowing you as I have come to, it sorrows me to say goodbye."

"But does it really have to be that way?"

"It does. For Daniel and I to unite with God means we must also let go of this world. We may briefly return, but not as we have before, not as we are now. The point is that but for you, both of you, Daniel and I would never have fulfilled our destiny. For that we are grateful beyond measure."

"But you're mistaken." David half rose, speaking with some urgency. "We haven't fulfilled your destiny yet, not completely. I mean, even though Angela and I are married, we don't have children, your children, our children, not yet anyway. Wasn't that the largest part of it?"

"No, Doctor Weis, our children already exist."

David furrowed his brow, not understanding what she meant.

"Let me explain," she said. "Though you may not know it, your wife has already conceived our twins. They've been inside of her and alive for nearly a fortnight, ever since the night of your marriage on Shelter Island. In nine months, the very children Daniel and I would have had will be yours. We will watch them grow, but less and less as time passes, and always from afar."

"But can't we still meet and talk sometimes?"

"I'm sorry, Doctor Weis." She pulled the silk floss and clipped it clean with her tiny scissor. "It cannot be so."

"What if I promised you this room won't ever be contaminated with modern things? What if I make Angela promise too?"

"Have faith, doctor," she said. "And go bravely into your new life, for everything is coming to completion as it was meant to."

Almira held up the embroidered braces. "Do you not see? After so many, many years, they are finished."

She pointed to one end. "Can you see that I've added two little birds?"

"Your birdies."

"Yes, they are happy little bluebirds."

David noticed the cross stitched date on Daniel's suspenders. It had always been 1841, but now read 1972.

"I also see that you've changed the date."

Almira read her own cross stitching again. "So I did. 1972. Queer as it sounds, I do believe that is the current year. Was I correct?"

"Yes," said David. "Correct." He knew she now understood her dislodged position in time, and though he drew some sense of professional accomplishment from this, his heart was desolate.

"My dear, dear doctor," said Almira. "Do give me your hand."

"Are you sure?" He thought touching a ghost was intolerable for them.

Palm upward, she held hers out. David placed his hand upon it. His skin felt cold, even clammy, but Almira's long, slender fingers pulsed with warmth and life.

"Let me tell you more," she said. "Doctor Weis, it is God that brought us together. I was trapped here, first by my own unwillingness to forgive God, and then by my need to correct my sins against Him. Meanwhile you were here because you denied God's very existence. We were perfectly suited to help each other. That is why we must treasure our friendship for what it was, and not mourn it for what it never could be."

David looked in her eyes. "God is real, isn't he?"

"Oh yes," she said. "Though beyond our understanding."

Never had he felt as close to Almira as he did now, and he would likely never again have the chance to express his thoughts to her.

David squeezed his eyes shut. Tears sprouted and rolled down his face, yet he could still feel his hand gripped tightly in hers.

"Ah, Doctor Weis. You see, you do know how to love after all. You've known it all along."

Chapter 49

September 18th, 1842

DeGroot and Sandborne worked outside on the street, loading Rebecca and Tildie's trunks. Inside, Harriet held little Betty close and gloated from the foot of the stairs, while Susannah Platt, the Skinner twins, and Emily Wilcox expressed heartfelt goodbyes at Rebecca's departure.

Mrs. Bright kissed Rebecca's cheeks and invited her to visit Albany soon. "It has been a privilege to have a young lady of your caliber in my home," she said, loud enough for Harriet to hear.

The sad mood in the carriage hung so thick no one spoke. Yet the clatter of hooves on Albany's cobbled streets could still be heard.

Amidst all the activity at the riverfront docks, Rebecca noticed a tall, impeccably attired figure stepping off the Columbia's gangplank. He wore a silk hat and was dressed entirely in black, save for his starched white shirt. As he came closer, Rebecca recognized his face.

"Mary, Phebe, y'all look. It's your father."

The sisters turned around and were face to face with him.

"Papa," they said together.

"What are you doing here in Albany?" Phebe said.

"I'm here on some very urgent and important business," said Mr. Gardiner. He kissed his daughters, then turned to Rebecca. "Young lady, if I may be so bold, you have your father completely under your spell. Thank goodness my girls know better."

Rebecca couldn't stop her features from betraying her bewilderment.

"Please allow me to explain," Mr. Gardiner said. "Last week, while in Washington on business, I dined with your Senator Calhoun. He delivered me detailed instructions from a Mr. Moses Carvalho, your father. Evidently, he is, like myself, on intimate terms with the senator. When Calhoun was last in Charleston, your father confided to him the content of your recent letters, and the consequences of his prior indiscretion with a bonded servant, a mulatto woman. According to the senator, your father was overcome with remorse over his efforts to disguise the facts all these years. Now that they are known to you, he wishes to correct the matter as far as is practicable."

Jack and Tildie approached, holding each other close.

Mr. Gardiner turned toward them. "Are you the quadroon girl, Matilda?"

"Yes, sir. I'm Matilda."

"Excellent." Mr. Gardiner drew a packet of papers from the tail of his frock coat. "I have here a certificate of emancipation made out in triplicate."

"What's all this mean? I'm not sure I understand."

"Matilda," Mr. Gardiner said. "You're free. You are now the master of your own life."

Tildie and Jack squeezed each other tighter.

"Sir," DeGroot asked, "are you sure?"

"My good man, of course I'm sure." Mr. Gardiner sounded taken aback and slightly insulted. "I drew up these documents myself just yesterday, in the presence of a judge, with all appropriate seals and signatures."

"This means I really free?"

"Quite free, though I suggest you do not travel to slave-holding states. Additionally, your father has established an account at the Bank of New York. It is in your name and, needlessly generous in my view, but that is quite beside the point. In light of your limited literacy, I have been designated as executor until such time as you should marry, at which point the account will naturally transfer to your husband."

Tildie accepted the papers cautiously and unfolded them as Jack looked on.

"That's me?" she pointed. "Matilda Carvalho?"

"Precisely," Mr. Gardiner said.

She looked up at Jack and smiled.

"There is here, as well, a letter for you from your father. Judging by its weight, he appears to have much he wished to impart."

Rebecca laid her hand on Tildie's forearm. "So, it's obvious things have changed—you're not saying goodbye to Jack, you're saying goodbye to me."

A cacophony of emotions erupted in Tildie's throat, but Rebecca silenced her.

"I'm going on to Philadelphia, but you're not coming with me. You're staying here with your future husband."

The horn of the Columbia sounded, signaling that all passengers must board immediately.

"Mr. DeGroot," said Rebecca, slipping her hand under Tildie's arm, "you do promise to look after my sister?"

"Don't you worry, miss. Matilda is in good hands with me."

"And you will never, ever mistreat her?"

"No, I could never do that. She's my dearest girl."

Mary and Phebe wept with joy, and for the first time in many months, Rebecca's dark eyes sparkled with delight. Somehow, miraculously, everything had resolved itself.

Then, what was happening hit her fully. Tildie had been by her side her entire life. Her companion and confidant every day and in every situation—as much a sister as any girl could ask for. She leaned into Tildie and kissed her cheek, then, overwhelmed, took her in her arms without reservation. When they stood apart, Tildie dropped her parasol and made to retrieve it. Rebecca stopped her.

"No. This time let me get it." Rebecca rose and handed the parasol back to Tildie. Her face now streaked with tears.

"Who's gonna take care of you, Miss Becca? Who's gonna braid your hair at night?"

"Don't worry about me. I'll learn to do for myself."

Tildie looked back and forth between Jack and Rebecca, she clearly looked torn between loyalty and love.

"I love you," Rebecca said to her sister. "And I'll miss you terribly. Goodbye, Tildie. I don't know if I'll ever come back to Albany, so please write to me soon, and tell me all about how you and Mr. DeGroot are getting on. Father and I will both want to know you are well."

Tildie lunged forward and squeezed her sister in her arms one last time. "I love you. I never said that to you before, but I do."

"Girls." Mr. Gardiner cleared his throat. "My client has engaged me to escort his daughter to Philadelphia. If we do not board the steamer at once, I'll be remiss in my duties as his attorney."

Rebecca composed herself and opened her parasol. "Mr. Sandborne, would you kindly return Miss Tildie's trunk to the carriage?"

A few minutes later, as the Columbia backed away from the pier, Rebecca and Mr. Gardiner stood on the upper deck, smiling down on the future Mr. and Mrs. DeGroot standing arm in arm. Even at this distance, Jack's bald head reflected the sunlight.

Mary and Phebe meanwhile leaned into each other. "Bon voyage, Papa," they called, waving their hankies in the air.

"Farewell Rebecca," said Phebe. "*Au revoir* and *adieu*."

Chapter 50

August 1976

"You know," **Angela said,** settling herself on the blanket, "once my position starts, we won't have much time for picnics with the kids, or any more vacations on Shelter Island."

David poured their two mugs full. "Yeah, Shelter Island...we've had some fun there, haven't we?" He took a sip. "We'll go back there next summer. In the meantime, we've got this spot right in our backyard."

Lounging side by side, he was happy to watch the lake and listen to their children playing.

"Isn't this nice," David said, then corrected himself, "No, it's more than nice."

"Oh, baby, it sure is." Angela sounded happy and calm. "It's funny how things work out, isn't it?"

By the time the twins came scampering up, with the dog in tow, the bottle of wine was about finished.

"Momma, look," said the girl.

The boy held up a small green object between his fingers. David leaned forward to take a look too.

"Wow," he said. "This is a genuine four-leafed clover. Good job, kids. Why don't you go see if you can find another one?"

Once they were gone adventuring again, he turned back to his wife and picked up her hand. "If I say something, would you promise to forget I said it?"

"That's a weird condition, but okay, sure."

"Well," said David. "I had a dream about Dr. Koenigsberg last night."

"No kidding. Koenigsberg. It's been a long time since I've heard that name."

"Yeah, I dreamed he took a drive up here. I was showing him around. It was great. We were sitting in the Quiet Room talking. Anyway, it got me thinking that maybe I should get back into psychotherapy."

"As a patient or as a therapist?"

A long time ago, **Joseph Covais** enjoyed a successful career producing precise replica clothing for museums, historic sites, and the movie industry. He was an avid collector of early American antiques – especially photography.

In his mid-30's, blindness presented Covais with a challenge. It was also an opportunity many of us don't get. He had to dismantle his life and rebuild it from the ground up. Today Joe is a psychotherapist, work he finds immensely rewarding, and teaches psychology, which he is surprised to find he loves.

A third career is as historian/writer. In 2011, Covais self-published *Battery*, a non-fiction account of the glider service in WWII and based on in-depth interviews he conducted with surviving veterans. The focus of his current historical research involves the unpublished personal papers of one of America's first daguerreotype artists. "

Today Joe lives in Winooski, Vt. He works as a psychotherapist with blind and visually impaired persons throughout Vermont, teaches psychology classes at St. Michael's College, writes novels, and welcomes correspondence from readers, through Facebook, Good-Reads, or through direct email at josephcovaisauthswor@gmail.com.

Made in the USA
Monee, IL
11 December 2022

20581274R00187